D1146568

Jostein Gaarder was born in Oslo in 1952. *Sophie's World*, the first of his books to be published in English, has been published in 40 languages and has been a bestseller in each of them.

By the same author

Sophie's World
The Christmas Mystery

The Solitaire Mystery

JOSTEIN GAARDER

Illustrations by
Hilda Kramer

Translated by
Sarah Jane Hails

PHŒNIX

A Phoenix paperback
First published in Great Britain by Phoenix House in 1996
This paperback edition published in 1997 by Phoenix,
a division of Orion Books Ltd,
Orion House, 5 Upper St Martin's Lanc, London WC2H 9EA

Published by arrangement with Farrar, Straus & Giroux Inc.,
19 Union Square West, New York, NY 10003

Originally published in Norwegian under the title *Kabalmysteriet*,
copyright © 1990 by H. Aschehoug & Co
(W. Nygaard), Oslo

Copyright © Jostein Gaarder 1990
Translation copyright © Sarah Jane Hails 1996

A CIP catalogue record for this book is available
from the British Library.

ISBN: 0 75380 000 4

Typeset by RefineCatch Limited, Bungay, Suffolk
Printed in England by Clays Ltd, St Ives plc

CONTENTS

♠ SPADES ♠

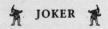 JOKER

. . . He stole into the village like a poisonous snake . . .

♦ DIAMONDS ♦

The Solitaire Mystery

In This Story You Will Meet

Hans Thomas, who reads the sticky-bun book on his way to the philosophers' homeland

Dad, who grew up in Arendal as the illegitimate child of a German Soldier, before running away to become a sailor

Mama, who has lost herself in the fashion world

Line, who is Hans Thomas's grandma

Grandpa, who was sent to the eastern front in 1944

The dwarf, who gives Hans Thomas a magnifying glass

A fat lady in the pub in Dorf

The old baker, who gives Hans Thomas a fizzy drink and four sticky buns in a paper bag

A fortune-teller and her extremely beautiful daughter, an American lady who splits herself in two, a Greek fashion agent, a Russian brain researcher, Socrates, King Oedipus, Plato, and a talkative waiter

In The Sticky-Bun Book You Will Also Meet

Ludwig, who came over the mountains to Dorf in 1946

Albert, who grew up as an orphan after his mother died

Baker Hans, who was shipwrecked in 1842 on his way from Rotterdam to New York, before he settled down as a baker in Dorf

Frode, who was shipwrecked with a large cargo of silver in 1790 en route from Mexico to Spain

Stine, who was engaged to Frode and was pregnant when he left for Mexico

The farmer Fritz André and *the storekeeper Heinrich Albrechts*

52 playing cards, including the Ace of Hearts, the Jack of Diamonds, and the King of Hearts

The Joker, who sees too deeply and too much

Six years have passed since I stood in front of the ruins of the ancient Temple of Poseidon at Cape Sounion and looked out across the Aegean Sea. Almost one and a half centuries have passed since Baker Hans arrived on the strange island in the Atlantic Ocean. And exactly two hundred years have passed since Frode was shipwrecked on his way from Mexico to Spain.

I have to go that far back in time to understand why Mama ran away to Athens . . .

I would really like to think about something else. But I know I have to try to write everything down while there is still something of a child in me.

I am sitting by the living-room window at Hisøy, watching the leaves drift from the trees outside. The leaves sail down through the air and come to rest like a loose carpet on the street. A little girl wades through the horse chestnuts, which bounce and scatter between the garden fences.

It's as though nothing fits together any more.

When I think about Frode's playing cards, it's as though all nature has come apart at the seams.

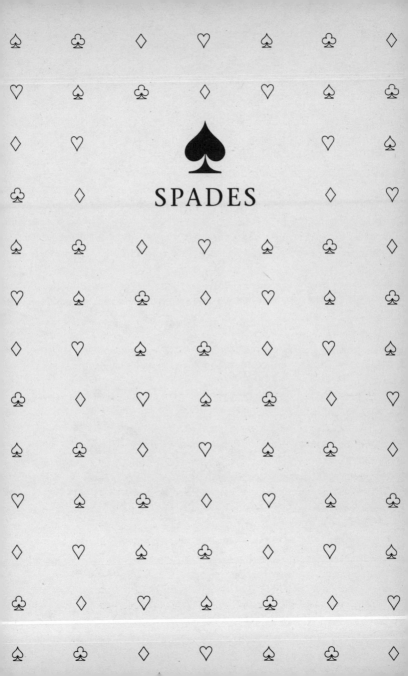

SPADES

ACE OF SPADES

*... a German soldier came
cycling along the country road ...*

The great journey to the homeland of the philosophers
began in Arendal, an old shipping town on the south
coast of Norway. We took the ferry, the *Bolero*, from Kristiansand to Hirtshals. I'm not going to say much about the trip
down through Denmark and Germany, because apart from
Legoland and the large dock area in Hamburg, we saw little more
than highways and farms. It was only when we got to the Alps
that things really began to happen.

Dad and I had a deal: I wasn't supposed to complain if we had
to drive a long time before stopping for the night, and he wasn't
allowed to smoke in the car. In return, we agreed to make lots of
cigarette stops. These cigarette stops are what I remember most
clearly from the time before we reached Switzerland.

The cigarette stops always began with Dad giving a little lecture
about something he'd been thinking about while he'd been driv-

ing and I'd been reading comics or playing solitaire in the back seat. More often than not, his lecture had something to do with Mama. Otherwise, he would go on about stuff which had fascinated him for as long as I'd known him.

Ever since Dad had returned from his life at sea, he had been interested in robots. Maybe that in itself wasn't so strange, but with Dad it didn't end there. He was convinced that one day science would be able to create artificial people. By this, he didn't just mean those dumb metal robots with red and green flashing lights and hollow voices. Oh no, Dad believed that science would one day be able to create real thinking human beings, like us. And there was more – he also believed that, fundamentally, human beings *are* artificial objects.

'We are dolls bursting with life,' he would say.

This sort of declaration often came after a little drink or two.

When we were in Legoland, he stood and stared at all the Lego people. I asked him if he was thinking about Mama, but he just shook his head.

'Just imagine if all this suddenly came alive, Hans Thomas,' he said. 'Imagine if these figures suddenly began to toddle around among the plastic houses. What would we *do* then?'

'You're crazy,' was all I could say. I was sure this kind of statement wasn't normal for fathers who took their children to Legoland.

I was about to ask for an ice cream. You see, I had learned that it was best to wait until Dad started to air his odd ideas before asking for something. I think he occasionally felt guilty for going on about things like this with his son, and when you feel guilty, you tend to be a little more generous. Just as I was about to ask for the ice cream, he said, 'Basically, we ourselves *are* such live Lego figures.'

I knew the ice cream was a sure thing now, because Dad was about to philosophise.

We were going all the way to Athens, but we weren't on a normal holiday. In Athens – or at least somewhere in Greece – we were going to try to find Mama. It wasn't certain that we'd find her, and even if we did find her, it wasn't certain she'd want to come home with us to Norway. But Dad said we had to try, because neither he nor I could bear the thought of living the rest of our lives without her.

Mama ran away from Dad and me when I was four years old. That's probably why I still call her Mama. Gradually Dad and I got to know each other better, and one day it just didn't seem right to call him Daddy any more.

Mama went out into the world to find herself. Both Dad and I realised that it was about time you found yourself if you'd managed to become the mother of a four-year-old boy, so we supported the actual project. I just could never understand why she had to go *away* to find herself. Why couldn't she sort things out at home, in Arendal – or at least be satisfied with a trip to Kristiansand? My advice to all those who are going to find themselves is: stay exactly where you are. Otherwise you are in great danger of losing yourself for ever.

So many years had passed since Mama left us that I couldn't really remember what she looked like. I just remembered that she was more beautiful than any other woman. At least that's what Dad used to say. He also believed that the more beautiful a woman is, the more difficulty she has finding herself.

I had been searching for Mama from the moment she disappeared. Every time I walked across the market square in Arendal, I thought I might suddenly see her, and every time I was in Oslo visiting Grandma, I looked for her along Karl Johan Street. But I never saw her. I didn't see her until Dad came in one day holding up a Greek fashion magazine. *There* was Mama – both on the cover and inside the magazine. It was pretty obvious from the pictures that she still hadn't found herself, because these were not pictures of my Mama: she was clearly trying to look like somebody else. Both Dad and I felt extremely sorry for her.

The fashion magazine had found its way to us after Dad's aunt

had been to Crete. There, the magazine with the pictures of
Mama had been hung up on all the newspaper stands. All you
had to do was toss a few drachmas on the counter, and the magazine was yours. I thought it was almost comical. We had been
looking for Mama for years, while all the time she'd been down
there posing and smiling to all the passersby.

'What the hell has she gone and got herself mixed up in?' Dad
asked, scratching his head. Nevertheless, he cut out the pictures
of her and stuck them up in his bedroom. He thought it was
better to have pictures of someone who looked like Mama than
to have none at all.

That was when Dad decided we had to go to Greece and find
her.

'We must try to tow her home again, Hans Thomas,' he said.
'Otherwise, I'm afraid she may drown in this fashion fairy tale.'

I didn't really understand what he meant by that. I had heard
of people drowning in big dresses lots of times, but I didn't know
it was possible to drown in a fairy tale. Now I know it is something everyone should be careful about.

When we stopped on the highway outside Hamburg, Dad started
to talk about his father. I had heard it all before, but it was different now with all the cars whizzing by.

You see, Dad is the illegitimate child of a German soldier. I am
no longer embarrassed to say it, because I know now that these
children can be just as good as other children. But that's easy for
me to say. I haven't felt the pain of growing up in a little southern Norwegian town without a father.

It was probably because we had arrived in Germany that Dad
started to talk again about what had happened to Grandma and
Grandpa.

Everyone knows that it wasn't easy to get food during the Second World War. Grandma Line knew this, too, the day she biked
up to Froland to pick cowberries. She was no more than seventeen years old. The problem was, she got a flat tyre.

That cowberry trip is the most important thing that has happened in my life. It might sound strange that the most important thing in my life happened more than thirty years before I was born, but if Grandma hadn't had a flat tyre that Sunday, Dad wouldn't have been born. And if he hadn't been born, then I wouldn't have stood a chance either.

What happened is as follows: Grandma got a flat tyre when she was up at Froland with a basketful of cowberries. Of course she didn't have a repair kit with her, but even if she'd had a thousand and one repair kits, she probably couldn't have fixed the bike herself.

That was when a German soldier came cycling along the country road. Although he was German, he was not particularly militant. On the contrary, he was very polite to the young girl who could not get home with her cowberries. Furthermore, he had a repair kit with him.

Now, if Grandpa had been one of those malicious brutes we readily believe all German soldiers occupying Norway at that time were, he could have just kept going. But of course that's not the point. No matter what, Grandma should have stuck her nose in the air and refused to accept any help from the German military.

The problem was that the German soldier gradually took a liking to the young girl who had run into bad luck. Her greatest misfortune, though, was actually his fault. But that happened a few years later ...

At this point in the story Dad used to light a cigarette.

The thing was, Grandma liked the German, too. That was her great mistake. She didn't just thank Grandpa for repairing her bike for her, she agreed to walk down to Arendal with him. She was both naughty and stupid, no doubt about it. Worst of all, she agreed to meet Unterfeldwebel Ludwig Messner again.

That's how Grandma became the sweetheart of a German soldier. Unfortunately, you don't always choose who you fall in love with. However, she should have chosen not to meet him again *before* she'd fallen in love with him. Of course she didn't do this, and consequently paid for it.

Grandma and Grandpa continued to meet each other secretly. If the people of Arendal had found out she was dating a German, it would have been the same as banishing herself to exile. Because the only way ordinary Norwegians could fight against the Germans was by having nothing to do with them.

In the summer of 1944, Ludwig Messner was sent back to Germany to defend the Third Reich on the eastern front. He wasn't even able to say a proper goodbye to Grandma. The moment he stepped onto the train at Arendal, he disappeared from Grandma's life. She never heard another word from him – even though for many years after the war she tried to track him down. After a while she felt pretty sure he had been killed in the fighting against the Russians.

Both the bike ride to Froland and everything that followed would probably have been forgotten if Grandma hadn't got pregnant. It happened just before Grandpa left for the eastern front, but she didn't know it until many weeks after he had gone.

Dad refers to what happened next as human devilry – and at this point he usually lights another cigarette. Dad was born just before liberation in May 1945. As soon as the Germans surrendered, Grandma was taken prisoner by the Norwegians, who hated all Norwegian girls who had been with German soldiers. Unfortunately, there were more than a few of these girls, but it was worse for those who'd had a child with a German. The truth was that Grandma had been with Grandpa because she loved him – and not because she was a Nazi. Actually, Grandpa wasn't a Nazi either. Before he'd been grabbed by the collar and sent back to Germany, he and Grandma had been making plans to escape to Sweden together. The only thing that stopped them was a rumour of Swedish border guards shooting German deserters who tried to cross the border.

The people of Arendal attacked Grandma and shaved her head. They also beat and kicked her, even though she was the mother of a newborn baby. One can honestly say that Ludwig Messner had behaved better.

With not so much as a hair on her head, Grandma had to travel to Oslo to stay with Uncle Trygve and Aunt Ingrid. It was no longer safe for her in Arendal. Although it was spring and the weather was warm, she had to wear a woollen hat, because she was as bald as an old man. Her mother continued to live in Arendal, but Grandma didn't return until five years after the war, with Dad in tow.

Neither Grandma nor Dad seeks to excuse what happened at Froland. The only thing you might question is the punishment. For example, how many generations should be punished for one offence? Naturally, Grandma must take her part of the blame for getting pregnant, and that is something she'll never deny. I think it's more difficult to accept that people believed it was right to punish the child, too.

I've thought a great deal about this. Dad came into the world because of a fall of Man, but can't everyone trace their roots back to Adam and Eve? I know the comparison stumbles a little. One case revolved around apples and the other around cowberries. But the inner tube which brought Grandma and Grandpa together does look a little like the snake that tempted Adam and Eve.

Anyway, all mothers know you can't go around your whole life blaming yourself for a child that is already born. Moreover, you can't blame the child. I also believe that the illegitimate child of a German soldier is entitled to be happy in life. Dad and I have disagreed slightly on this particular point.

Dad grew up not only as an illegitimate child but also as an illegitimate child of the enemy. Although the adults in Arendal stopped beating the 'collaborators', the children continued to persecute the unfortunate innocents. Children are very clever at learning devilry from adults. This meant that Dad had a tough childhood. By the time he was seventeen years old, he couldn't take any more. Although he loved Arendal like everyone else, he was forced to start a life at sea. He returned to Arendal seven years later, having already met Mama in Kristiansand. They moved into an old house on Hisøy Island, and that is where I was born on February 29, 1972. Of course, in some way I have to bear my part of the blame for what happened up at Froland as well. This is what is known as original sin.

Having experienced a childhood as the illegitimate child of a German soldier and then spent many years at sea, Dad had always enjoyed a strong drink or two. In my opinion he enjoyed them a little too much. He claimed that he drank to forget, but here he was mistaken. For when Dad drank, he always started to talk about Grandma and Grandpa, and his life as the illegitimate child of a German soldier. Sometimes he would start to cry as well. I think the alcohol just made him remember all the better.

After Dad had told me his life story again, on the highway outside Hamburg, he said, 'And then Mama disappeared. When you started nursery school, she got her first job as a dance teacher. Then she started modelling. There was quite a lot of travelling to Oslo, and a couple of times to Stockholm as well, and then one day she didn't come home. The only message we got from her was a letter saying she'd found a job abroad and didn't know when she'd be back. People say this sort of thing when they're away a week or two, but Mama's been gone more than eight years ...'

I'd heard this many times before as well, but then Dad added, 'There's always been somebody *missing* in my family, Hans Thomas. Someone has always got lost. I think it's a family curse.'

When he mentioned the curse, I was a little scared. But then I thought about it in the car and realised he was right.

Between us, Dad and I were missing a father and a grandfather, a wife and a mother. And there was even more which Dad must definitely have had in mind. When Grandma was a little girl, her father had been killed by a falling tree. So she had also grown up without a proper father. Maybe that's why she ended up having a child by a German soldier who would go to war and die. And maybe that's why this child married a woman who went to Athens to find herself.

TWO OF SPADES

*... God is sitting in
heaven laughing because people don't
believe in Him ...*

At the Swiss border we stopped at a deserted garage with
only one petrol pump. A man came out of a green house
and he was so small he had to be a dwarf or something.
Dad got out a gigantic map and asked him the best way over the
Alps to Venice.

The little man pointed at the map and replied in a squeaky
voice. He could speak only German, but Dad interpreted for me
and said the little man thought we should spend the night in a
small village called Dorf.

The whole time he spoke, the little man looked at me as
though I was the world's first and only child. I think he particularly liked me, because we were exactly the same height. As we
were about to drive away, he came hurrying over with a little
magnifying glass with a green cover.

'Take this,' he said. (Dad translated.) 'I cut this once from some old glass I found embedded in the stomach of a wounded roe deer. You'll need it in Dorf, indeed you will, my boy. Because I'll tell you something: as soon as I saw you, I knew that you might need a little magnifying glass on your journey.'

I started to wonder whether the village of Dorf was so small that you needed a magnifying glass to find it. But I shook his hand and thanked him for the gift before getting in the car. Not only was his hand smaller than mine, it was also a lot colder.

Dad rolled down the window and waved to the dwarf, who waved back with both his short arms.

'You come from Arendal, *nicht wahr*?' he said as Dad started the Fiat.

'That's right,' said Dad, and drove off.

'How did he know we came from Arendal?' I asked.

Dad looked at me in the rear view mirror. 'Didn't you tell him?'

'Nope!'

'Oh yes, you did,' Dad insisted. 'Because I certainly didn't.'

I knew that I hadn't said anything, and even if I had told him that I came from Arendal, the little man wouldn't have understood, because I didn't speak a single word of German.

'Why do you think he was so small?' I asked when we were on the highway.

'Don't you know?' said Dad. 'That guy is so small because he is an artificial person. He was made by a Jewish sorcerer many hundreds of years ago.'

Of course I knew that he was only joking; nevertheless I said, 'So he was several hundred years old, then?'

'Didn't you know that either?' continued Dad. 'Artificial people don't get old like us. It's the only advantage they can brag of. But it's pretty significant, because it means they never die.'

As we drove on, I took out the magnifying glass and checked to see whether Dad had any head lice. He didn't, but he had some ugly hairs on the back of his neck.

*

After we had crossed the Swiss border, we saw a sign for Dorf. We turned off onto a small road which began to climb up into the Alps. The area was virtually uninhabited; only a Swiss chalet or two lay dotted among the trees on the high mountain ridges.

It soon began to grow dark, and I was about to fall asleep in the back seat when I was suddenly woken by Dad stopping the car.

'Cigarette stop!' he cried.

We stepped out into the fresh Alpine air. It was completely dark now. A star-filled sky hung above us like a carpet, electric with thousands of tiny lights, each one a thousandth of a watt.

Dad stood by the roadside and peed. Then he walked over to me, lit a cigarette, and pointed up to the sky.

'We are small things, my boy. We are like tiny little Lego figures trying to crawl our way from Arendal to Athens in an old Fiat. Ha! On a pea! Beyond – I mean beyond this seed we live on, Hans Thomas – there are millions of galaxies. Every single one of them is made up of hundreds of millions of stars. And God knows how many planets there are!'

He tapped the ash from the end of his cigarette.

'I don't believe we are alone, son; no, we are not. The universe is seething with life. It's just that we never get an *answer* to whether we're alone. The galaxies are like deserted islands without any ferry connections.'

You could say a lot about Dad, but I'd never found him boring to talk to. He should never have been satisfied with being a mechanic. If it had been up to me, he would have been employed by the government as a national philosopher. He once said something similar himself. We have departments for this and that, he said, but there's no Department of Philosophy. Even large countries think they can manage without that kind of thing.

Being hereditarily tainted, I sometimes tried to take part in Dad's philosophical discussions, which arose just about every time he wasn't talking about Mama. This time I said, 'Even though the universe is huge, it doesn't necessarily mean that this planet is a pea.'

He shrugged, threw his cigarette butt onto the ground, and lit a new cigarette. He'd never really cared about other people's opinions when he talked about life and the stars. He was too wrapped up in his own ideas for that.

'Where the hell do the likes of us come from, Hans Thomas? Have you thought about that?' he said, instead of really answering me.

I had thought about it many times, but I knew he wasn't really interested in what I had to say.

So I just let him talk. We had known each other for such a long time, Dad and I, that I had learned it was best that way.

'Do you know what Grandma once said? She said she'd read in the Bible that God is sitting in heaven laughing because people don't believe in Him.'

'Why?' I asked. It was always easier to ask than to answer.

'Okay,' he began. 'If a God has created us, then He must regard us as something artificial. We talk, argue, and fight, leave each other and die. Do you see? We are so damned clever, making atom bombs and sending rockets to the moon. But none of us asks where we come from. We are just here, taking our places.'

'And so God just laughs at us?'

'Exactly! If *we* had managed to make an artificial person, Hans Thomas, and this artificial person started to talk – about the stock market or horse racing – without asking the simplest and most important question of all, namely how everything had come to be – yes, then we'd have a good laugh, wouldn't we?'

He laughed that laugh now.

'We should've read a little more from the Bible, son. After God created Adam and Eve, He went around the garden and spied on them. Well, literally speaking. He lay in wait behind bushes and trees and carefully followed everything they did. Do you understand? He was so enthralled with what He'd made, He was unable to keep His eyes off them. And I don't blame Him. Oh no, I understand Him well.'

Dad stubbed out his cigarette, and with that the cigarette stop was over. I thought, in spite of everything, I was lucky to be able to take part in thirty or forty of these cigarette stops before we reached Greece.

When we got back in the car I took out the magnifying glass the mysterious little man had given me. I decided to use it to investigate nature more closely. If I lay on the ground and stared long enough at an ant or a flower, maybe I'd spy some of nature's secrets. Then I'd give Dad some peace of mind as a Christmas present.

We drove higher and higher up into the Alps, and more and more time passed.

'Are you sleeping, Hans Thomas?' Dad asked after a while. I would have been, the moment he asked, if only he hadn't asked.

So as not to lie, I said no, and at once I was even more awake.

'You know,' he said, 'I'm beginning to wonder whether that little fellow tricked us.'

'So it wasn't true, then, that the magnifying glass was in a roe deer's stomach?' I mumbled.

'You're tired, Hans Thomas. I'm talking about the road. Why should he send us into the wilderness? The highway went over the Alps, too. It's now forty kilometres since I last saw a house – and even farther since I saw a place where we could spend the night.'

I was so tired I didn't have the strength to answer. I just thought that I might hold the world record in loving my father. He shouldn't have been a mechanic, no way. Instead, he should have been allowed to discuss the mysteries of life with the angels in heaven. Dad had told me that angels are much smarter than people. They aren't as clever as God, but they understand everything people understand, without having to stop and think.

'Why the hell would he want us to drive to Dorf?' Dad continued. 'I bet you he's sent us to the village dwarfs.'

That was the last thing he said before I fell asleep. I dreamed about a village full of dwarfs. All of them were very nice. They all talked at the same time about everything, but none of them could say where in the world they were or where they had come from.

I think I remember Dad lifting me out of the car and carrying me to bed. There was the smell of honey in the air. And a lady's voice said, *'Ja, ja. Aber natürlich, mein Herr.'*

THREE OF SPADES

... a little strange to decorate the forest floor so far away from people ...

When I woke up the next morning, I realised that we'd arrived in Dorf. Dad was fast asleep in the bed next to me. It was past eight o'clock, but I knew he needed to sleep a little longer, because no matter how late it was, he always had a little drink before he went to bed. He was the only one who called it 'a little drink'. I knew these drinks could be pretty big, and quite numerous, too.

From the window I could see a large lake. I got dressed at once and went downstairs. I met a fat woman who was so friendly she tried to talk to me, even though she couldn't speak a word of Norwegian.

She said 'Hans Thomas' several times. Dad must have presented me to her when I'd been asleep and he'd carried me up to the room. I understood that much.

I walked across the lawn in front of the lake and tried out a crazy Alpine swing. It was so high I could swing up above the rooftops. While I played on the swing I observed the little Alpine village. The higher I swung, the more of the landscape I could see.

I began to look forward to Dad waking up – he was sure to go wild when he saw Dorf in full daylight. You see, Dorf was a typical doll's village. Between high, snow-crested mountains there were a few shops lining a few narrow streets. When I swung high into the sky, it was like peeping down at one of the villages from Legoland. The guest-house was a three-storeyed white building with pink shutters and lots of tiny coloured-glass windows.

Just as I was beginning to grow bored with the swing, Dad appeared and called me in for breakfast.

We went into what must have been the world's smallest dining room. There was only enough space for four tables, and as if that wasn't bad enough, Dad and I were the only guests. There was a large restaurant beside the dining room, but it was closed.

I guessed that Dad felt guilty for sleeping longer than I, so I asked for a fizzy drink for breakfast instead of Alpine milk. He gave in at once, and in return he ordered a 'viertel'. It sounded mysterious, but when it was poured into his glass, it looked suspiciously like red wine. I understood we wouldn't be driving on until the next day.

Dad said that we were staying at a Gasthaus. It meant 'guesthouse', and apart from the windows it didn't look very different from any other guest-house. It was called the Schöner Waldemar, and the lake was called the Waldemarsee. If I wasn't mistaken, they were both named after the same Waldemar.

'He fooled us,' Dad said after drinking some of his viertel.

I knew at once he meant the little man. No doubt he was the one called Waldemar.

'Have we driven a roundabout way?' I asked.

'Did you say a roundabout way? It's just as far from here to Venice as it was from the garage. In kilometres, that is. It means that all that driving we did after we asked for directions was a complete waste of time.'

'Well, I'll be damned!' I said. Having spent so much time with Dad, I'd started to pick up some of his sailor's talk.

'I only have two weeks of my holiday left,' he went on, 'and we can't count on meeting Mama as soon as we roll into Athens.'

'Why couldn't we drive on today?' I had to ask. I was just as eager to find Mama as he was.

'And how did you know we wouldn't be driving today?'

I couldn't be bothered to answer that, I just pointed at his viertel.

He began to laugh. He laughed so loudly and raucously that the fat lady had to laugh, too, although she had no idea what we were talking about.

'We didn't get here until after one o'clock in the morning,' he said, 'so I think we deserve a day to recover.'

I shrugged. I was the one who hadn't liked the fact that we had to drive and drive without *staying* anywhere, so I felt I couldn't protest. I just wondered whether he really had thought of 'recovering' or whether he'd planned to use the rest of the day to hit the bottle.

Dad started to rummage around in the Fiat for some luggage. He hadn't bothered to take out so much as a toothbrush when we'd arrived in the middle of the night.

When the boss had finished putting the car in order, we agreed to go for a long walk. The lady in the guest-house showed us a mountain with a wonderful view, but with it already being late morning, she thought it was a bit too far for us to walk up *and* down.

That was when Dad got one of his bright ideas. What do you do when you want to walk *down* a high mountain but you can't be bothered to climb up? You ask if there is a road to the top of the mountain, of course. The lady told us that there was, but if we drove up and walked down, wouldn't we have to walk *up* the mountain to fetch the car afterwards?

'We'll take a taxi up and walk down,' said Dad. And that's exactly what we did.

The lady called for a taxi, and although the taxi driver thought we were completely crazy, Dad waved some Swiss francs about and the driver did as Dad said.

The landlady obviously knew the terrain much better than the little man from the garage. Neither Dad nor I had ever seen such a fantastic mountain or view, even though we came from Norway.

Far down below, we spied a little pond beside a microscopic cluster of tiny dots. It was Dorf and the Waldemarsee. Although it was the middle of summer, the wind blew straight through our clothes on the top of the mountain. Dad said we were much higher above sea level than we could be on any mountain at home in Norway. I thought that was pretty impressive, but Dad was disappointed. He confessed he'd planned this trip to the top of the mountain purely because he'd hoped we'd be able to see the Mediterranean Sea. I think he'd imagined that he might be able to *see* what Mama was doing down there in Greece.

'When I was at sea, I was used to the complete opposite,' he said. 'I could stand on deck for hours and days without catching a glimpse of land.'

I tried to imagine what that would be like.

'It was much better,' Dad added, as though he'd read my thoughts. 'I've always felt cooped up when I can't see the sea.'

We started to walk down the mountain. We followed a path between some tall leafy trees and I could smell honey here, too.

At one point we rested in a field and I took out the magnifying glass while Dad lit a cigarette. I found an ant creeping along a little twig, but it wouldn't stay still, so it was impossible to study. Then I shook the ant off and studied the twig instead. It looked pretty impressive when it was enlarged, but I didn't learn any more about it.

All at once we heard the rustle of leaves. Dad jumped up as though he was afraid some dangerous bandits would be roaming around up here; but it was only an innocent roe deer. The deer stood still for a few seconds staring straight at us before it sprang off into the woods again. I looked across at Dad and realised that he and the deer had been equally scared by each other. Since then, I've always thought of Dad as a roe deer, but it's something I've never dared to say aloud.

Even though Dad had drunk a viertel at breakfast, he was in good shape this morning. We ran down the mountainside and didn't stop until we suddenly came across a whole battery of white stones lined up in their own little field between the trees. There were several hundred; they were all smooth and round, and none of them was bigger than a lump of sugar.

Dad stood scratching his head.

'Do you think they grow here?' I asked.

He shook his head and said, 'I smell the blood of a Christian man, Hans Thomas.'

'But isn't it a little strange to decorate the forest floor so far away from people?'

He didn't answer right away, but I knew he agreed with me.

If there was one thing Dad couldn't stand, it was to be unable to explain something he experienced. In situations like this, he reminded me a bit of Sherlock Holmes.

'It reminds me of a graveyard. Each little stone has its allotted space of a few square centimetres ...'

I thought he was going to say something about the people of Dorf burying some tiny Lego people here, but that would be going a bit far, even for Dad.

'It's probably just some children who bury beetles here.' This was clearly for the lack of a better explanation.

'Possibly,' I said, crouching over a stone with the magnifying glass in my hand. 'But the beetles would hardly have laid the white pebbles.'

Dad laughed nervously. He put his arm around my shoulder,

and we continued down the mountain at a slightly slower tempo.

We soon came to a log cabin.

'Do you think somebody lives here?' I asked.

'Of course!'

'How can you be so sure?'

He pointed to the chimney, and I saw a thin trail of smoke rising from it.

Just down from the cabin we drank some water from a pipe which stuck out from a little stream. Dad called it a water pump.

FOUR OF SPADES

*. . . what I held in
my hands was a little book . . .*

By the time we got back down to Dorf, it was already late afternoon.

'It'd be good to have a meal now,' said Dad.

The large restaurant was open, so we didn't have to creep into the little dining room. A number of locals sat around one of the tables with tankards of beer.

We ate sausages and Swiss sauerkraut, and for dessert we had a kind of apple pie with whipped cream.

After we'd finished eating, Dad stayed at the table 'to taste the Alpine brandy', as he put it. I thought this was *so* boring to watch that I took a fizzy drink and went up to our room. Here I read for the last time the same Norwegian comic books I had read ten or twenty times before. Then I began to play solitaire. I started a seven-card game twice, but both times I got stuck almost as soon as I'd dealt out the cards, so I went back down to the restaurant.

I thought I'd try to get Dad up to the room before he got too drunk to tell stories from the seven seas, but he clearly hadn't finished tasting the Alpine brandy. Moreover, he'd started to speak German with some of the locals.

'You can go for a walk and look round the town,' he told me.

I thought it was mean of him not to come with me. But today – today I'm glad I did as he said. I think I was born under a luckier star than Dad.

To 'look round the town' took exactly five minutes, it was so small. It consisted of one main street, called Waldemarstrasse. The people of Dorf weren't very inventive.

I was pretty angry with Dad for sitting around drinking Alpine brandy with the locals. 'Alpine brandy!' Somehow it sounded better than alcohol. Once Dad had said it wasn't good for his health to stop drinking. I went around repeating this sentence to myself many times before I understood it. Normally people say the opposite, but Dad can be thought of as a rare exception. He wasn't the illegitimate child of a German soldier for nothing.

All the shops in the village were closed, but a red van drove up to a grocery shop to make a delivery. A Swiss girl played ball against a brick wall, and an old man sat on a bench under a large tree smoking his pipe. But that was it! Although there were a lot of fine fairy-tale houses here, I thought the little Alpine village was incredibly boring. I couldn't understand why I needed a magnifying glass either.

The only thing that kept me in a good mood was knowing we would be driving on the next morning. Some time in the afternoon or evening we would reach Italy. From there we would drive through Yugoslavia to Greece ... and in Greece we might find Mama. Thinking about it gave me butterflies in my stomach.

I walked across the street to a little bakery. It was the only shop window I hadn't looked in. Next to a tray of old cakes was a glass bowl with one lonely goldfish inside. There was a big chip in the upper edge of the bowl, about the same size as the magnifying glass I'd got from the mysterious little man at the garage. I pulled the magnifying glass out of my pocket, removed its cover, and examined it closely. It was just a bit smaller than the chip in the bowl.

The tiny orange goldfish was swimming round and round inside the glass bowl. It probably lived on cake crumbs. I thought that maybe a roe deer had tried to eat the goldfish, but it had taken a bite from the bowl instead.

All of a sudden the evening sun shone through the little window and lit up the glass bowl. Then I saw the fish wasn't just orange, it was red, yellow, and green. Both the glass and the water in the bowl were tinted by the fish now, all the colours from a paintbox at once. The more I stared at the fish, the glass, and the water, the more I forgot where I was. For a few seconds I thought I was the fish swimming around inside the bowl and the fish was outside gazing at me.

As I stared at the fish in the glass bowl, I suddenly noticed an old man with white hair standing behind the counter inside the bakery. He looked down at me and waved for me to come inside.

I thought it was a little odd that this bakery should be open in the evening. First I glanced back at the Schöner Waldemar to see if Dad had finished drinking his Alpine brandy, but when I didn't see him I opened the door to the bakery and stepped inside.

'*Grüss Gott!*' I said politely. It was the only thing I'd learned to say in Swiss-German, and it meant 'praise be to God,' or something like that.

I could tell at once that the baker was a kind man.

'Norwegian!' I said, beating my chest so he'd understand I didn't speak his language.

The old man leaned over a wide marble counter and stared into my eyes.

'Reallich?' he said. 'I have also lived in Norway. Many, many years ago. Now I have almost all my Norwegian forgotten.'

He turned round and opened an old refrigerator. He took out a bottle, opened it, and put it on the counter.

'Und you like fizzy drinks,' he said. '*Nicht wahr?* There you go, my *junger* friend. It is a *sehr* good fizzy drink.'

I placed the bottle to my lips and took a few gulps. It tasted even better than the drink I'd had at the Schöner Waldemar. I think it had a pear flavour.

The white-haired old man bent over the marble counter again and whispered, 'It tastes good, yes?'

'Delicious,' I replied.

'*Jawohl,*' he whispered again. 'It *is* a *sehr* good drink. And there is anozer fizzy drink to be found here in Dorf. It is even besser. But that soda isn't sold over counter. *Verstehst* you?'

I nodded. He whispered so strangely I was almost scared. But then I looked up into his blue eyes, and they were truly kind.

'I come from Arendal,' I said. 'Dad and I are on our way to Greece to find Mama. Unfortunately, she's got lost in the fashion world.'

He looked at me sharply. '*Sagst* you Arendal, my friend? And got lost? There are perhaps others who have the same done. I have *auch* some years in that *grimme Stadt* lived. But they have probably me there forgotten.'

I looked up at him. Had he really lived in Grimstad? That was our neighbouring town. Dad and I used to go there by boat during the summer.

'That's not . . . that far from Arendal,' I stuttered.

'No, no. And I knew that a *junger* jack one day here to Dorf would come. To collect the treasure, my friend. Now it is no longer just mine.'

Suddenly I heard Dad calling me. I could tell by his voice he'd had plenty of Alpine brandy.

'Thank you very much for the drink,' I said. 'But I have to go now, Dad's calling.'

'*Vater ja. Aber natürlich*, my friend. Wait *doch* a little. While you were here at the fish looking, a tray of buns in the oven I put. I saw you had the magnifying glass. Then I knew that you the right jack were. You will *verstehen*, my *sohn*, you will *verstehen* . . .'

The old baker disappeared into a back room. A minute later he returned with four freshly baked sticky buns, which he put into a paper bag.

He gave me the bag and said sternly, '*Nur* an important ding you must promise me. You will hide the biggest sticky bun till last and eat it when you are completely alone. You must never say anything to anyone else. *Verstehst* you?'

'Of course,' I said. 'And thank you very much.'

The next moment I was back out on the street. Everything happened so fast I don't remember anything before I met Dad between the little bakery and the Schöner Waldemar.

I told him I'd got a fizzy drink and four sticky buns from an old baker who'd emigrated from Grimstad. Dad probably thought I was just making it up, but he ate one of the sticky buns on the way back to the guest-house. I ate two. I hid the biggest sticky bun in the bag.

Dad fell asleep as soon as he lay down on the bed. I lay awake thinking about the old baker and the goldfish. In the end, I was so hungry I got out of bed and fetched the bag with the last sticky bun. I sat on a chair in the dark and bit into the bun.

Suddenly my teeth hit something hard. I tore away the bits of bun and discovered an object the size of a matchbox. Dad lay snoring on his bed. I turned on a light by the chair.

What I held in my hands was a little book. On the cover was written: *The Rainbow Fizz and the Magic Island*.

I began to leaf through the book. Although it was extremely small, it had over a hundred pages of minuscule writing. I turned to the first page and tried to read the tiny letters, but it was absolutely impossible. Then I remembered the magnifying glass I'd got from the little man at the garage. I fetched my jeans, found the magnifying glass in the green cover in one of the pockets, and put it over the letters on the first page. They were still very small, but as soon as I leaned over the magnifying glass, they were just big enough for me to read.

FIVE OF SPADES

... I heard the old
man walking around in the attic ...

D ear Son,
I must be allowed to call you that. I am sitting here writing
my life story, knowing that one day you'll come to the village. Maybe you'll wander by the bakery in Waldemarstrasse and
stand in front of the goldfish bowl. You won't even know why you've
come, but I know you'll come to Dorf to carry on the story of the
Rainbow Fizz and the magic island.

I am writing this in January 1946, and I am still a young man.
When you meet me in thirty or forty years time, I will be old, with
white hair. So I am also writing for a day to come.

The paper I am writing on is like a life raft, my unknown son. A life
raft can drift with the wind and rain before sailing towards the ocean
in the distance. But some rafts sail a totally different course. They sail
towards the land of tomorrow. From there, there is no return.

How do I know you are the one to carry the story further? I will be able to tell when you come towards me, son. You will carry the sign.

I am writing in Norwegian so you will understand, but also so that the people of Dorf cannot read the story of the dwarfs. If that were to happen, the secret of the magic island would be a sensation, but a sensation is always the same as a piece of news, and a piece of news never lives long. It captures attention for one day, then it is forgotten. But the story of the dwarfs must never drown in the temporary sparkle of the news. It is better for only one person to know the secret of the dwarfs, rather than for everybody to forget it.

I was one of the many who sought a new place to live after the terrible war. Half of Europe was immediately transformed into a refugee camp. A large part of the world was under the shadow of an exodus. But we weren't only political refugees; we were lost souls looking for ourselves.

I, too, had to leave Germany to build a new life for myself, but there weren't so many possibilities of escape for a non-commissioned officer of the Third Reich.

I didn't just find myself in a broken nation. I had brought home a broken heart from the land in the north. The whole world lay strewn about me in pieces.

I knew I couldn't live in Germany, but I couldn't travel back to Norway either. In the end, I managed to get myself over the mountains to Switzerland.

I roamed around for several weeks in a state of confusion, but in Dorf I soon met the old baker Albert Klages.

I was on my way down from the mountains when, exhausted by hunger and many long days of wandering, I suddenly saw a small village. Hunger made me run like a hunted animal down through the dense woodland, and I soon collapsed in front of an old wooden cabin. There I heard the humming of bees and could smell the sweet aroma of milk and honey.

The old baker must have managed to carry me inside the cabin. When I awoke on a bunk, I saw a man with white hair sitting in a rocking chair, smoking a pipe, and when he saw that I had opened my eyes, he came and sat next to me at once.

'You've come home, dear son,' he said comfortingly. 'I knew that one day you'd come to my door. To collect the treasure, my boy.'

I must have fallen asleep again. When I next awoke, I was alone in the cabin. I got up and went out onto the front steps. Here, I found the old man sitting bent over a stone table. On the heavy tabletop was a beautiful glass bowl. Inside the bowl swam a colourful goldfish.

It immediately struck me how odd it was that a little fish from far away could swim around so happily here, high up in the mountains, in the middle of Europe. A piece of the living ocean had been lifted up to the Swiss Alps.

'*Grüss Gott!*' I greeted the old man.

He turned round and looked up at me kindly.

'My name is Ludwig.'

'And I am Albert Klages,' he replied.

He went inside the cabin, but soon came out into the sunshine carrying some bread, cheese, milk, and honey.

He pointed down to the village and told me that it was called Dorf, and that he owned a little bakery there.

I lived with the old man a few weeks, and I soon began to join him in the bakery. Albert taught me to bake bread and sticky buns, pastries and all kinds of cakes. I'd always heard that the Swiss were great bakers.

Albert was particularly happy to have some help stacking the heavy sacks of flour.

I also wanted to meet other people from the village, and so I would sometimes visit the old pub called the Schöner Waldemar.

I think the locals took a liking to me. Although they understood that I had been a German soldier, none of them asked me any questions about my past.

One evening someone in the pub started to talk about Albert, who had been so kind to me.

'He has a screw loose,' said the farmer Fritz André.

'But so did the previous baker,' continued the old shopkeeper Heinrich Albrechts.

When I joined in the conversation and asked them what they meant, they answered evasively at first. I had drunk a few carafes of wine, and I could feel my cheeks glowing.

'If you can't give me a direct answer, then you can at least take back your malicious gossip about the man who bakes the bread you eat!' I spat out.

Nothing more was said about Albert that evening, but a few weeks later Fritz piped up again. 'Do you know where he gets all his gold fish from?' he asked. I had noticed that the village locals showed particular interest in me because I lived with the old baker.

'I didn't know there was more than one,' I replied truthfully. 'And he probably bought that from a pet shop, in Zürich perhaps.'

The farmer and the shopkeeper both started to laugh.

'He has lots more,' said the farmer. 'Once my father was out hunting, and on his way home he came across Albert airing his goldfish. He had them out in the sunshine all together, and there were more than just a few of them, mark my words, baker boy.'

'He's never been outside Dorf either,' added the shopkeeper. 'We are exactly the same age, and as far as I know, he's never left Dorf.'

'Some people say he's a wizard,' whispered the farmer. 'They claim he doesn't only bake bread and cakes, but he *makes* these fish himself. One thing is sure: he didn't catch them in Waldemarsee.'

I also began to wonder whether Albert was really hiding a big secret. A couple of sentences constantly rang in my ears: 'You've come home, dear son. I knew that one day you'd come to my door. To collect the treasure, my boy.'

I didn't want to hurt the old baker's feelings by repeating any of the villagers' gossip. If he *was* hiding a secret, I was sure he would tell me when the time was right.

For a long time I thought the reason there was so much gossip about the old baker was simply that he lived on his own high above the village itself. But there was also something about the old house which got me thinking.

As soon as you stepped into the house, you were in a large living room with a fireplace and a kitchen corner. There were two doors leading from the living room, one to Albert's bedroom and the other to a little bedroom I'd been given the use of when I had arrived in Dorf. The rooms didn't have particularly high ceilings, but when I observed the house from the outside, it was obvious that there must be a large attic. Moreover, from the crest of the hill behind the house, I could see a little window in the slate roof.

It was strange that Albert had never said anything about this attic, and he was never up there either. This is probably why I thought of the attic whenever my friends mentioned Albert.

Then one evening I happened to come home late from Dorf, and I heard the old man walking around in the attic. I was so surprised – and possibly a little scared, too – that I immediately ran outside to fetch some water from the pump. I took my time, and when I went back inside, Albert was sitting in his rocking chair, smoking his pipe.

'You're late,' he said, but I felt as though he was thinking about something completely different.

'Were you up in the attic?' I asked. I didn't know how I dared ask, but it just slipped out.

He seemed to sink into his chair, but then he looked up with the same kind face he had when he had taken care of me that day many months ago, when I had collapsed with exhaustion outside the old house.

'Are you tired, Ludwig?' he asked.

I shook my head. It was a Saturday evening. The next day we could sleep until the sun woke us.

He got up and threw some logs onto the fire.

'Then we'll sit together tonight,' he said.

SIX OF SPADES

... a drink which is more
than a thousand times better ...

I was just about to fall asleep over the magnifying glass and the sticky-bun book. I realised I had read the beginning of a great fairy tale, but it didn't occur to me that this fairy tale had anything to do with me. I tore a piece from the paper bag that the buns had been in and used it as a bookmark.

I had once seen something similar in Danielsen's bookstore in the market square in Arendal. It was a tiny book of fairy tales inside a box. The difference was that that book's writing was so big there wasn't room for more than fifteen or twenty words on each page. Of course, this being so, there was no chance of it being a great fairy tale either.

It was past one in the morning. I put the magnifying glass in one of my jeans pockets and the sticky-bun book in the other and dived into bed.

Dad woke me up early the next morning. We had to hurry and

get back on the road, he said, otherwise we would never make it to Athens in time. He was slightly irritated because I'd dropped so many sticky bun crumbs on the floor.

Crumbs! I thought. So the sticky-bun book hadn't been just a dream. I pulled on my jeans and could feel something hard in both pockets. I told Dad that I'd been so hungry in the middle of the night I'd eaten the last sticky bun. I hadn't wanted to turn on any lights, that's why there were so many crumbs on the floor.

We hurriedly packed our things and loaded them into the car before we dashed into the dining room for breakfast. I glanced into the empty restaurant where Ludwig had once sat drinking wine with his friends.

After breakfast we said goodbye to the Schöner Waldemar. As we drove past the shops in Waldemarstrasse, Dad pointed to the bakery and asked if that was where I'd got the buns. I didn't have to answer his question, though, because at that moment the white-haired baker appeared on the steps and waved. He waved at Dad, too, and Dad waved back.

We were soon back on the highway. I sneaked out the magnifying glass and the sticky-bun book from my jeans pockets and started to read. Dad asked me a couple of times what I was doing. First I said I was checking to see whether there were any fleas or lice in the back seat, but the second time he asked, I said I was thinking of Mama.

Albert sat back down in his rocking chair, found some tobacco in an old chest, filled his pipe, and lit it.

'I was born here in Dorf in 1881,' he began. 'I was the youngest of five children. That was probably why I was the one most attached to Mother. It was usual in Dorf for boys to stay at home with their mother until they were seven or eight years old, but as soon as they turned eight, they joined their fathers at work in the fields and woods.

'I remember all those long, happy days I walked around the kitchen hanging on to her skirts. The whole family gathered together only on Sundays. That's when we would go for long walks, spend more time eating dinner, and play dice games in the evening.

'Then misfortune fell on our family. When I was four years old, Mother was struck down by tuberculosis. We lived with the sickness in our house for many years.

'Of course, as a little boy I didn't understand everything, but I remember that Mother was always having to sit down to take a rest, and gradually she was confined to her bed for long periods of time. Sometimes I would sit by her bed and tell her stories I made up myself.

'I once found her bent over the kitchen bench having a terrible coughing attack. When I saw that she had coughed up blood, I went into a terrible rage and started to break everything I found in the kitchen. Cups and saucers and glasses, everything I came across. That must have been the first time I realised she was going to die.

'I also remember Father coming in to me early one Sunday morning, before the rest of the house had woken up.

' "Albert," he said, "it is time we talked, because Mother doesn't have long to live."

' "She's not going to die," I cried in fury. "You're lying!"

'But he wasn't. We had a few more months together. Even though I was only a young boy, I grew used to living with the thought of death, long before it arrived. I saw how Mother grew paler and thinner, and how she had a constant fever.

'I remember the funeral most of all. My two brothers and I had to borrow mourning clothes from friends in the village. I was the only one who didn't cry; I was so angry with Mother for leaving us that I didn't shed a single tear. Since then I've always thought the best medicine for sorrow is anger . . .'

The old man looked up at me – as though he knew I was also carrying a great sorrow.

'In this way, Father had to support five children,' he went on. 'In the beginning we managed pretty well. In addition to working on the little farm, Father was the village postmaster. There weren't more than two or three hundred people living in Dorf at that time. My oldest sister, who was only thirteen years old when Mother died, looked after the house. The others helped on the farm, while I – being too small to be useful – went around by myself most of the time. It wasn't uncommon for me to sit by my mother's grave and cry, but I hadn't forgiven her for dying.

'However, it wasn't long before Father started to drink. At first it was only at the weekends, but it soon became every single day. The postmaster job was the first to go; then the farm started to fall apart. Both my brothers left for Zürich before they were fully grown men. I continued to wander about on my own.

'As I grew older, I was often teased because my father was "on the grape", as they called it. If he was found stone drunk in the village, he was sure to be put to bed. I was the one to be punished. I felt I was the one who constantly had to pay for Mother's death.

'In the end I found a good friend, Baker Hans. He was a white-haired old man who had run the village bakery for a whole generation, but because he had not grown up in Dorf he was always regarded as a stranger. In addition, he was a quiet man, so no one in the village felt they knew him.

'Baker Hans had been a sailor, but after many years at sea he had settled down in the village as a baker. On the rare occasions when he walked round the bakery in just his undershirt, he exposed four enormous tattoos on his arms. We thought this alone made Baker Hans a bit mysterious, as no other man in Dorf had a tattoo.

'I particularly remember the tattoo of a woman sitting on a big anchor, under which was written MARIA. There were many stories about this Maria. Some people said she had been his sweetheart, but she'd died of tuberculosis before she was twenty years old. Others said Baker Hans had killed a German woman called Maria and that's why he'd settled down in Switzerland ...'

Albert seemed to look at me as if he knew that I, too, had run away from a woman. He doesn't think I've killed her, does he? I thought to myself.

But then he added: 'There were also some who said Maria was the name of a ship he had sailed on, which had been wrecked somewhere in the great Atlantic Ocean.'

With that Albert got up and fetched a big piece of cheese and some bread. He brought out two glasses and a bottle of wine.

'Am I boring you, Ludwig?' he asked.

I shook my head vigorously, and the old baker continued.

'Being the "orphan" I was, I sometimes stood in front of the bakery on Waldemarstrasse. I was often hungry and thought it helped my hunger just to look at all the bread and cakes. Then one day Baker Hans waved me into the bakery and gave me a big slice of currant cake. From that day on I had a friend, and this is where my story begins, Ludwig.

'From then on I was always visiting Baker Hans. I think he quickly noticed how lonely I was, and how I had to take care of myself. If I was hungry, he would give me a piece of freshly baked bread or some cake, and sometimes he opened a fizzy drink. In return, I started to run small errands for him, and before I turned thirteen years old, I was a baker's apprentice. But that was after many long years, by which time everything else had come to light and I had become his son.

'Father died the same year: he really did drink himself to death. Until the very end, he talked about how he wanted to meet Mother again in heaven. Both my sisters had married far away from Dorf, and I've never heard from my brothers since then . . .'

At this point Albert poured the wine. He walked across to the fireplace and knocked the ash out of his pipe, refilled it with tobacco, and lit it. He blew large, heavy clouds of smoke into the room.

'Baker Hans and I were companions for each other, and once he was my protector, too. Four or five boys started to bully me right outside the bakery. They threw me to the ground and punched me: at least, that's how I remember it now. I had learned long before why this kind of thing happened. It was punishment because Mother was dead and Father a drunkard. But that day Baker Hans came charging out onto the street, and I will never forget that sight, Ludwig. He fought to free me and beat every single one of them; not one escaped without a scratch. He may have been more aggressive than he needed to be, but since that day none of the people of Dorf have dared to bother me.

'Well now, this fight was a turning point in my life in more ways than one. Baker Hans dragged me into the shop, brushed off his white coat, and opened a bottle, which he placed on the marble counter in front of me.

' "Drink!" he ordered.

'I did as he said, and I already felt my score had been settled.

' "Does it taste good?" he asked, almost before I'd had the chance to swallow the first mouthful of the sweet drink.

' "Yes, thank you."

' "But if that tastes good," he continued, almost trembling, "then I promise you that one day I will offer you a drink which is more than a thousand times better."

'Of course, I thought he was only joking, but I never forgot his promise. There was something about the way he said it, and something about the situation. His cheeks were still red from what had happened out on the street. Moreover, Baker Hans was no joker . . .'

Albert Klages started to cough and splutter now. I thought he'd got some smoke caught in his throat, but he was just a bit over-excited. He looked across the table at me with a pair of heavy brown eyes.

'Are you tired, my boy? Should we continue another evening?'

I took another sip of wine and shook my head.

'I was just twelve years old at this time,' he said pensively. 'The days carried on as before, except that nobody dared to lay a hand on me now. I was always dropping in at the baker's. Sometimes we talked together, but now and then he just gave me a piece of cake and sent me on my way. Like everyone else, I discovered that he could be quiet, but he could also tell exciting stories about his life at sea. In this way I learned about foreign lands.

'I always visited Baker Hans in his bakery. Otherwise, I would never meet him. However, one cold winter's day, as I sat throwing stones across the frozen Waldemarsee, he suddenly appeared beside me.

' "You're growing up, Albert," he said simply.

' "I'm going to be thirteen in February," I replied.

' "Mmm. It'll do. Tell me – do you think you're big enough to keep a secret?"

' "I'll keep all the secrets you tell me until I die."

' "I thought so. And that's important, my boy, because I don't think I have that long to live."

' "Oh yes, you do," I said at once. "You have loads of time."

'Suddenly I felt as cold as the snow and ice around me. It was the second time in my young life that I had been given news of a death.

'He took no notice of my words. Instead, he said, "You know where I live, Albert. I would like you to come to my house tonight." '

SEVEN OF SPADES

... a mysterious planet ...

My eyes were sore after spelling my way, letter by letter, through this long section in the sticky-bun book. The letters were so tiny that I sometimes had to stop and wonder whether I was also making a little bit up myself.

I sat for a while staring at the high mountaintops we passed, thinking about Albert, who'd lost his mother and who'd had a father who liked his drink.

After a while, Dad said, 'We're getting close to the famous St Gotthard Tunnel. I think it cuts right through the huge mountain range you see ahead.'

He told me the St Gotthard Tunnel was the world's longest road tunnel. It was more than 16 kilometres long, and had been open only a few years. But before that – for more than a hundred years – there had been a railway tunnel, and before that, monks and other travellers had taken the St Gotthard Pass on their way between Italy and Germany.

'So there have been people here before us,' he concluded. The next moment we were inside the long tunnel.

The trip through the tunnel took almost a quarter of an hour. On the other side we passed a little town called Airolo.

'Oloria,' I said. It was a kind of game I'd played in the car all the way from Denmark. I read all the names and road signs backwards to see if they hid a secret word or something. Sometimes I was luckier than others. 'Roma,' for example, became 'amor,' and I thought that was rather fitting.

'Oloria' wasn't too bad either. It sounded like the name of a fairy-tale country. If I squinted my eyes a little, it was as though I were driving through this country now.

We drove down into a valley with small farms and stone walls. We soon crossed a river called Ticino, and when Dad saw it, his eyes began to water. That hadn't happened since we strolled along the docks in Hamburg.

He braked sharply and pulled off the road. He jumped out of the car and stood pointing down at the river running through the steep-sided valley.

By the time I'd got out, he'd already managed to light a cigarette.

'We've reached the sea at last, my boy. I can smell the tar and the seaweed.'

Dad was always coming out with remarks like this, but nevertheless, this time I was scared he'd finally flipped. What particularly worried me was that he said nothing else. It was as though he had nothing on his mind but to make it clear that we had reached the sea.

I knew we were still in Switzerland, which had no coastline, and even though I hadn't a clue about geography, the high mountainsides were solid evidence that we were a long way from the sea.

'Are you tired?' I asked.

'Nope,' he said, pointing down to the river again. 'But I'm

afraid I haven't told you much about the boat traffic in Central Europe, and I'm going to do that right away.'

I must have looked as though I'd fallen from the moon, because he added, 'Relax, Hans Thomas. There aren't any pirates here.'

He pointed at the mountains and continued: 'We've just gone through the St Gotthard massif. Many of Europe's longest rivers flow from here. The Rhine collects its first drops here, the source of the Rhône is also here – as is the Ticino's, which joins the great Po further downstream before running out into the Adriatic Sea.'

It began to dawn on me why he'd suddenly started to talk about the sea, but to confuse me even more he said, 'I said the source of the Rhône was here.' He pointed to the mountains again. 'That river flows through Geneva and down through France before it eventually spills into the Mediterranean a few miles west of Marseille. Then there's the Rhine; it flows through Germany and Holland before it eventually empties into the North Sea. But there are many other rivers as well, you know, which drink their first gulps up here in the Alps.'

'So do boats sail along these rivers?' I asked. I thought I'd stay one step ahead of him.

'You can be sure of that, my boy. But they don't just sail *along* the rivers. They sail *between* them, too.'

He'd lit himself another cigarette, and once again I wondered whether he was totally out of his mind. Sometimes I worried that the alcohol was corroding his brain.

'For example, if you sail along the Rhine,' he said, 'in a way you are sailing along the Rhône, the Seine, and the Loire. And along many other important rivers, for that matter. In this way you have access to all the large city ports of the North Sea, the Atlantic Ocean, and the Mediterranean.'

'But aren't there high mountains separating these rivers?' I asked.

'Yes,' Dad continued. 'And mountains are really perfectly all right as long as you can sail between them.'

'What *are* you talking about?' I said, interrupting him. Sometimes I got irritated when he started to talk in riddles.

'Canals,' he said. 'Didn't you know that you can sail from the Baltic to the Black Sea without being near either the Atlantic Ocean or the Mediterranean?'

I just shook my head in despair.

'You end up in the Caspian Sea: in other words, in the heart of Asia,' he whispered excitedly.

'Is that true?'

'Yup! It's as true as the St Gotthard Tunnel. It's amazing.'

I stood looking down at the river, and now I thought I, too, could smell the faint tang of tar and seaweed.

'What do you learn at school, Hans Thomas?' Dad asked.

'To sit still,' I replied. 'It's so difficult that we spend years learning to do it.'

'Okay ... But do you think you'd have sat still if the teacher had told you about the sea routes in Europe?'

'Probably,' I said. 'Yes, I'm quite sure.'

And with that the cigarette stop was over. We drove on, following the Ticino River. The first place we passed was Bellinzona, a large town with three huge fortresses from the Middle Ages. After Dad had given a little lecture on the Crusades, he said, 'You know I'm very interested in outer space, Hans Thomas. Well, I'm particularly interested in planets – most of all living planets.'

I didn't say anything. Both he and I knew he was interested in that kind of thing.

'Did you know,' he continued, 'that a mysterious planet has just been discovered where millions of intelligent beings are loafing around on two legs peering out over the planet through a pair of bright lenses?'

I had to admit this was completely new to me.

'The little planet is held together by a complicated network of tracks where these clever guys constantly roll around in colourful wagons.'

'Is that true?'

'Yes it is! On this planet these mysterious creatures have also built enormous buildings which are more than a hundred storeys tall. And underneath these constructions they've dug long tunnels which they can flit around in, in electric things moving on rails.'

'Are you quite sure?' I asked.

'Yes, quite sure.'

'But . . . why have I never heard of this planet?'

'Well,' Dad said, 'first of all, it was discovered only recently, and second, I fear that I am the only one who has discovered it.'

'Where is it, then?'

At this point Dad stepped on the brake and pulled off the road.

'*Here*,' he said, and slapped his palm down on the dashboard. 'This is the remarkable planet, Hans Thomas. And we are those intelligent guys rolling around in a red Fiat.'

I sat for a few seconds sulking because he'd fooled me. But then it occurred to me how incredible this planet is, so I forgave him.

'People would have gone absolutely wild if the astronomers had discovered *another* living planet,' Dad concluded. 'They just don't let themselves be amazed by their own.'

He sat for a long time without saying anything, so I took the opportunity to read more of the sticky-bun book.

It wasn't easy to separate all the bakers in Dorf from each other. But I soon understood that Ludwig was the one who had written the sticky-bun book, and Albert was the one who had told him about the time he was a boy and went to visit Baker Hans.

EIGHT OF SPADES

... like a whirlwind from foreign lands ...

Albert Klages lifted his glass to his lips and took a mouthful of wine.

When I looked at his old face, it was strange to imagine that this person was the neglected little boy who'd lost his mother on her sickbed. I tried to imagine the special friendship which had developed between him and Baker Hans.

I had been lonely and forlorn when I had come to Dorf, but the man who had taken me in had once been just as exhausted. Albert put his glass back down on the table and raked about in the fire with a poker before he continued.

'Everyone in the village knew Baker Hans lived in a wooden cabin above Dorf. There were many rumours about what it was like there, but I don't think anyone had been inside his place. So it wasn't surprising that I had butterflies in my stomach as I walked between the high banks of snow up to Baker Hans's that winter evening. I was the very first person to visit the mysterious baker . . .

'A white full moon rose above the mountains in the east, and the first stars had already appeared in the night sky.

'As I walked up the last little hill, I remembered what Baker Hans had said about me one day tasting a fizzy drink a thousand times better than the one I'd had after the big fight. Did this drink have anything to do with the big secret?

'I soon spied the house up on the ridge, and as I'm sure you understand, Ludwig, that house was the very house we're sitting in now.'

'I nodded quickly, and the old baker continued: 'I passed the water pump, hurried over the snow-covered courtyard, and knocked on the door. I heard Baker Hans call, "Come in, my son!"

'Now, you have to remember I was only twelve years old at the time, and I still lived at home on the farm with my father. So it felt a bit strange to be addressed as another man's son.

'I stepped inside, and it was like slipping into another world. Baker Hans sat in a deep rocking chair, and all over the room there were glass bowls with goldfish inside. In every corner a little piece of rainbow danced.

'But there were not only goldfish here. I stood for a long time staring at objects I had never seen before. It took many years before I could put into words what I saw there.

'There were ships in bottles and conch shells, Buddha figures and precious stones, boomerangs and wooden dolls, old rapiers and swords, knives and pistols, Persian cushions and South American carpets made of llama wool. I particularly noticed a strange glass figure of an animal with a little pointed head and six legs. It was like a whirlwind from foreign lands. I might have heard of some of the things I saw, but this was long before I had seen a photograph.

'The whole atmosphere in the little cabin was totally different from the way I had imagined it to be. It was as though I were no longer at Baker Hans's; suddenly I was visiting an old seafarer. Oil lamps were lit around the room, and these were so different from the paraffin lamps I was used to seeing, they must have come from his life at sea.

'The old man asked me to sit down in a chair beside the fire, and it was exactly the same chair you're sitting in now, Ludwig. Do you understand?'

I nodded again.

'Before I sat down, I walked around the cosy room looking at all the goldfish. Some of them were red, yellow, and orange; others were green, blue, and violet. I had seen a goldfish like these only once before. That had been on a little table in the back room of Baker Hans's bakery. I had often stood staring at the tiny fish swimming back and forth inside the glass bowl while Baker Hans made dough.

"What a lot of goldfish you have," I exclaimed as I walked across the room towards him. "Are you going to tell me where you caught them?"

'He chuckled and said, "All in due course, my boy, all in due course. Tell me – would you like to be the baker in Dorf one day when I am gone?"

'Although I was only a child, the idea had already occurred to me. I didn't have anything in my life except Baker Hans and his bakery. Mother was dead, Father had stopped asking about my comings and goings, and all my brothers and sisters had moved away from Dorf.

"I've already decided to stay in the bakery trade," I replied formally.

"I thought as much," said the old man. "Hmm . . . You will have to look after my fish as well. And there's even more. You'll be the keeper of the secret of Rainbow Fizz."

"Rainbow Fizz?"

"Yes, that and everything else, my boy."

"Tell me about Rainbow Fizz," I said.

'He raised his white eyebrows and whispered, "It has to be tasted, my boy."

"Can't you tell me what it tastes like?"

'He shook his old head in despair.

"A normal fizzy drink tastes of orange or pear or raspberry – and that's that. That isn't the case with Rainbow Fizz, Albert. You taste all those flavours at the same time with this drink, and you even taste fruits and berries you've never been near with your tongue."

"Then it must be good," I said.

"Hah! It's more than just good. You can taste a normal fizzy drink only in your mouth ... first on your tongue and the roof of your mouth, then a little bit down your throat. You can taste Rainbow Fizz in your nose and head, down through your legs, and out through your arms."

"I think you're pulling my leg," I said.

"You think so?"

'The old man looked almost dumbfounded, so I decided to ask something which was easier to answer.

"What colour is it?" I asked.

'Baker Hans started to laugh. "You're full of questions, aren't you, boy. And that's good, but it's not always easy to answer. I have to *show* you the drink, you see."

'Baker Hans got up and walked over to a door which led into a little bedroom. Inside, there was a glass bowl with a goldfish in it. The old man pulled out a ladder from underneath the bed and leaned it up against the wall. I noticed a little trapdoor in the ceiling which was locked with a heavy padlock.

'The baker climbed the ladder and opened the trapdoor to the attic with a key which he fished out of his shirt pocket.

"Come here, my boy," he said. "No one but me has been here for more than fifty years."

'I followed him up into the attic.

'Moonlight streamed in through a little window in the roof. It fell upon old chests and ships' bells lying under a cover of dust and spider's webs. But it wasn't only the moon illuminating the dark attic. The moonlight was blue, but there was also a bright shimmer, in all the colours of the rainbow.

'Baker Hans made his way across the attic floor. He stopped at the far end and pointed towards a corner. An old bottle was standing on the floor under the slanting roof. A light shone from the bottle which was so dazzlingly beautiful that at first I had to cover my eyes. It was a clear glass bottle, but the contents were red, yellow, green, and violet – or all these colours at once.

'Baker Hans picked up the bottle, and the contents glittered like liquid diamonds.

"What is it?" I whispered timidly.

"The old baker's face was serious. "This, my boy, is Rainbow Fizz. These are the last drops to be found in the whole world."

"And what's that?" I asked, pointing down at a small wooden box containing a pile of dusty old playing cards. They had almost disintegrated. The eight of spades lay on the top of the heap. I could only just make out a number eight in the left-hand corner of the card.

'Baker Hans put his finger to his lips and whispered, "They're Frode's playing cards, Albert."

"Frode?"

"Yes, Frode. But we'll hear that story another evening. Now you and I are going to take this bottle down to the living room."

'With the bottle in his hand, the old man started to walk across the floor. He looked like a pixie with a lantern; the only difference was that this lantern didn't know whether it wanted to shine red, green, yellow, or blue. Small specks of colour splashed across the room – like the light from a hundred tiny dancing lanterns.

'When we were back downstairs in the living room, he put the bottle on the table in front of the fireplace. The exotic objects in the room were coloured by the contents of the bottle. The Buddha figure became green, an old revolver became blue, and a boomerang became red like blood.

"*Is* that Rainbow Fizz?" I asked again.

"Yes, the last drops. And it's just as well, Albert, because this is a drink which is so terribly good, I wouldn't like to say what might happen if it were sold over the counter."

'He got up and fetched a little glass; then he poured a couple of drops into it. They lay on the bottom of the glass and glittered like snow crystals.

"That's enough," he said.

"Don't I get any more?" I asked, surprised.

'The old man shook his head. "A little taste is more than enough. The taste of just one drop of Rainbow Fizz will last for many hours."

"So maybe I can drink a drop now, and another drop early tomorrow morning," I suggested.

'Baker Hans shook his head in despair. "No, no. One drop now –
and no more drops ever again. You will find this drop so good you
will want to steal the rest. That's why I have to lock it up in the attic
again as soon as you leave. When I've told you about Frode's playing
cards, you'll think yourself lucky I didn't give you the whole bottle."

"Have you tasted it yourself?"

"Yes, once. But that was more than fifty years ago."

'Baker Hans got up from his chair by the fire, took the bottle with
the liquid diamonds, and put it in the little bedroom.

'When he returned, he placed one hand on my shoulder and said,
"Drink now. This is the greatest moment of your life, my boy. You will
always remember it, but this moment will never ever return."

'I raised the little glass to my mouth and drank the glittering drops
that lay in the bottom. As soon as the first drop tickled the tip of my
tongue, a wave of desire washed through my body. At first I tasted all
the best flavours I had tasted previously in my young life; then a
thousand other flavours surged through my body.

'Baker Hans had been right about the taste starting from the tip of
my tongue. But I could also taste strawberry, raspberry, apple, and
banana in my arms and my legs. In the tip of my little finger I could
taste honey, in one of my toes I tasted preserved pears, and in the
small of my back confectioner's custard. I could smell the scent of my
mother all over my body. It was a smell I had forgotten, though I had
missed it ever since she'd died.

'When the first storm of flavour eased, it was as though the whole
world was in my body; yes, as if *I* was the whole world. I suddenly felt
that all the woods and lakes, mountains and fields were part of my
body. Although my mother was dead, it was as though she were out
there somewhere ...

'When I looked at the green Buddha figure, it seemed to laugh. I
glanced at the two swords hanging crossed on the wall, and now
they appeared to fence. The ship in the bottle which I had spotted as
soon as I had entered Hans's cabin was on top of a large cupboard. I

now felt as though I were standing on board the old sailing ship, rushing towards a lush island in the distance.

"Was it good?" I heard a voice say. It was Baker Hans. He leaned over and ruffled my hair.

"Mmm . . ." was all I could reply. I didn't know what to say.

'And so it is today. I can't say what Rainbow Fizz tasted like; it tasted like everything. I just know I still get tears in my eyes when I think of how good it was.'

NINE OF SPADES

*. . . he saw peculiar things
that everyone else was blind to . . .*

Dad had kept trying to talk to me while I read about Rainbow Fizz, but that drink was so good I couldn't put the sticky-bun book down. Now and then, to be polite, I glanced out of the window when Dad commented on the view.

'Wow!' I'd say. Or: 'Beautiful!'

One of the things Dad pointed out while I continued to sneak around Baker Hans's attic was that all the signs and names were written in Italian. We were driving through the Italian part of Switzerland, and the names were not the only things that were different. Even while I was reading about Rainbow Fizz, I had noticed the valley we drove through had flowers and trees which really belonged to countries from the Mediterranean regions.

Dad – who'd been all over the world – started to comment on the vegetation.

'Mimosa,' he said. 'Magnolia! Rhododendron! Azalea! Japanese cherry tree!'

We saw a number of palm trees, too – long before we'd crossed the Italian border.

'We're not far from Lugano,' Dad said, as I put the book down.

I suggested we spend the night there, but Dad shook his head. 'The agreement was, we would cross the Italian border first. It's not that far now, and it's still early afternoon.'

As a consolation, we had a long stop in Lugano. First of all we nosed around the streets and in the various gardens and parks the town was full of. I took the magnifying glass with me and made a few botanical investigations, while Dad bought an English newspaper and smoked a cigarette.

I found two very distinct trees. One had large red flowers, while the other had rather small yellow ones. The flowers had totally different forms as well; nevertheless, these two trees must have been of the same family, because when I studied the leaves from the two trees closely under the magnifying glass, I discovered the veins and fibres of the leaves were almost identical.

We suddenly heard a nightingale. It chirped, whistled, twittered, and peeped for so long and so beautifully I almost started to cry. Dad was equally impressed, but only laughed.

It was so hot that I got two ice creams without having to coax Dad into philosophising. I tried to get a big cockroach to walk along the ice-cream stick, so I could put it under the magnifying glass, but this particular cockroach had a hopeless fear of the doctor.

'They jump out as soon as the thermometer teeters over thirty degrees,' Dad said.

'And they jump away again as soon as they see an ice-cream stick,' I replied.

Before getting back in the car, Dad bought a pack of cards. He did this as often as other people might buy a magazine. He wasn't particularly interested in playing cards, and he didn't play solitaire either – I was the only one who did that. So I'd better explain about these packs of cards.

Dad worked as a mechanic in a large garage in Arendal. Apart from going back and forth to work, he'd always been utterly absorbed by the eternal questions. The bookshelves in his room were overflowing with books about different philosophical subjects. But he also had a pretty normal hobby. Well – exactly how normal it was, is, of course, open to discussion.

Lots of people collect different things like stones, coins, stamps, and butterflies. Dad also had a passion for collecting. He collected jokers. This was something he'd done long before I'd known him; I think it began when he was at sea. He had a drawerful of different jokers.

He mainly went about it by asking for the joker from people playing cards. He would walk over to complete strangers sitting at a café, or by the dockside, playing cards and say that he was a passionate collector of jokers and could he have the joker if they didn't need it in the game. Most of them plucked out the joker and gave it to him right away, but a lot of them looked at him as though they were about to say 'it takes all kinds.' Some politely said no to the request, others refused in a bolder fashion. I sometimes felt like a Gypsy child who'd been involuntarily drawn into some kind of begging operation.

Of course, I wondered how this unique hobby had begun. In this way, Dad had managed to collect a card from all the packs of cards he came across. Therefore, his hobby seemed related to collecting a postcard from all the corners of the world. It was also clear that the joker was the only card he could collect. For example, he couldn't collect the nine of spades or the king of clubs, because interrupting a high-spirited bridge party and asking for the king of clubs or the nine of spades just wasn't done.

The whole point was that there are usually *two* jokers in a pack of cards. We had found up to three and four, but generally there were two. Moreover, there aren't many games requiring the joker, and on the rare occasions it is used, you can get by with just one. But Dad was interested in jokers for a deeper reason.

The fact was, Dad considered himself a joker. He rarely said it straight out, but I had known for a long time that he saw himself as a joker in a pack of cards.

A joker is a little fool who is different from everyone else. He's not a club, diamond, heart, or spade. He's not an eight or a nine, a king or a jack. He is an outsider. He is placed in the same pack as the other cards, but he doesn't belong there. Therefore, he can be removed without anybody missing him.

I think Dad felt like a joker when he grew up as the illegitimate child of a German soldier in Arendal. But there was even more: Dad was also a joker in being a philosopher. He always felt he saw peculiar things that everyone else was blind to.

So when Dad bought this pack of cards in Lugano, it wasn't for the pack itself. Something made him particularly curious to see what the joker of *this* pack of cards looked like. He was so excited he opened the package right away and pulled out one of the jokers.

'Just as I thought,' he said. 'I've never seen this one before.'

He put the joker in his shirt pocket, and now it was my turn.

'Do I get the pack of cards?'

Dad handed the rest of the pack to me. This was an unwritten law: when Dad bought a pack of cards, he kept the joker – never more than one – and gave the rest of the cards to me if I asked for them before he'd disposed of them elsewhere. In this way, I'd collected nearly a hundred packs of cards. Because I was an only child – and didn't have a mother at home – I really liked playing solitaire, but I wasn't an avid collector, so I began to feel I had enough packs of cards. Sometimes Dad would simply buy a pack of cards, snatch the joker, and throw the rest away. It was almost like peeling a banana and throwing away the skin.

'Garbage!' he might say as he took the good from the bad and tossed the remains in the bin.

He generally got rid of the garbage, however, in a more compassionate way. If I didn't want the cards, he'd find some other children and give the pack of cards to them without saying a word. In this way, he paid mankind back for all the jokers he had

gone around bumming off casual cardplayers. I thought mankind got a good deal.

When we started the car again, Dad confided in me that the
scenery was so beautiful here he wanted to make a little detour.
Instead of following the highway from Lugano to Como, we
drove along Lake Lugano. We crossed the Italian border after having driven halfway along the lake.

I soon understood why Dad had chosen this route. Just after
we'd left Lake Lugano, we came to a much larger lake with a lot of
boat traffic. It was Lake Como. From here we drove through a
little town called Menaggio. Oigganem, I said. We drove along
the large lake for several miles before we arrived in Como later
that evening.

While we drove, Dad continued to name all the trees we saw.

'Stone pine,' he said. 'Cypress, olive, fig.'

I didn't know where he got all the names from. I had heard a
couple of them before, but all the others he could have just made
up, for all I knew.

In between all the impressions from the landscape around us, I
read more from the sticky-bun book. I was eager to find out
where Baker Hans had got the delicious Rainbow Fizz. And all the
goldfish, for that matter.

Before I started to read, I made sure to start a game of solitaire,
so I had a kind of explanation as to why I was so quiet. I had
promised the nice baker in Dorf to keep the sticky-bun book a
secret between the two of us.

TEN OF SPADES

*. . . like distant islands I would
never reach under this boat's sail . . .*

As I wandered home from Baker Hans's that night, the taste of Rainbow Fizz lingered in my body. A sudden taste of cherry would warm the outer rim of my ear, or a touch of lavender would brush across my elbow. But then a bitter rhubarb flavour might also sharply bite into one of my knees.

The moon had gone down, but above the mountains there was a sparkling shower of fiery stars – as though they were being shaken from a magic salt cellar.

I thought I was a little human being on earth. But now – with the Rainbow Fizz still inside me – it wasn't something I just thought. I felt, through my entire body, as though this planet was my home.

Already I understood why Rainbow Fizz was a dangerous drink. It had awakened a thirst which could never be completely quenched. I already wanted more.

When I reached Waldemarstrasse, I saw Father. He came staggering out of the Schöner Waldemar. I went over to him and told him I'd been to visit the baker. He got so angry he boxed my ears.

When everything else was so good, this blow hurt me even more and I immediately began to cry. Then Father started to cry, too. He asked me if I could ever forgive him, but I didn't reply, I just followed him home.

The last thing Father said before he fell asleep was that Mother was an angel and brandy was the devil's curse. I think that was the last thing he *said* to me before the alcohol drowned him for good.

Early the next morning I stopped off at the bakery. Neither Baker Hans nor I said anything about the Rainbow Fizz. It didn't really belong down here in the village – it belonged to another world completely. But we both knew that we now shared a deep secret.

If he had asked me again if I could keep the secret, I would have been deeply offended. But the old baker knew he needn't ask.

Baker Hans went into the bakery behind the shop to make some pastry, so I sat on a stool and stared at the goldfish. I never got tired of looking at it. Not only did it have many beautiful colours, it swam back and forth inside the bowl and made small fidgety dives up and down in the water – driven by a peculiar inner desire. It had small living scales all over its body. It had black dots for eyes which never shut. Only its little mouth constantly opened and closed.

Every little animal is an individual, I thought to myself. This goldfish swimming round and round inside the glass bowl lives only this once, and one day when it comes to the end of its life, it will never return.

When I was about to go out into the street again – as I usually did after visiting Baker Hans in the morning – the old man turned to me and said, 'Are you coming this evening, Albert?'

I nodded without saying anything.

'I still haven't told you about the island ... and I don't know how many days I have left to live,' he added.

I turned and threw my arms round his neck.

'You're not allowed to die,' I cried. 'You'll never be allowed to die!'

'All old people must be allowed to die,' he replied. He held on tightly to my skinny shoulder. 'But it's good to know there is someone to carry on from where the old leave off.'

When I walked up to Baker Hans's cabin that night, he met me by the water pump.

'Now it is back in its place,' he said.

I knew he meant the Rainbow Fizz.

'Will I ever taste it again?' I had to ask.

The old man snorted and said, 'No, never!'

He was strict and authoritative now. But I knew he was right. I had understood that I would never taste the mysterious drink again.

'The bottle will now remain in the attic,' he continued. 'And it shan't be taken down again before more than half a century has passed. A young man will knock on your door – and then it will be his turn to taste the golden brew. In this way, what is left in the bottle will flow through many generations. And some day – some day the remarkable stream will flow right into the land of tomorrow. Do you understand, son? Or am I talking too much like an adult?'

I said that I understood, and we went inside the cabin with all the wonderful things from all the corners of the world. We sat by the fire, as we had done the night before. There were two glasses on the table and Baker Hans poured blueberry juice from an old decanter.

I was born in Lübeck one cold winter's night in January 1811 [he began]. It was in the middle of the Napoleonic Wars. Father was a baker like myself, but I decided at an early age to go to sea. The truth was, I had to. There were eight of us, and it wasn't easy to support us all with Father's little bakery. As soon as I turned sixteen – in 1827 – I signed on to a large sailing ship in Hamburg. It was a full-rigged ship from the Norwegian town of Arendal and it was called the *Maria*.

The *Maria* was my home and my life for more than fifteen years. But then – in the autumn of 1842 – we sailed from Rotterdam to New York with a general cargo. We had a skilled crew, but on this occasion both the compass and octant fooled us. I think we took too southerly a course when we left the English Channel. We must have sailed towards the Mexican Gulf. How this happened is still a mystery to me.

After seven or eight weeks in open water, by all accounts we should have been in port, but there was no land in sight. We may have been somewhere south of Bermuda. Then one morning a storm brewed. The wind grew stronger throughout the day, and soon there came a full-blown hurricane.

I don't remember exactly what happened, but the ship must have capsized from one of the hurricane's mighty blows. I have only a few broken memories from the shipwreck itself, everything happened so fast. I remember the ship turning over and taking in water, and I remember one of my mates being washed overboard and being lost in the sea. But that's all. The next thing I recall is waking up in a lifeboat. And now – now the sea was completely calm.

I still don't know how long I was unconscious. It could have been a few hours or many days. My reckoning of time begins again from when I woke up in the lifeboat. Since then I have found out that the ship went down without a trace of either the boat or the crew. I was the only one to survive.

The lifeboat had a small rig, and I found an old sailsheet under the floorboards at the front of the bow. I hoisted the sail and tried to navigate by the sun and the moon. I reckoned I must be somewhere on the east coast of America, and I tried to hold a westerly course.

I lay drifting about on the sea like this for more than a week, with nothing to eat but biscuits and water. I never saw so much as a ship's mast.

I particularly remember the last night. The stars glittered above me like distant islands I would never reach under this boat's sail. It was strange to think I was under the same sky as Mother and Father back home in Lübeck. Although we could see the same stars, we were so infinitely far apart from each other. Because stars don't gossip, Albert. They don't care how we live our lives on earth.

Mother and Father would soon hear the sad news that I had gone down with the *Maria*.

Early the next morning, as the sky above me cleared and the morning blushed forth across the horizon, I suddenly caught sight of a little dot in the distance. At first I thought the dot was a bit of dust in my eye, but although I rubbed my eye and cried, the dot stayed as immovable as before. I finally realised it must be an island.

I tried to steer the boat closer, but at the same time I felt it strain against a strong current pouring out from the little island I could hardly see. I loosened the sail, found a pair of solid oars, sat with my back to my destination, and put the oars into the rowlocks.

I rowed and rowed without stopping, but it seemed as though I didn't move an inch. The endless ocean in front of me would be my grave if I didn't reach the island. Almost a day had passed since I had drunk the last of the water ration. I struggled for hours, and the palms of my hands were soon bloody from the strokes of the oars, but the island was my last chance.

After I had rowed furiously for several laborious hours, I turned round and looked in the direction of the small dot. It had now grown into an island with clear contours, and I could see a lagoon with palm trees. But I still hadn't reached my goal; I still had a tough job ahead of me.

At last I was rewarded for my pains. Well into the day, I rowed into the lagoon and felt the soft nudge of the boat hitting shore.

I climbed out of the boat and pushed it up on the beach. After all the long days at sea, it was like a fairy tale to feel solid ground under my feet.

I ate the last ration of biscuits before I pulled the boat up between the palm trees. The first thing I thought about was whether the island had water.

Although I had saved myself by landing on a tropical island, I wasn't that optimistic. The island seemed so terribly small that I thought it must be uninhabited. From where I stood, I could see how it curved over. I could very nearly see over the top of it.

There weren't many trees, but from the crown of a palm tree I suddenly heard a bird singing more beautifully than any bird I had ever heard before. It probably sounded so exceptionally beautiful because it was the very first sign that, despite everything, there was life on the island. Having spent many years at sea, I was sure this was not a seabird.

I left the boat and followed a narrow path to get closer to the bird in the tree. The island seemed to grow, the deeper I moved into it. I realised there were more trees here, and I heard more birds singing further inland. At the same time – I think I must have made a mental note of it just then – I realised that many of the flowers and bushes were different from any I had seen before.

From the beach I had seen only seven or eight palm trees, but I now saw that the little path I was following continued between some tall rosebushes – and then twisted on towards a small group of palm trees up ahead.

I hurried towards those trees – now I would find out just how big the island was. As soon as the palm-tree crowns were above my head, I could see they formed the gateway to some dense woodland. I turned round. There lay the lagoon I had sailed into. To my left and right the Atlantic Ocean glittered like gold in the bright daylight.

I stopped thinking. I just had to see where this forest ended, and so I ran in between the trees. When I emerged on the other side, steep hillsides rose around me. I could no longer see the sea.

JACK OF SPADES

... like polished chestnuts ...

I had read as much of the sticky-bun book as my eyes could take before I started to see double. I hid it under my comic books in the back seat, and stared out across Lake Como.

I wondered what the connection could be between the magnifying glass and the little book the baker in Dorf had baked inside the sticky bun. It was a riddle in itself how anyone could possibly write anything so small.

When we drove into the town of Como at the end of Lake Como, it was already getting dark. This didn't necessarily mean it was late at night, because at this time of year it got dark in Italy earlier than it did at home in Norway. It got dark an hour earlier in the evening with each day we drove southwards.

As we drove around the lively town, the streetlights came on, and I suddenly caught sight of a fairground. For the first time since the beginning of our trip, I put all my energy into getting my way.

'We're going to that fairground over there,' I said at first.

'We'll see,' Dad replied. He'd started to look around for a suitable place to spend the night.

'Nope!' I said. 'We have to go to the fair.'

He finally agreed, on condition that we found a place to stay first. He also insisted on having a beer before he was willing to negotiate further. So there was no chance of *driving* to the fair afterwards.

Luckily, we found a hotel only a stone's throw away from the fair. Mini Hotel Baradello was its name.

'Olledarab Letoh Inim,' I said.

Dad asked me why I'd suddenly started to talk Arabic. I pointed to the hotel sign and he began to laugh.

After we'd carried our things up to the hotel room and Dad had drunk his beer in the lobby, we set off for the fair. On the way, Dad ran into a little shop and bought himself two miniature bottles of something strong to drink.

The fair was pretty good, but the only things I managed to get Dad to try were the House of Horrors and the Ferris wheel. I also went on a corny roller-coaster with loops.

From the top of the Ferris wheel we could look out over the whole town, and even far across Lake Como. Once when we reached the top, the wheel stopped and we were left rocking back and forth as new passengers came on. As we swayed between heaven and earth, I suddenly saw a little man standing on the ground below, looking up at us.

I jumped up out of my chair, pointed at the little man, and said, 'There he is again!'

'Who?'

'The dwarf ... the one who gave me the magnifying glass at the garage.'

'Don't be silly!' Dad said, but he looked down at the ground all the same.

'It's him!' I insisted. 'He's got exactly the same hat, and you can see quite clearly that he's a dwarf.'

'There are lots of dwarfs in Europe, Hans Thomas. There are lots of hats, too. Now sit down.'

I was absolutely positive it was the same dwarf, and it was quite obvious he was looking at us. When the gondola started to tip down towards the ground again, I watched him dash as quick as lightning behind some booths and disappear.

I was no longer interested in the things at the fair. Dad asked me if I wanted to drive a radio-controlled car, but I politely said no, thank you.

'I just want to have a look around,' I explained.

What I didn't say was that I was looking for the dwarf. Dad must have been a bit suspicious, because he was unusually eager to pack me off on merry-go-rounds and various fun rides.

A couple of times as we walked about the fair Dad turned his back to the crowd and had a swig from one of the two miniature bottles he'd bought. I think he'd rather have done this when I was inside the House of Horrors or something.

At the centre of the fairground was a five-sided tent. The word SIBYLLA was written on the tent, but I read the letters back to front.

'Allybis,' I said.

'What?'

'There!' I said, pointing.

'Sybilla,' said Dad. 'It means fortune-teller. Perhaps you want your fortune told?'

There was no doubt about it: I headed straight for the tent.

A beautiful girl about my age was sitting in front of the entrance. She had long black hair and dark eyes; she was probably a Gypsy. She was so beautiful to look at, I got butterflies in my stomach.

Unfortunately, the girl was more interested in Dad. She looked up at him and asked in very broken English, 'Will you see your future, sir? Only 5,000 lire.'

Dad unfolded some bills, pointed at me, and gave the girl the money. Just at that moment an old woman stuck her head out of the tent. She was the fortune-teller. I was a bit disappointed that the girl who took the money wasn't going to read my fortune.

I was then shoved into the tent. A red lamp hung from the canvas. The fortune-teller had sat down in front of a round table. On the table was a large crystal ball and a goldfish bowl with a little silvery fish inside. There was also a pack of cards.

The fortune-teller pointed towards a stool and I sat down. If I hadn't known Dad was standing outside with a miniature bottle in his hand, I would have felt very nervous.

'Do you speak English, my dear?' she asked at first.

'Of course,' I replied.

She now picked up the pack of cards and pulled out a card. It was the jack of spades, and she placed it on the table. Then she asked me to choose twenty cards. When I had done that, I was told to shuffle them. I did as she said, and then I was told to place the jack of spades in the middle of the pile. When that was done, the fortune-teller placed the twenty-one cards on the table, all the while staring straight into my eyes.

The cards were arranged in three rows, seven in each. She pointed to the top row and told me it represented the past, the middle showed the present, and the bottom row the future. In the middle row the jack of spades reappeared, and she now laid it beside a joker.

'Amazing,' she said softly. 'A very special spread.'

Not a lot happened for a while; I wondered whether the twenty-one cards were so special that she'd been hypnotised by them, but then she began to speak.

She pointed to the jack of spades in the middle row and looked at the surrounding cards.

'I see a growing boy,' she said. 'He is far away from home.'

So far I wasn't that impressed; you didn't have to be a Gypsy to know I wasn't from Como.

But then she said, 'Are you not happy, my dear?'

I didn't answer, and the woman looked down at the cards again.

She now pointed to the row which told of the past. The king of spades lay among a number of other spades.

'Many sorrows and obstacles in the past,' she said.

She picked up the king of spades and said it was Dad. He had had a bitter childhood, she continued. Then she said all sorts of things, of which I understood only about half. She frequently used the word 'grandfather'.

'But where is your mother, dear son?'

I said she was in Athens, but regretted it at once, because I'd helped her. She could very well be bluffing.

'She has been away for a very long time,' the fortune-teller continued. She pointed to the bottom row of cards. The ace of hearts lay to the far right, far away from the king of spades.

'I think this is your mother,' she said. 'She is a very attractive woman ... wearing beautiful clothes ... in a foreign country far away from the land in the north.'

She continued to tell my fortune like this, and I never understood more than about half of it. When she started to talk about the future, her dark eyes shone like polished chestnuts.

'I have never seen a spread like this,' she said once again.

She pointed to the joker, which lay beside the jack of spades, and said, 'Many great surprises. Many hidden things, my boy.'

Then she got up and nervously tossed her head. The last thing she said was 'And it is so close ...'

And with that the session was over. The fortune-teller followed me out of the tent, hurried straight over to Dad, and whispered some words of truth in his ear.

I ambled along behind her, and then she put her hand on my head and said, 'This is a very special boy, sir ... Many secrets. God knows what he will bring.'

I think Dad was about to laugh. Maybe it was to stop himself from bursting out laughing that he gave the woman yet another note.

Even when we'd moved well away from the tent, the fortune-teller was still standing there watching us.

'She read cards,' I said.

'Really? You asked for the joker, didn't you?'

'You're absolutely crazy,' I replied moodily. His question was like swearing in church. 'Who are the Gypsies around here – us or them?'

Dad laughed harshly. I could tell by his tone that both his bottles were empty.

When we got back to the hotel room, I got him to tell me a couple of old tales from the seven seas.

He had sailed for many years on oil tankers between the West Indies and Europe, and he had got to know the Gulf of Mexico and towns like Rotterdam, Hamburg, and Lübeck like the back of his hand. But the ships also made other voyages, taking Dad to ports in all corners of the world. We had already visited Hamburg; we'd trudged around the dock area there for half a day. Tomorrow we'd be in another town with a port Dad had visited as a young boy: Venice. And when we eventually reached Athens, he had plans to visit Piraeus.

Before we'd started out on our long journey, I'd asked him why we couldn't simply fly. Then we would have had more time to find Mama in Athens. But Dad said the whole point of the trip was to get Mama home, and it was easier to push her into the Fiat than drag her into a travel agency and buy a plane ticket for her.

I suspected he wasn't so sure he'd find her, and if he didn't, then he wasn't going to be cheated out of a proper holiday. If the truth be known, Dad had wanted to visit Athens ever since he was a boy. When he was in Piraeus, which is only a few kilometres from Athens, the captain hadn't allowed him to visit the ancient town. In my opinion, that captain should have been demoted to ship's boy.

Lots of people travel to Athens to study ancient temples. Dad wanted to visit Athens, first and foremost, because this was where the great philosophers had lived.

Mama running away from me and Dad was bad enough, but Dad thought it was like a slap in the face when she'd decided to travel to Athens as well. If she was going to try to find herself in a country which Dad also wanted to visit – then they might as well have gone there and worked it out together.

After Dad had told a couple of juicy stories from his life at sea, he fell asleep. I lay in bed thinking about the sticky-bun book and the strange baker in Dorf.

I regretted hiding the sticky-bun book in the car. Now I couldn't find out how Baker Hans had spent the night after the shipwreck.

Before I fell asleep, I thought about Ludwig and Albert and Baker Hans. They'd all had a tough time before becoming bakers in Dorf. What linked them together was the secret of the Rainbow Fizz and all the goldfish. Baker Hans had also mentioned something about a man called Frode, who'd had some strange playing cards . . .

Unless I was completely mistaken, it all had something to do with Baker Hans's shipwreck.

QUEEN OF SPADES

*... these butterflies made a
sound like birdsong ...*

D ad woke me unusually early the next morning. There can't have been so many drops in the small bottles he'd bought on his way to the fair, after all.

'We're going to Venice today,' he announced. 'We'll leave at sunrise.'

As I jumped out of bed, I remembered that I'd dreamed about the dwarf and the fortune-teller from the fair. In my dream, the dwarf had been a wax figure in the House of Horrors, but he had suddenly come alive because the dark-haired Gypsy lady had stared deeply into his eyes once when she and her daughter had been there, too. In the dead of night, the little man had crept out of the tunnel, and now he wanders around Europe in constant fear that someone will recognise him and send him back to the House of Horrors. If they did that, he would turn back into a lifeless wax figure.

Dad was ready to go before I'd managed to get the strange dream out of my head and put on my jeans. I was beginning to look forward to reaching Venice. We would see the Adriatic for the first time in our long journey. It was a sea I'd never seen before, and Dad hadn't seen it since he was a sailor. From Venice our journey would take us through Yugoslavia to Athens.

We went down to the dining room and ate the dried-up breakfast you get everywhere south of the Alps. We were in the car by seven o'clock, and just as we were setting off the sun peeped above the horizon.

'We're going to have that bright star in front of us all morning,' Dad said, putting on his sunglasses.

The route to Venice went through the famous Valley of the Po, which is one of the most fertile areas in the whole world. The reason for this, of course, is all the fresh Alpine water.

One moment we were driving past dense orange and lemon groves; the next moment we were surrounded by cypress, olive, and palm trees. In wetter areas we drove past wide rice fields lined with tall poplar trees. Red poppies grew everywhere along the roadside, and they were so brightly coloured that from time to time I had to rub my eyes.

Later that morning we reached the top of a hill and looked down over a plain so rich in colour that an unfortunate landscape painter would have had to use his entire paintbox to produce a truthful painting.

Dad parked the car, jumped out onto the roadside, and lit a cigarette while he gathered his thoughts for one of his typical mini-lectures.

'All this bursts through each spring, Hans Thomas. Tomatoes and lemons, artichokes and walnuts – tons of greenery. How do you think this black earth pumps it all out?'

He stood gazing at the work of creation.

'What impresses me most,' he continued, 'is that everything comes from one single cell. Several million years ago a little seed appeared which split in two, and as time passed, this little seed changed into elephants and apple trees, raspberries and orangu-tans. Do you follow me, Hans Thomas?'

I shook my head, so he carried on. It was a comprehensive lecture about the origin of different plant and animal species, and in conclusion he pointed to a butterfly which had taken off from a blue flower and explained that this butterfly was able to live in peace, here in the Po Valley, because the dots on its wings looked like the eyes of a wild animal.

On the rare occasion Dad stood deep in thought during a cig-arette stop instead of overloading his defenceless son with his philosophical lectures, I would take out the magnifying glass from my jeans pocket and make biological investigations. I also used the magnifying glass when I sat in the back seat and read the sticky-bun book. I felt that nature and the sticky-bun book were equally rich in secrets.

For many miles Dad remained deep in thought behind the steering wheel. I knew that at any moment he might come out with some important truth about the planet we lived on, or about Mama, who'd suddenly left us. But nothing was more important now than reading the sticky-bun book.

I was relieved that I had managed to land on something more than just a meagre reef in the sea. But there was more: the island seemed to contain an unfathomable secret. It appeared to grow in size the further I moved into it – as though it unfolded in every direction with each step I took. It widened out on all sides as though something was pouring out from its inner depths.

I followed the path further into the island, but it soon split in two and I had to choose which path to follow. I hurried along the path to the left; then that also divided in two. I went on, always heading left.

The path slipped into a deep crevasse between two mountains, and here some enormous turtles crawled among the craters; the biggest turtles were over two metres long. I had heard about turtles

this big, but I had never seen any myself. One of them stretched its
head out from under its shell and peeped up at me as though it
wanted to welcome me to the island.

I continued my wandering all day. I saw new woods, valleys, and
mountain plateaus, but never again did I see the sea. It was as
though I'd entered a magical land, a reversed labyrinth where the
paths never came to an end.

Late in the afternoon I came to an open area with a large lake
sparkling freshly in the afternoon sun. I immediately threw myself
onto the bank of the lake and drank away my thirst. It was the first
time for many weeks I had drunk anything other than ship's water.

It had been a long time since I'd washed myself, too. I tore off my
tight sailor's uniform and dived in. The water was refreshing after I'd
walked about all day in the sweltering tropical heat, and only now
did I realise how sunburnt my head was after I had sat unprotected in
the lifeboat.

I dived deeply a few times, and when I opened my eyes under the
water, I saw a multitude of goldfish in all the colours of the rainbow.
Some were as green as the plants by the edge of the lake, some were
as blue as gemstones, others had a glorious shine of red, yellow, and
orange. At the same time they each had a touch of every colour
imaginable.

I crawled onto land again and lay in the evening sun to dry. I felt a
hunger chase through my body, and I noticed a thicket laden with
clusters of yellow berries the size of strawberries. I had never seen any
berries like them, but I guessed they were edible. They tasted like a
cross between a nut and a banana. When I was full, I put on my
clothes and finally fell asleep, exhausted, on the shore of the large
lake.

I woke with a start early the next morning, before the sun had come
up. It was as though a solid ray of consciousness shot through my
body.

I've survived the shipwreck! I thought to myself. This really
dawned on me only now, and I felt reborn.

A rugged mountain landscape rose to the left of the lake. It was covered with yellow grass and some red, bell-shaped flowers which swayed gently in the cool morning breeze.

Before the sun had appeared in the sky, I was on top of a mountain ridge. I couldn't see the sea from here either . . . I gazed across a vast country, a continent. I had been in both North and South America before, but I couldn't be on either of these continents now. There wasn't a trace of human existence anywhere.

I stood on the mountaintop until the sun began to rise in the east. Red as a tomato, but shimmering like a mirage, it rose over a plain in the distance. Because the horizon was so low, the sun was bigger and redder than I'd ever seen it before – yes, even at sea.

Was it the same sun as the one shining on Mother and Father's house at home in Lübeck?

I continued to roam all morning from one landscape to the next. At around midday, when the sun stood high in the sky, I found myself in a valley filled with yellow rosebushes. Enormous butterflies flew among the bushes. The largest had wingspans the size of a crow's, but they were infinitely more beautiful. They were all deep blue, but on their wings they had two large blood-red stars – I thought they looked like flowers in flight. It was as though some of the island's flowers had suddenly broken free from the ground and learned to fly. However, the strangest thing was that these butterflies made a sound like birdsong. They whistled a gentle flute melody, only with a slightly different pitch. Soft haunting flute music floated through the valley – as though all the flautists in a large orchestra were tuning their instruments before a concert. Now and then they struck me with their soft wings; it was like being brushed with velvet. They gave off a scent which was heavy and sweet, like an expensive perfume.

A torrential river ran through the valley. I decided to follow the river so as not to roam aimlessly around the big island. This way I was sure to reach the sea sooner or later, or so I thought. It wasn't that simple, as I discovered later in the afternoon when the great wide valley came to an end. At first it narrowed like a funnel; finally it hit a massive rock face.

I couldn't understood it. How could a river turn and flow back on itself? When I got down into the gorge, I could see that the river continued through a mountain tunnel. I walked up to the entrance and peered inside. The water flattened out and created an underground canal.

In front of the entrance to the mountain some large frogs were jumping around the water's edge. They were the size of rabbits. When they all croaked at the same time, they made a terrible racket. That nature could produce such enormous frogs was totally new to me.

Some fat anole lizards crept through the wet grass, and some even bigger geckos. Although I had never seen them quite so big, I was used to seeing these kinds of creatures, having been in so many ports all over the world. But I had never seen so many different colours. The reptiles on this island were red, yellow, and blue.

I discovered it was possible to walk along the edge of the canal inside the tunnel. All I had to do was creep inside and see how far I could get.

There was a soft blue-green light inside the mountain. The water hardly moved. I saw some scores of goldfish twitching in the crystal-clear water here, too.

After a while, I heard a faint rumbling sound further along the tunnel. As I moved forward, the sound gradually grew louder and louder, like the thunder of kettledrums. I was nearing an underground waterfall. I'm going to have to turn round after all, I thought to myself. But before I reached the edge of the waterfall, a bright light filled the place.

I looked up and saw a tiny opening in the rock wall. I scrambled up to it. The view was so blindingly beautiful that my eyes began to water.

I only just managed to wriggle out through the hole. I stood up, and before me lay a valley so green and fertile that I no longer missed the sea.

As I made my way down the hillside, I came across all kinds of different fruit trees. Some of them bore apples and oranges and other familiar fruits. But there were also fruits and berries in this valley that I had never seen before. The biggest trees bore long, plumlike fruits. Some of the slightly smaller trees bore green fruits the size of tomatoes.

The ground was carpeted with different flowers, each kind more fantastic than the previous one. There were bellflowers, cowslips, and crown flowers. Small rosebushes grew all over the place, with tight garlands of purple-coloured dwarf roses. Bees buzzed around these bushes. They were almost as big as the sparrows in Germany. Their wings shone like glass in the bright afternoon sun, and I could smell the strong aroma of honey.

I continued a little way down the valley. That's when I saw the moluks . . .

Both the bees and the butterflies had made me look twice, but although they were much larger and more beautiful than their relations back home in Germany, they *were* bees and butterflies. It was the same with the frogs and reptiles. But now – now I saw some large white animals which were so different from anything I'd seen or heard about, I had to rub my eyes.

There was a flock of about twelve to fifteen of them. They were the size of horses and cows, but their heads were much smaller and more pointed, they had thick white hides which resembled pigskin – and they all had six legs. Now and then they stretched their heads towards the sky and said 'Brash, brash!'

I wasn't scared. The six-legged animals looked as dopey and kind as the cows in Germany. But their presence made it clear that I wasn't in a country drawn on any map. It was as spooky as meeting a person without a face.

Naturally, it took much longer to read the tiny letters in the sticky-bun book than to read normal letters. Every little letter had to be singled out from the multitude and combined with the others. By the time I'd read about the six-legged animals on the magic island, it was already late in the afternoon, and now Dad turned off the wide *autostrada*.

'We'll have a meal in Verona,' he said.

'Anorev,' I replied. I had read the sign.

As we drove towards the town, Dad told me the terribly sad story of Romeo and Juliet, who couldn't be together because their two families were always at war with each other. The young couple – who had to pay with their lives for their forbidden love – had lived in Verona many hundreds of years ago.

'It sounds a bit like Grandma and Grandpa,' I said, and Dad laughed heartily. He'd never thought of that before.

We ate antipasto and pizza at a big outdoor restaurant. Before driving on, we walked around the streets, and Dad bought a pack of cards with fifty-two half-naked women on them from a souvenir shop. Needless to say, he picked out the joker pretty quickly, but this time he kept the whole pack of cards.

I think he was a little embarrassed, because the ladies in the pack were even more flimsily dressed than he'd imagined. At any rate, he quickly put the cards in his breast pocket.

'It is really quite amazing that there are so many women,' he said, more to himself than to me. Since he had to say something.

Of course, it was a dumb comment, seeing as half the world's population are women. What he probably meant was that there were a lot of *naked* women, since they're not quite as common.

If that was what he meant, I totally agreed. I thought it was a bit much to group fifty-two models in one pack of cards. Whatever the reason, it was a bad idea, because you can't play cards with a pack made up only of women. True enough, the king of spades, the four of clubs, and so on were printed in the upper left-hand corner, but if you were going to play with cards like these, you'd probably sit staring at the ladies rather than concentrating on the game.

The only man in the pack was the joker. On this occasion, it was a Greek or Roman statue with a billygoat's horn. He was naked as well, but then so are all old statues.

When we were back inside the Fiat, I kept thinking about the strange cards.

'Have you ever thought that you could find yourself a new wife, instead of spending half your life trying to find the one who hasn't found herself?' I asked.

At first he laughed out loud, but then he replied, 'I agree that it is a bit of a mystery. There are five billion people living on this planet. But you fall in love with one particular person, and you won't swap her for any other.'

No more was said about that pack of cards. Although there were fifty-two different women doing everything they could to look their best, I realised that Dad thought the pack was missing one important card. It was that card we were going to find in Athens.

KING OF SPADES

... *close encounter of the*
fourth kind ...

When we eventually arrived in Venice, towards evening, we had to leave the car in a large carpark before we were allowed to enter the town itself, because Venice doesn't have a single proper street. On the other hand, it has 180 canals, more than 450 bridges, and thousands of motorboats and gondolas.

From the carpark we took the waterbus to the hotel, which was beside the Grand Canal, the biggest canal in Venice. Dad had booked a room from the hotel in Como.

We dumped our luggage in the smallest and ugliest hotel room we'd stayed in during the whole trip, and went out and strolled along the canals and over some of the numerous bridges.

We were to stay in this city of canals for two nights before continuing our journey, and I knew that there was a strong chance Dad would revel in the city's selection of alcoholic drinks.

After eating dinner in Piazza San Marco, I persuaded Dad to pay for a little trip in a gondola. Dad pointed to where he wanted to go on a map, and the gondolier splashed off. The only thing that wasn't as I expected was that he didn't sing a note. It didn't bother me, though, because I'd always thought singing gondoliers sounded like cats meowing.

Something happened as we splashed along which Dad and I have never agreed on. Just as we were about to go under a bridge, a familiar face peeped over the top of the railing above us. I was positive it was the little man from the garage, and this time I disliked the surprise meeting. I realised we were actually being followed.

'The dwarf!' I exclaimed, jumping up in the boat and pointing at him.

Today I can understand why Dad got angry, because the whole gondola very nearly capsized.

'Sit down!' Dad ordered. But when we had passed under the bridge, he turned around and looked, too. Only now the dwarf was long gone – just like at the fair in Como.

'It was him, I saw him,' I said, and then I started to cry. I'd had a scare when the gondola almost tipped over. Moreover, I was sure Dad didn't believe me.

'You're just imagining it, Hans Thomas,' he said.

'But it *was* a dwarf!'

'It could well have been, but it wasn't the same one,' he protested, even though he hadn't caught so much as a glimpse of him.

'So you think all Europe is full of dwarfs?'

That question must have hit the nail on the head, because Dad now sat in the gondola smiling smugly.

'Possibly,' he said. 'We're all strange dwarfs, really. We are mysterious small people who suddenly jump out from bridges in Venice.'

The gondolier, whose expression hadn't changed, dropped us off at a place where there were lots of little restaurants. Dad bought me an ice cream and a fizzy drink, and ordered a coffee and something called Vecchia Romagna for himself. When the coffee arrived, I wasn't surprised to discover that it was served with a brown drink in an elegant glass that looked like a goldfish bowl.

After two or three of these glasses, Dad looked me straight in the eyes, as though he'd decided to tell me his darkest secret.

'You haven't forgotten our garden at home on Hisøy Island?' he began.

I couldn't be bothered to answer such a dumb question, and he didn't expect an answer either.

'Okay,' he continued, 'now listen very carefully, Hans Thomas. Let us imagine you're out in the garden one morning – and you discover a little Martian between the apple trees. We'll say he's a little shorter than you, but whether he's yellow and green I'll leave to your imagination.'

I nodded dutifully. There was no point in protesting about the choice of topic.

'The stranger stands and stares at you – as you do at people from another planet,' Dad went on. 'The question is, how would *you* react?'

I was about to say I would invite him for an earth breakfast, but then I replied truthfully that I would probably be so terrified I'd scream.

Dad nodded; he was clearly pleased with my answer. At the same time I could see he had more on his mind.

'Don't you think you'd also wonder who the little chap was and where he came from?'

'Of course,' I said.

He tossed his head and appeared to assess all the people in the square.

'Has it never struck you that you are a Martian yourself?' he asked.

I'd expected to hear something along these lines, but all the same I had to grab hold of the table to stop myself from falling off the chair I was sitting on.

'Or earth-dweller, if you like,' he continued. 'It doesn't matter at all what we call the planet we live on. The point is that you are also a two-legged human being crawling around on a planet in the universe.'

'Just like that Martian,' I added.

Dad nodded. 'Although you may not stumble across a Martian in the garden, you might stumble across yourself. The day that happens, you'll probably also scream a little. And that'll be perfectly all right, because it's not every day you realise you're a living planet dweller on a little island in the universe.'

I understood what he meant, but it wasn't easy to add anything to the conversation. The last thing he said about Martians was 'Do you remember we saw a film called *Close Encounters?*'

I nodded. It was a crazy film about some people who discovered a flying saucer from another planet.

'To see a spaceship from another planet is called a close encounter of the first kind. If you also *see* the two-legged beings come out of the spaceship, that's called a close encounter of the second kind. But one year after we saw *Close Encounters*, we saw another film ... '

'And that was called *Close Encounters of the Third Kind,*' I said.

'Exactly. That was because they touched those strange humanoids from another solar system. It is this direct contact with the unknown which is called close encounters of the third kind. Okay?'

'Okay.'

He sat for a while, looking across the square with all the cafés.

'But you know, Hans Thomas, you've experienced a close encounter of the *fourth* kind.'

I must have looked like a living question mark.

'Because you *are* one of those space beings yourself,' Dad said emphatically. He put his coffee cup down on the table with such a loud clatter we were both amazed it didn't break. 'You *are* this mysterious creation, and feel it inside.'

'You should have been given government funding as a philosopher' was all I said, and these words came straight from my heart.

When we got back to the hotel that evening, we found a huge cockroach on the floor. It was so big its shell crackled as it walked.

'Sorry, pal, but you can't sleep here tonight,' Dad said as he bent down. 'We booked a double room, and there's only room for the two of us. More to the point, we're the ones paying the bill.'

I thought he'd gone crazy, but then he glanced up at me and said, 'This is too fat for us just to kill it, Hans Thomas. It's so big it has to be called an individual, and you never beat individuals to death, even if you do feel a little uncomfortable in their presence.'

'Are we just going to let it paddle around the floor while we sleep, then?'

'Nope! We'll escort it out.'

And he did just that. Dad started to herd the cockroach out of the hotel room. He lined up the suitcases and bags to create a long passage across the floor. Then he began to tickle the cockroach's behind with a match to get it moving. After about half an hour it was in the corridor outside the little hotel room. At that point Dad felt he'd done enough, so he didn't follow the uninvited guest down to the lobby.

'And now we'll turn in for the night,' he said as he closed the door behind him. The moment he lay down on his bed he fell fast asleep.

I left the bedside light on and continued to read from the sticky-bun book as soon as I was sure Dad had stamped his passport at the border to dreamland.

CLUBS

ACE OF CLUBS

... exactly the same figures
you'd find on playing cards ...

had been walking through the lush garden all afternoon when I suddenly saw two human figures in the distance. My heart jumped for joy.

I was saved. Maybe I had arrived in America after all.

As I walked over to them, it suddenly occurred to me that we would probably not be able to understand each other. I spoke only German, some English, and a little Norwegian, which I'd picked up after being on board the *Maria* for four years, but the inhabitants of the island undoubtedly spoke a completely different language.

As I gradually drew nearer, I could see they were bent over a small, tilled patch of ground. At this point I also realised that they were much shorter than I. Were they children?

When I came closer, I saw that they were gathering some bright roots in a basket. They suddenly turned round and looked up at me. Slightly on the chubby side, the two men were no taller than my chest. They both had brown hair and greasy, nut-brown skin. They were dressed in identical dark-blue uniforms. The only difference was that one of them had three black buttons on the sleeve of his uniform and the other had only two.

'Good afternoon,' I said in English.

The little men put down the tools they'd been holding and stared at me with blank expressions.

'Do you speak English?' I asked.

They just threw their arms into the air and shook their heads.

Instinctively I spoke to them in my own language. And now the man with three buttons on his uniform replied in fluent German. 'If you have more than three marks, you're allowed to beat us, but we earnestly beg you not to.'

I was so taken aback, I was at a loss for words. At the heart of a deserted island in the Atlantic Ocean I was spoken to in my own mother tongue. But that was only part of it. I didn't understand what he meant by the three marks.

'I come in peace,' I said for safety's sake.

'So you should, too, otherwise the King will punish you.'

The King! So I wasn't in North America after all.

'I would very much like to have a word with the King,' I said.

Now the one with two buttons joined in the conversation. 'Which King do you want to have a word with?'

'Didn't your friend say the King would punish me?'

The two-buttoned man turned to the three-buttoned man and whispered, 'It's as I thought. He doesn't know the rules.'

The three-buttoned man looked up at me.

'There's more than just one King,' he said.

'Oh really? How many are there?'

The two men sneered. They clearly thought I'd asked some pretty stupid questions.

'There's one for each suit.' The two-buttoned man sighed in despair.

It was only now that I really noticed how small they were. They were no bigger than dwarfs, yet their pint-size bodies had quite normal proportions. At the same time, I wondered whether these Lilliputian people were mentally retarded.

I was about to ask how many 'suits' there were, to find out how many Kings there were on the island, but I decided to skip that question.

'What's the name of the most powerful King?' I asked instead.

They looked at each other again and shook their heads.

'Do you think he's trying to trick us?' the one with two buttons asked.

'Don't know,' said the one with three, 'but we have to answer.'

The two-buttoned man brushed away a fly that had landed on his greasy cheek and said, 'As a rule, a black King is allowed to beat a red King, but it is also possible for a red King to hit the black.'

'That's rather brutal,' I said.

'Those are the rules.'

We suddenly heard a loud crash in the distance. It sounded as if some glass was being broken. Both dwarfs turned in the direction of the noise.

'Idiots!' exclaimed the man with two buttons. 'They break more than half of what they make.'

While they stood for a moment with their backs to me, I made a disturbing discovery: two black clubs were drawn on the back of the one with two buttons on his jacket. The other had three clubs. They were exactly the same figures you'd find on playing cards. This suddenly made the conversation I'd become entangled in slightly less absurd.

When they turned around again, I decided to try a totally new tack.

'Are there many people living on this island?' I enquired.

But they looked at each other with puzzled expressions now, too.

'He asks a lot of questions,' one of them said.

'Yes, he's rude,' said the other.

I thought this conversation was worse than if we hadn't understood each other's language at all, because although I understood every single word they said, I couldn't grasp what they *meant*. It would almost have been better if we'd used sign language.

'How many are you?' I tried again, and now I was getting impatient.

'You can see for yourself that we are Two and Three,' replied the one with the three of clubs on his back. 'If you need glasses, you'd better talk to Frode, because he's the only one who knows how to cut glass.'

'How many are *you*, by the way?' asked the other one.

'There's only one of me,' I said.

The one with two buttons on his jacket turned to the one with three and whistled loudly.

'Ace!' he said.

'Then we've lost,' replied the other, dumbfounded. 'He'll beat the King, too.'

With that he took out a miniature-sized bottle from his inside pocket. He took a swig of a sparkling drink and passed the bottle to his companion, who also drank thirstily from the bottle.

'But isn't Ace a lady?' exclaimed the one with three buttons.

'Not necessarily,' said the other. 'The Queen is the only one who is always a lady. He might be from another pack.'

'Nonsense! There aren't any other packs. And Ace is a lady.'

'Maybe you're right. But he needed only four buttons to beat us.'

'Us, yes, but not our King, you know that. So he *has* fooled us!'

They continued to drink from the little bottle, and their eyes grew heavier and heavier. Then, without warning, the two-buttoned man's body started to twitch all over. He looked me straight in the eyes and said, '*The goldfish does not reveal the island's secret, but the sticky bun does.*'

With that they both lay down on the ground, mumbling, 'Rhubarb ... mango ... kurberry ... dates ... lemon ... honya ... shuka ... coconut ... banana ...'

They continued to say the names of all sorts of fruits and berries, I had heard only a few of the names before. Finally they rolled onto their backs – and fell asleep instantly.

I tried to kick them awake, but they didn't stir.

Once again I was left alone. It occurred to me that the island might be a sanctuary for the incurably mentally ill and the substance which the two men drank from the bottle was a kind of sedative. If this was the case, then a doctor or a nurse would soon be along to accuse me of upsetting the patients.

I started to walk back across the field. A dumpy man soon came toward me. He was dressed in the same dark blue uniform, except that he had a double-breasted jacket with a total of ten buttons. He had the same greasy brown skin.

'*When the master sleeps, the dwarfs live their own lives,*' he exclaimed, waving his arms about and glancing at me shiftily.

He's mad, too, I thought to myself.

I pointed to the two men who were lying asleep a little way off. 'It looks as though the dwarfs have fallen asleep, too,' I said.

With that he hurried on his way. Although he ran as fast as his short legs could carry him, he didn't get very far very fast. He fell down several times and got up again, got up and fell down. I had plenty of time to count the ten clubs on his back.

I soon came to a narrow cart track. I had not followed it very far before I witnessed a terrible uproar. At first I heard a thundering sound right behind me. It sounded like horses' hooves getting closer and closer. I turned around quickly and jumped to the side.

The six-legged animals I had seen earlier that day were coming towards me. Riders were sitting on two of them. A dwarf ran behind them swinging a long stick in the air. All three men wore the same dark blue uniforms. I noticed they had double-breasted jackets with four, six, and eight black buttons respectively.

'Stop!' I cried, as they charged past me on the path.

Only the one on foot, the man with eight buttons, turned round and slowed his pace a little.

'*After fifty-two years the shipwrecked grandson comes to the village,*' he shouted in a frenzy.

With that, the dwarfs and the six-legged animals were gone. I noticed that the dwarfs had the same number of clubs on their backs as they had buttons on their double-breasted jackets.

Tall palm trees with tight clusters of yellow fruit the size of oranges grew along the roadside. Under one of the trees was a cart half-filled with the yellow fruit. It was a bit like the cart that Father used to transport his bread at home in Lübeck, but it was not a normal horse hitched to the front of the cart underneath the palm tree. Here, one of the six-legged animals was used as a workhorse.

Only when I walked round to the front of the cart did I discover a dwarf sitting under the tree. Before he spotted me, I noticed his jacket had a simple fastening with five buttons. Otherwise it was identical to the other uniforms. All the dwarfs I had seen so far had one other thing in common: their round heads were covered with thick brown hair.

'Good afternoon, Five of Clubs!' I said.

He glanced up at me with a look of indifference. 'Good after –'

He stopped in mid-sentence and sat staring up at me without saying a word.

'Turn round,' he said eventually.

I did as he asked. When I turned back to face him, he was sitting scratching his head with a pair of chubby fingers.

'Trouble!' he sighed, and waved his arms in the air.

The next minute two fruits were thrown down from the tall palm tree. One of them landed in the Five of Clubs's lap; the other narrowly missed my head.

I wasn't surprised to see the Seven and Nine of Clubs come climbing down from the tree a few seconds later. I had now met the whole lot of them, from Two to Ten.

'We tried to knock him out with the shuka fruit,' said the Seven.

'But he jumped aside just as we threw it,' said the Nine.

They sat down under the tree, beside the Five.

'Okay, okay,' I said. 'I'll forgive you all, but first you'll have to answer some simple questions. If not, I'll wring all your necks. Is that understood?'

I managed to scare them enough to keep them sitting in silence under the tree. I looked into their dark brown eyes in turn.

'Right – who are you?'

With that they stood up one after the other and each recited a crazy sentence:

'*The baker conceals the treasures from the magic island,*' said the Five.

'*The truth lies in the cards,*' said the Seven.

'*Only a lonesome joker sees through the delusion,*' concluded the Nine.

I shook my head.

'I thank you for this information,' I said. 'But who are you?'

'Clubs,' replied the Five at once. He'd obviously taken the threat seriously.

'Yes, that is clear. But where do you come from? Did you all just fall from the sky – or did you sprout from the ground like clover leaves?'

They quickly glanced at one another. Then the Nine of Clubs said, 'We come from the village.'

'Oh really? And how many of these ... um ... field workers like you live there?'

'None,' said the Seven of Clubs. 'I mean, just us. Nobody is identical to us.'

'I see, you can't really expect that either. But all in all – how many fieldworkers live on this island?'

They quickly looked at each other again.

'Come on!' said the Nine of Clubs. 'Let's beat it!'

'But are we allowed to beat him?' asked the Seven of Clubs.

'I said, let's *beat it*, not beat him!'

With that they threw themselves into the cart. One of them whacked the white animal on the back, and it now ran off as fast as its six legs could carry it.

I had never felt so powerless. Of course I could have stopped them. I could undoubtedly have wrung their necks as well. But none of it would have made me any the wiser.

TWO OF CLUBS

... He waved two tickets
in the air ...

T he first thing I thought about when I woke up in the little hotel room in Venice was Baker Hans, who'd met the strange dwarfs on the magic island. I fished the magnifying glass and the sticky-bun book out of my jeans.

As soon as I had turned on the light, however, and was about to start reading, Dad let out a lion's roar and was awake as fast as he usually fell asleep.

'The whole day in Venice.' He yawned. The next minute he was out of bed.

I had to smuggle the sticky-bun book back into my pocket under the blanket. I had promised the old baker in Dorf that everything in it would remain a secret between him and me.

'Are you playing hide-and-seek?' Dad asked.

'I'm looking to see if there are any cockroaches here,' I answered.

'And you need a magnifying glass for that ?'

'They might have babies,' I replied. Of course, it was a dumb answer, but I couldn't think of anything better in time. To be safe I added, 'You never know, there might be some dwarf cockroaches living here.'

'You never know,' said Dad, and disappeared into the bathroom.

The hotel we were staying at was so basic it didn't even serve breakfast. This suited us just fine, because the night before we'd already discovered a cosy outdoor café which served breakfast between 8 and 11 a.m.

It was pretty quiet outside, both on the Grand Canal and along the wide pavements banking the canal. At the restaurant we ordered juice and scrambled eggs, toast and orange marmalade. On our trip, this breakfast was the only exception to the rule that it is best to eat breakfast at home.

It was during this meal that Dad got another of his bright ideas. At first he stared into space, and I suddenly thought the dwarf had reappeared.

'Now you stay here, Hans Thomas. I'll be back in five minutes,' he said.

I didn't have a clue what he was up to, but I'd been in similar situations before. When Dad got an idea, almost nothing could stop him.

He disappeared through a big glass door on the other side of the square. When he returned, he sat down and ate the rest of his scrambled eggs without saying a word.

Then he pointed to the shop he'd just been in and asked, 'What's written on that poster over there, Hans Thomas ?'

'Sartap-Anocna,' I read backwards.

'Ancona-Patras, yes.'

He dipped a piece of toast in his coffee before putting it into his mouth. It was amazing that he managed to get it in, since the whole of his mouth was one big grin.

'And what about it ?' I asked. Both words were Greek to me, whether I read them one way or the other.

He now looked straight into my eyes. 'You've never been to sea with me, Hans Thomas. You've never been on a proper sailing trip.'

He waved two tickets in the air and continued : 'It's not right for an old seaman to *drive* around the Adriatic. And I'll be damned if we're going to be landlubbers any longer. Now we roll the Fiat on board a huge boat – then we sail to Patras on the west coast of the Peloponnese. It's just a few miles from there to Athens.'

'Are you sure ?'

'Damn right, I'm sure,' he said.

It was probably because he'd soon be back at sea that he was swearing so freely.

So we didn't end up spending a whole day in Venice after all. The boat to Greece sailed that evening from Ancona, which was almost 250 miles away.

The only thing Dad insisted on taking in before he got behind the wheel was a study of Venice's famous art of glassblowing.

To melt the glass you need open space for the fires. As a precaution against fire hazards, the Venetians had moved the town's glass manufacture onto a small island in the lagoon. This was in the Middle Ages. The island is called Murano.

Dad insisted we go via this place to the carpark before starting our trip. We just had to collect our luggage from the hotel.

On Murano we started by visiting a museum which had glass in all sorts of colours and designs from hundreds of years ago. Afterwards we were able to see a glass workshop where they blew pitchers and glass bowls right in front of our eyes. What they made was then put on sale, but Dad said we'd leave the business side of the visit to the rich Americans.

From the glassblowers' island we took a waterbus back to the carpark, and by one o'clock we were again on the *autostrada* heading for Ancona, 250 miles south of Venice.

The road followed the Adriatic coast all the way, and Dad sat whistling and enjoying himself all the more now that he had constant eye contact with the wet element.

Our route took us over a ridge of hills with an excellent view of the sea. Dad stopped the car and started to comment on the sailing boats and merchant ships we could see.

In the car he told me a lot I didn't know about Arendal's history as a shipping town. Off the top of his head, he mentioned the dates and the names of the large sailing ships. I learned the difference between schooners, brigs, barques, and full-rigged ships. He told me about the first ships to sail from Arendal to America and the Gulf of Mexico. I also found out that the first steamship to visit Norway came to Arendal. It was a specially adapted sailing ship which was fitted with a steam engine and a paddle. It was called the *Savannah*.

As for Dad, he'd been on board a tanker, built in Hamburg and owned by Kuhlnes Shipping Company in Bergen. The ship weighed over 8,000 tons and had a crew of forty.

'The tankers are much bigger today,' he said. 'But the crews have been reduced to eight or ten men. Everything is run by machines and technology. So life at sea has become a memory, Hans Thomas – I mean *the life* itself. In the next century there'll be some idiots sitting with remote controls steering everything from land.'

If I understood him correctly, life at sea was something which had gradually faded away from as early as the end of the sailing ship era, 150 years ago.

While Dad talked about life at sea, I took out a pack of cards. I plucked out all the clubs from two to ten and spread them out next to me on the car seat.

Why did all the dwarfs on the magic island have clubs drawn on their backs? Who were they – and where did they come from? Would Baker Hans find someone he could talk to properly about the country he'd come to? My head buzzed with unanswered questions.

And the Two of Clubs had said something that was hard to

forget : *'The goldfish does not reveal the island's secret, but the sticky-bun does.'* Could it be the baker's goldfish in Dorf he'd babbled about ? And the bun – could it be the same sticky-bun that I'd got in Dorf ? The Five of Clubs had said, 'The baker conceals the treasures from the magic island.' But how could the dwarfs whom Baker Hans had met in the middle of the previous century know anything about this ?

Dad sat for a good twenty miles whistling shanties he'd learned as a sailor. Then I sneaked the sticky-bun book out again and read on.

THREE OF CLUBS

... a bit of a threesome ...

I continued in the direction in which the three fieldworkers had fled. The cart track twisted its way between some tall, leafy trees. The bright afternoon sunshine seemed to turn the leaves on the trees into living sparks.

In a clearing in the woods I came across a large wooden house. Black smoke rose from two chimneys. From a distance I saw a figure dressed in pink slip into the house.

It soon became clear that the wooden house was missing one whole wall, and I could look in at something which took me so much by surprise, I had to lean against a tree to keep my balance. On a large floor without any dividing walls was a kind of factory. It wasn't long before I understood this had to be a glassblowers' workshop.

The roof was held up by thick beams. There were some big white stone tubs over three or four massive wood-burning ovens. A red-hot glowing liquid bubbled in the tubs, giving off a greasy steam. Three female figures, the same size as the fieldworkers but dressed in pink, ran between the tubs. They dipped some long tubes into the substance in the tubs and blew glass into all sorts of designs. At one end of the large floor there was a heap of sand, and at the other end finished glassware was stacked on shelves along the wall. In the middle of the floor was a metre-high pile of broken glass bottles, glasses, and bowls.

Once again I had to ask myself where I was. If I ignored their uniforms, the fieldworkers could just as easily have lived in a Stone Age society. Yet now the island appeared to have a refined glass industry.

The women running the glassworks were dressed in dark pink dresses. They had almost white complexions and all three had long, straight, silver-coloured hair.

I quickly noticed, to my horror, that all the dresses had diamond symbols on the front. They were exactly the same diamond symbols you find on playing cards. One of them had three diamonds, another had seven, and the third had nine. The diamonds were silver-coloured.

The three women were so busy blowing glass that it took a long time before they noticed me, even though I was standing right in front of the large opening. They skipped back and forth across the big floor and moved their arms so lightly and gently they seemed almost weightless. I wouldn't have been any more surprised if one of them had started to float up to the ceiling.

Suddenly the one with seven diamonds on her dress saw me. I was about to run away, but when she looked up she got so confused she dropped a glass bowl onto the floor. When it smashed it was too late to escape, because now they were all looking at me.

I went in, bowed politely, and said hello in German. Then they glanced at each other and smiled so widely their white teeth shone in the light from the glowing ovens. I walked towards them, and they gathered round me.

'I hope it's all right if I pay a little visit,' I said.

They looked at each other again and smiled even wider. They all had deep blue eyes. They were so alike they must have been from the same family. Perhaps they were sisters.

'Do you understand what I'm saying?'

'We understand all normal words!' said the Three of Diamonds in a little, doll-like voice.

They all started to talk at the same time, and two of them curtsied. The Nine of Diamonds even came over to me and held my hand. I was surprised that her delicate hand was so icy, because here inside the glass workshop it was anything but cold.

'What lovely glass you blow,' I said, and then they bubbled with laughter.

These girl glassblowers were perhaps friendlier than the hot-headed fieldworkers, but they were just as unapproachable.

'But who has taught you the art of glassblowing?' I asked. I took it for granted they hadn't taught themselves.

Nobody answered me now either, but the Seven of Diamonds immediately went and fetched a glass bowl which she presented to me.

'There you are!' she said.

And the girls began to laugh again.

Amid all this friendliness, it wasn't so easy to carry out my real mission. If I didn't find out the meaning of all these strange little people soon, I'd go out of my mind.

'I have just arrived on the island,' I began again, 'but I have no idea where in the world I am. Can you tell me something about this place?'

'We can't talk –' said the Seven of Diamonds.

'Does somebody forbid you to?'

All three of them shook their heads, so their silver hair fluttered in the light from the ovens.

'We are good at blowing glass,' said the Nine of Diamonds. 'But we're not good at thinking. That's why we're not too good at talking either.'

'You're a bit of a threesome,' I said, which made the three girls burst out laughing again.

'We're not all *three*,' said the Seven of Diamonds. She started to play with her dress and added, 'Can't you see we're all different numbers?'

'Idiots!' It slipped out of me, and they cowered together.

'Please don't get angry,' said the Three of Diamonds. 'We get sad and unhappy very easily.'

I wasn't sure whether I believed her. She smiled so convincingly that I thought it would take a lot more than a little anger to break that smile, but I took note of the warning.

'Are you really as scatterbrained as you say?' I asked.

They nodded formally.

'I would really like –' began the Nine of Diamonds, but then she put her hand over her mouth without saying any more.

'Yes?' I asked in a friendly voice.

'I would really like to think a thought which is so difficult I can't think it, but I can't.'

I pondered over what she had said and realised that *that* must be difficult for anyone to master.

Suddenly the Three of Diamonds started to cry.

'I wou . . .' she sobbed.

The Nine put her arm around her, and the Three continued. 'I would really like to wake up . . . but I *am* awake.'

She expressed my thoughts exactly.

The Seven of Diamonds gazed up at me with a distant look in her eyes. Then she said very seriously, '*The truth is that the master glass-blower's son has made fun of his own fantasies.*'

It wasn't long before all three of them were standing on the floor sniffling. One of them grabbed a big glass pitcher and smashed it on the floor on purpose. Another started to pull her silver-coloured hair. I realised my visit was over.

'Please excuse me for disturbing you,' I said quickly. 'Goodbye!'

I was now absolutely positive I'd come to a sanctuary for mentally disturbed people. I was also convinced that at any time some nurses dressed in white would show up and take me to task for walking round the island causing anxiety and unrest among the patients.

All the same, there were some things I didn't understand. The first was the size of the island's inhabitants. As a sailor I had travelled to many lands, and I knew there was no country in the whole world where the people were so small. The fieldworkers and the girl glass-blowers also had hair of different colours, so they couldn't be that closely related.

Was it possible that at some time a worldwide epidemic had broken out, making people both smaller and more stupid – and those who were struck down in this way were placed on this island so as not to infect others? If this was so, then I would soon be just as small and stupid myself.

The second thing I didn't understand was the categorisation of diamonds and clubs as in a pack of cards. Was this how the doctors and nurses organised their patients?

I continued along the cart track, which now passed between some tall trees. The forest floor had a light green carpet of moss. Blue flowers, which reminded me of forget-me-nots, grew everywhere. The sun slipped in only through the very tops of the trees. The branches lay like a golden canopy above the landscape.

After I'd been there a while, a bright figure appeared between the tree trunks. It was a thin young woman with long fair hair. She was wearing a yellow dress and wasn't much taller than the other dwarfs on the island. Now and then, she bent down and picked a blue flower. Then I saw that she had a big blood-red heart on her back.

As I gradually moved closer, I heard her humming a sorrowful melody.

'Hello!' I whispered when I was a few yards away from her.

'Hello!' she said, and stood up. She said it as naturally as if we had met each other before.

I thought she was so pretty I didn't quite know where to look.

'You sing beautifully,' I finally managed to say.

'Thank you . . .'

I unconsciously ran my fingers through my hair. For the first time since I'd arrived on the island, I thought about my appearance. I hadn't shaved for more than a week.

'I think I am lost,' she now said.

She tossed her little head and looked quite bewildered.

'What's your name?' I asked.

She stood for a moment, smiling knowingly. 'Can't you see I'm the Ace of Hearts?'

'Yes, of course . . .' I paused a moment before I continued. 'And that's what I find rather remarkable.'

'Why?'

She bent down and picked another flower. 'Who are you, by the way?'

'My name's Hans.'

She stood thinking. 'Do you think it's stranger to be the Ace of Hearts than to be Hans?'

This time I was at a loss for an answer.

'Hans?' she went on. 'I think I have heard something like that before. Or maybe it's something I've just imagined . . . It is so terribly far away . . .'

She bent down and picked another blue flower. Then it was as though she had a kind of epileptic fit. Quivering at the mouth she said, '*The inner box unpacks the outer box at the same time as the outer box unpacks the inner.*'

It was as though she wasn't really saying this meaningless sentence. I got the impression the words just tumbled out of her, without her understanding what she said. As soon as she had said the sentence, she was herself again, and now she pointed to my sailor's uniform.

'But you're completely blank,' she said, alarmed.

'You mean I don't have anything drawn on my back?'

She nodded. Then she tossed her head sharply. 'You do know you're not allowed to hit me?'

'I would never hit a lady,' I replied.

Two big dimples appeared in her cheeks. I thought she was angelically beautiful, like a fairy. When she smiled, her green eyes shone like emeralds, and I couldn't take my eyes off her.

At once a worried expression clouded her face. 'You're not a trump, are you?' she blurted out.

'Oh no, I'm just an able-bodied seaman.'

With that, she slipped away behind a tree trunk and was gone. I tried to follow her, but it was as though she'd disappeared into thin air.

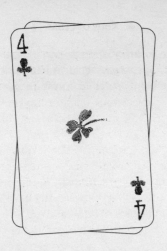

FOUR OF CLUBS

*. . . one huge lottery where
only the winning tickets are visible . . .*

I put the sticky-bun book down and stared out across the Adriatic Sea.

What I had just read raised so many questions I didn't quite know where to begin.

The dwarfs on the magic island seemed more and more mysterious the more I read about them. Baker Hans had now met the club dwarfs and the diamond dwarfs. He'd also met the Ace of Hearts but she'd suddenly disappeared.

Who were all these dwarfs? How had they come to be – and where did they come from?

I was sure the sticky-bun book would eventually answer all my questions. But there was something else: the diamond dwarfs had been blowing glass in a glass workshop. This was even more bizarre, considering I had just visited a glass workshop myself.

I was pretty sure there must be some kind of relationship

between my own journey through Europe and what was in the sticky-bun book. But what I read in the sticky-bun book was something Baker Hans had told Albert many many years ago. Could there be a mysterious relationship between my life on earth and the big secret which Baker Hans, Albert, and Ludwig had shared?

Who was the old baker I met in Dorf? Who was the little man who gave me the magnifying glass – and, moreover, who kept popping up on our journey through Europe? I was convinced there must be a connection between the baker and the dwarf – even if they weren't aware of it themselves.

I couldn't tell Dad about the sticky-bun book – or at least not until I had finished reading it. Nevertheless, it was good to have a philosopher in the car.

We had just passed Ravenna when I asked, 'Do you believe in coincidences, Dad?'

He looked at me in the mirror. 'Do I *believe* in coincidences?'

'Yeah!'

'But a coincidence is something which happens totally coincidentally. When I won ten thousand crowns in the lottery, my ticket was pulled out of thousands of other tickets. Of course I was happy with the result, but it was sheer luck that I won.'

'Are you sure about that? Have you forgotten we found a four-leaf clover that morning? And if you hadn't won the money, we might not have been able to afford the trip to Athens.'

He just grunted, but I continued. 'Was it just as coincidental that your aunt travelled to Crete and suddenly discovered Mama in the fashion magazine? Or was that *intended?*'

'You're asking me whether I believe in fate,' he said. I think he was pleased his son was interested in philosophical questions. 'The answer is no.'

I thought about the girl glassblowers – and the fact that I had visited a glass workshop just before I read about the glass workshop in the sticky-bun book. Moreover, I thought about the dwarf who'd given me a magnifying glass just before I got a book with tiny writing, and about what happened when Grandma's bike got a flat tyre at Froland – and everything that followed.

'I don't think you can call it a coincidence that I was born,' I said.

'Cigarette stop!' Dad announced. I must have said something which made one of his mini-lectures shoot out from the filing cabinet.

He parked on a hill with a splendid view over the Adriatic.

'Sit down!' he ordered when we were out of the car, and pointed to a large stone.

'Thirteen forty-nine,' was the first thing he said.

'The Black Death,' I replied. I had a pretty good knowledge of history, but I had no idea what the Black Death had to do with coincidences.

'Okay,' he said, and off he went. 'You probably know that half Norway's population was wiped out during the great plague. But there's a connection here I haven't told you about.'

When he began like this, I knew it was going to be a long lecture.

'Did you know that you had thousands of ancestors at that time?' he continued.

I shook my head in despair. How could that possibly be?

'You have two parents, four grandparents, eight great-grandparents, sixteen great-great-grandparents – and so on. If you work it out, right back to 1349 – there are quite a lot.'

I nodded.

'Then came the bubonic plague. Death spread from neighbourhood to neighbourhood, and the children were hit worst. Whole families died, sometimes one or two family members survived. A lot of your ancestors were children at this time, Hans Thomas. But none of *them* kicked the bucket.'

'How can you be so sure about that?' I asked in amazement.

He took a drag on his cigarette and said, 'Because you're sitting here looking out over the Adriatic.'

Once again he had made such an astounding point I didn't

really know how to respond. But I knew he was right, because if just one of my ancestors had died as a child, then he wouldn't have been my ancestor.

'The chances of one single ancestor of yours not dying while growing up is one in several billion,' he went on, and now the words flowed out of him like a waterfall. 'Because it isn't just about the Black Death, you know. Actually *all* your ancestors have grown up and had children – even during the worst natural disasters, even when the child mortality rate was enormous. Of course, a lot of them have suffered from illness, but they've always pulled through. In a way, you have been a millimetre from death billions of times, Hans Thomas. Your life on this planet has been threatened by insects, wild animals, meteorites, lightning, sickness, war, floods, fires, poisoning, and attempted murders. In the battle of Stiklestad alone you were injured hundreds of times. Because you must have had ancestors on both sides – yes, really you were fighting against yourself and your chances of being born a thousand years later. You know, the same goes for the last world war. If Grandpa had been shot by good Norwegians during the occupation, then neither you nor I would have been born. The point is, this has happened billions of times through history. Each time an arrow has rained through the air, *your* chances of being born have been reduced to the minimum. But here you are, sitting talking to me, Hans Thomas! Do you see?'

'I think so,' I said. At least I think I understood how important it was that Grandma got a flat tyre at Froland.

'I am talking about one long chain of coincidences,' Dad continued. 'In fact, that chain goes right back to the first living cell, which divided in two, and from there gave birth to everything growing and sprouting on this planet today. The chance of *my* chain not being broken at one time or another during three or four billion years is so little it is almost inconceivable. But I have pulled through, you know. Damn right, I have. In return, I appreciate how fantastically lucky I am to be able to experience this planet together with you. I realise how lucky every single little crawling insect on this planet is.'

'What about the unlucky ones?' I asked at this point.

'They don't *exist!*' he almost roared. 'They were never born. Life is one huge lottery where only the winning tickets are visible.'

He sat for a long time looking out across the sea.

'Should we get going?' I asked after a couple of minutes.

'Nope! Now just sit still, Hans Thomas, because there's more.'

He said it as though it were not really him speaking. Maybe he saw himself as a radio receiver simply catching the radiowaves coming to the set. That's probably what people call inspiration.

While he waited for the inspiration, I fished out the magnifying glass from my jeans pocket and put it over a red bug which was scurrying back and forth on a rock. Under the magnifying glass it turned into a monster.

'It's the same with all coincidences,' Dad piped up again. I stopped playing with the magnifying glass and looked up at him. When he sat for a while gathering his thoughts like this before he began to talk, I knew something important was on its way.

'Let's take a simple example: I think about a friend just before he calls me on the telephone or arrives on the doorstep. Many people think a coincidence like this is due to something supernatural. But I think about this friend even if he doesn't ring the doorbell. Moreover, he calls me quite often, without me having thought about him at all. *Comprendo?*'

I nodded.

'The thing is, people collect those instances when both things happen at the same time. If they find some money just when they need it badly, they believe it is due to something "supernatural". They do that even when they constantly go around broke. In this way, a mass of wild rumours begins to buzz about various "supernatural" experiences which aunts and uncles all over the world have had. People are so interested in this sort of thing, there are soon a lot of stories. But only the winning tickets are visible here, too. It's not that strange that I have a drawerful of jokers when *I collect* them!'

He let out a sigh of exhaustion.

'Have you ever tried sending in an application?' I asked at this point.

'What on earth are you babbling about?' he barked.

'To be a government philosopher.'

He laughed out loud, but then he said in a slightly more subdued tone, 'When people are interested in the "supernatural", they suffer from a remarkable blindness. They don't see the most mysterious thing of all – that the world exists. They are more interested in Martians and flying saucers than in the whole of this puzzling creation which is unfolding at our feet. I don't think *the world* is a coincidence, Hans Thomas.'

He finally leaned over me and whispered, 'I think the whole universe is intended. You'll see there is some kind of purpose or other behind all the myriads of stars and galaxies.'

I thought this was yet another informative cigarette stop, but I still wasn't convinced that everything to do with the sticky-bun book was coincidental. Perhaps it *was* just coincidence that Dad and I had been on Murano just before I read about the diamond dwarfs. It might also be sheer coincidence that a magnifying glass was put in my hand just before I received a sticky-bun book with microscopic writing. But the fact that *I* was the one to get the sticky-bun book – that was something which must be intentional.

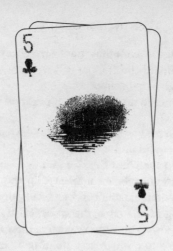

FIVE OF CLUBS

*... it had already become
a bit difficult to play cards ...*

When we arrived in Ancona that evening, Dad was so quiet he almost scared me. While we sat in the car and waited to drive on board, he just stared at the ship without saying a word.

It was a big yellow ship called the *Mediterranean Sea*.

The trip to Greece took two nights and one day. The boat sailed at nine o'clock in the evening. After the first night, we had the whole of Sunday at sea, and provided we weren't taken by pirates we would have our feet on Greek soil by eight o'clock on Monday morning.

Dad had found a brochure about the boat, and now he said, 'It is 18,000 tons, Hans Thomas. So it isn't a washtub. It does 17 knots and has room for over one thousand passengers and three hundred cars. There are various shops, restaurants, bars, sun-decks, discotheques, and casinos. And there's even more. Did you know this ship has a swimming pool on deck? Not that that means anything, that's not the point; I just wondered whether you knew. And one other thing: are you terribly upset that you didn't get the chance to drive through Yugoslavia?'

'Swimming pool on deck?' was my only comment.

I think both Dad and I understood there was nothing more to be said. All the same, he added, 'I had to book a cabin, you know. And I had to decide between a cabin inside the boat or a proper cabin on the outside of the boat with extensive windows and views of the sea. Which do you think I picked?'

I knew he'd picked the one on the outside – and I knew he understood that I knew this. That's why I just said, 'What was the difference in price?'

'Some lire, yes. But I don't coax my son to sea with me just to lock him up in a broom closet.'

He didn't get the chance to say any more, because we were now being waved on board the boat.

As soon as we had parked, we found the way to the cabin. It was on the second from top deck and was beautifully furnished with huge beds, curtains and lamps, lounge chairs and tables. People walked back and forth on the gangway outside the window.

Although the cabin had wide windows and was rather grand in itself, we agreed – without so much as a word being spoken – to go out for a bit. Before we left the cabin, Dad fished out a little hip flask and poured himself a drink.

'To your good health!' he said, even though I had nothing to drink a toast with or was aware of any problem with my health.

I knew he must be pretty exhausted after having driven all the way from Venice. Maybe, too, he had itchy feet, because he was stretching his sea legs on board a large boat after so many years on land. I was also happier than I had been for a long time. Nevertheless – or maybe that's exactly why – I commented on his bottle management.

'Do you *have* to drink every single evening?'

'Yes, I do' he said, and burped, and no more was said. But he had his thoughts, and I had mine. So it was better to come back to this matter later.

By the time the ship's bell rang for departure, we knew our way around the boat. I was a little disappointed to find the swimming pool closed, but Dad asked about it right away and found out it would be open early the next morning.

We went up onto the sundeck and stood leaning over the handrail until we could no longer see land.

'Right,' said Dad. 'We are now *at sea*, Hans Thomas.'

Following this well-thought-out remark, we went down to the restaurant for dinner. After we had eaten, we agreed to play a game of canasta in the bar before going to bed. Dad had a pack of cards in his inside pocket. Luckily it wasn't the one with all the ladies.

The boat was crawling with people from all corners of the world. Dad said many of them were Greeks.

I was dealt the two of spades and the ten of diamonds. When I picked up the ten, I already had two other diamonds in my hand.

'Girl glassblowers!' I exclaimed.

Dad opened his eyes wide. 'What did you say, Hans Thomas?'

'Nothing . . .'

'Didn't you say "girl glassblowers"?'

'Well, yes!' I now replied. 'I was talking about those women at the bar. They're sitting holding their drinks as though that's the only thing they've done all their lives.'

I thought I was pretty clever to get myself out of that one. But it had already become a bit difficult to play cards. It was almost like playing with the cards Dad had bought in Verona. When I placed the five of clubs on the table, I could only think of the little fieldworker whom Baker Hans had met on the strange island. When a diamond was put on the table, I saw before me some graceful female figures with pink dresses and silver hair. And when Dad threw down the ace of hearts on the table and carried away the six and the eight of spades in a sneaky trick, I shouted, 'There she is!'

Dad shook his head and said that it was time to hit the sack. He had just one important mission to accomplish before we left the bar. We weren't the only ones playing cards there. On the way out, he went round to some of the tables, bumming a few jokers. Actually, I thought it was a bit cowardly that he always did this when he was leaving a place.

It had been a long time since Dad and I had played cards. We did it much more when I was younger, but after a while Dad's passion for jokers had killed the old joy of playing. Otherwise, he was an expert when it came to card tricks. But his greatest feat was that he had once played a game of solitaire which took many days to win. To get pleasure from a game of solitaire like that, not only do you have to be patient, you also have to have a great deal of time.

When we got back to the cabin, we stood for a while looking out over the sea. We *saw* nothing, because it was pitch black, but we knew the blackness we were looking out on was the sea.

When a group of whining Americans passed the window on the walkway outside, we drew the curtains and Dad lay down on the bed. He'd obviously had enough sleeping draught – he dropped off instantly.

I lay on my bed, feeling the rocking of the boat on the sea. After a while I took out the magnifying glass and the sticky-bun book and read more about all the amazing things Baker Hans had told Albert, whose mother had died on her sickbed.

SIX OF CLUBS

*... as though he had to make sure
I was a real human being made of
flesh and blood ...*

I continued through the woods. It wasn't long before I reached a clearing. Wooden houses lay huddled together at the foot of a flower-covered hillside. A road, which was crawling with tiny people no bigger than those I had already met, wound its way between the houses. Further up the hill sat a small house all by itself.

There were probably no local officials here whom I could turn to, but I had to try to find out where on earth I was.

One of the first houses in the village was a tiny bakery. Just as I passed it, a fair-haired lady appeared in the doorway. She was wearing a red dress with three blood-red hearts on the chest.

'Freshly baked bread!' she said, blushing and smiling warmly.

The smell of fresh bread was so irresistible I went straight into the little bakery. I hadn't tasted bread for more than a week, and here pastries and loaves of bread were piled high on a wide counter along one of the walls.

A trail of smoke from a baker's oven seeped in from a cramped back room, and now another lady dressed in red entered the little shop. She had five hearts on her chest.

Clubs work in the fields and look after the animals, I thought to myself. Diamonds blow glass. Aces go around in beautiful dresses picking flowers and berries. And the hearts – they bake bread. Now I only needed to find out what the spades did; then I would have some sort of overview of the whole solitaire game.

I pointed to one of the loaves of bread. 'Can I have a taste?' I asked.

The Five of Hearts leaned over a simple counter made of wooden logs. On it was a glass bowl with a solitary goldfish inside. She looked me straight in the eyes.

'I don't think I've spoken to you for a few days,' she said with a puzzled expression.

'That's right,' I replied. 'I've just fallen from the moon. I've never been particularly good at talking. It's really because I find it difficult to think, and when you're not able to think, then there's not much point in talking either.'

I had already learned from experience that it did not help to speak clearly with these dwarfs. Maybe I would get along better if I expressed myself as incomprehensibly as they did.

'Did you say from the moon?'

'Yes, from the moon.'

'Then you must surely need a piece of bread,' said the Five of Hearts laconically – as though to fall from the moon was as plausible as to stand in front of a counter baking bread.

So it was as I thought. As long as I followed my notes, it wasn't so difficult to be on the same wavelength as these little people.

But then – in a sudden attack of intensity – she leaned over the counter and whispered excitedly, '*The future lies in the cards.*'

The next minute she was herself again, and she broke off a big piece of bread and stuck it in my hand. I put it straight in my mouth and went out onto the narrow street. The bread tasted slightly more sour than what I was used to, but it was good to chew on and filled me up just as well as other bread.

Out on the street I saw that all the dwarfs had small hearts, clubs, diamonds, or spades on their backs. They were dressed in four different costumes or uniforms. The hearts were in red, the clubs in blue, the diamonds in pink, and the spades in black.

Some were a bit taller than others. These were dressed as Kings, Queens, and Jacks. Both the Kings and the Queens had crowns on their heads; the Jacks carried a sword in a belt around their waists.

As far as I could see, there was only *one* of each kind. I saw only one King of Hearts, one Six of Clubs, and one Eight of Spades. There were no children here – and no old people either. All these tiny people were adult dwarfs in the prime of life.

After a while, the dwarfs noticed me, but then they quickly turned away, as though it didn't concern them that there was a stranger visiting the village.

Only the Six of Clubs – who'd been riding one of the six-legged animals earlier that day – came up to me in the street and rattled off one of the meaningless sentences the dwarfs were constantly coming out with: '*Sun princess finds her way to the ocean,*' he said. The next minute he'd turned the corner of the street and was gone.

I started to feel dizzy. I had obviously come to a society with an ingenious caste system. It was as though the people on this island had no lawbook to follow, only a pack of cards.

As I walked round the miniature village, I got the uncomfortable feeling of having ended up between two cards in a game of solitaire which just went on and on, without ever being completed.

The houses were low wooden cabins. Oil lamps made of glass hung outside, and I recognised these from the glass workshop. They weren't lit, and although the shadows had begun to grow long, the village continued to be bathed in the golden evening sun.

Numerous glass bowls with goldfish inside stood on benches and cornices. I also saw bottles of varying sizes everywhere. Some lay littering the streets between the houses, and one or two of the dwarfs walked around with a pocket-sized bottle in their hand.

One of the houses was much bigger than the others; it looked more like a warehouse. I could hear loud bangs coming from inside, and when I peeped through an open door I saw a carpentry workshop. There were four or five dwarfs bustling about, busily putting together a large table. They all had uniforms similar to the field-workers' blue ones, the only difference being that these uniforms were completely black – and they had symbols of spades on their backs, whereas the field workers had clubs. With that, the puzzle was solved: spades worked as carpenters. Their hair was as black as coal, but their skin was much paler than that of the clubs.

The Jack of Diamonds was sitting on a little bench in front of one of the cabins, studying the reflection of the evening sun in his sword. He was wearing a long pink jacket and a pair of wide-legged green trousers.

I went over to him and bowed respectfully.

'Good evening, Jack of Diamonds,' I said, attempting to sound cheerful. 'Can you tell me which King is in power at the moment?'

The Jack stuck his sword back in its sheath and stared at me with a glazed look in his eyes.

'The King of Spades,' he said shortly. 'Because tomorrow it is Joker. But it's not allowed to discuss the cards.'

'That's a shame, because I really need to ask you to show me where the island's highest official is.'

'Sdrac eht ssucsid ot dewolla ton si ti,' he said.

'What did you say?'

'Sdrac eht ssucsid ot dewolla ton si ti,' he repeated.

'I see. And that means?'

'Selur eht wollof tsum uoy taht!'

'Really?'

'Ees uoy!'

'You don't say?'

I looked at his little face closely. He had the same shiny hair and pale skin as the diamonds at the glass workshop.

'You'll have to excuse me, but I don't know that language,' I said. 'Is it by any chance Dutch?'

The little Jack now looked up at me smugly.

'Only Kings, Queens, and Jacks know the art of speaking both ways. Seeing as you don't understand this, you are below me.'

I thought it over. Did the Jack mean he'd been talking backwards?

'Ees uoy' . . . That was 'you see.' Then twice he had said, 'Sdrac eht ssucsid ot de wolla ton si ti.' If I began from the very end, it was 'It is not allowed to discuss the cards.'

'It is not allowed to discuss the cards.' I said.

He was on his guard now.

'Neht uoy od yhw?' he asked hesitantly.

'Uoy tset ot!' I replied confidently.

Now he looked like the one who had just fallen from the moon.

'I asked if you knew which King was in power at the moment, just to see if you could stop yourself from answering,' I continued. 'But you couldn't manage that, so you broke the rules.'

'That is the most impudent thing I have ever heard,' he declared.

'Oh yes, and I can certainly be a lot more impudent.'

'Taht si woh dna?'

'My father's name is Otto,' I replied. 'Can you say that name the other way round?'

He looked at me.

'Otto,' he said.

'That's right. Can you say it the other way round as well?'

'Otto,' he said again.

'Yes, I can hear that,' I continued, 'but can you say it the *other* way?'

'Otto, Otto!' snarled the Jack.

'It was a good try anyway,' I said to calm him down. 'Shall we try something else?'

'Neht no emoc!' replied the Jack.

'Pull up.'

'Pull up,' said the Jack.

I just waved my hand and said, 'And now say the same thing backwards.'

'Pull up, pull up!' said the Jack.

'Thank you, that's enough. Can you translate a whole sentence as well?'

'Esruoc fo!'

'Then I want you to say, "Red rum sir is murder," I said.

'Red rum sir is murder!' said the Jack at once.

'Yes, right, and now the other way.'

'Red rum sir is murder!' he said again.

I shook my head. 'You're just mimicking me. That's probably because you can't say it the other way round.'

'Red rum sir is murder! Red rum sir is murder!' he shouted again.

I felt a bit sorry for him, but I wasn't the one who had started the tricks.

Now the little Jack pulled his sword out of its sheath and took a swing at a bottle, sending it crashing against a cabin wall. Some hearts who were passing by stopped and stared, but then quickly turned away.

Again I thought the island had to be an asylum for the incurably mentally ill. But why were they so small? Why did they speak German? And above all – why were they divided into suits and numbers like a pack of cards?

I decided not to let the Jack of Diamonds out of my sight until I got some kind of explanation for what everything meant. I just had to be careful not to express myself too clearly, because the one thing these dwarfs had difficulty understanding was clear speech.

'I've just landed here,' I said. 'But I thought the country was as uninhabited as the moon. Now I'd really like to know who you all are and where you come from.'

The Jack took a step back and said defeatedly, 'Are you a new Joker?'

'I didn't know Germany had a colony in the Atlantic Ocean,' I continued. 'Although I've been in many lands, I'm afraid I have to admit this is the first time I have seen people so small.'

'You *are* a new Joker. Bother! As long as no more show up. It can't possibly be necessary for each suit to have its own Joker.'

'Don't say that! If the Jokers are the only ones who know the art of holding a proper conversation, then this game of solitaire would be solved much more quickly if everyone were a Joker.'

He tried to shoo me away with his hands.

'It is terribly strenuous to have to relate yourself to all sorts of possible questions,' he said.

I knew this would be difficult, so I tried again. 'You see, you're all shuffling around on an amazing island in the Atlantic Ocean. Wouldn't it be reasonable, therefore, if you had an explanation for how you'd all got here?' I asked.

'Pass!'

'What did you say?'

'You've upset the game, you hear. I am passing!'

Now he took out a little bottle from his jacket pocket and gulped down the same sparkling liquid as the clubs had drunk. When he had put the cork back in the bottle, he stretched out one of his arms and said loudly and masterfully, as though he were reading the beginning of a poem, '*Silver brig drowns in foaming sea.*'

I shook my head and sighed in despair. He'd probably fall asleep soon. Then I'd have to try to find the King of Spades on my own. At the same time, I sensed I wouldn't get much further with him.

Then I suddenly remembered something one of the dwarfs had said.

'I'll have to go and see if I can find Frode . . .' I muttered to myself.

With that the Jack of Diamonds suddenly sprang to life. He jumped up off the bench he'd been sitting on and raised his right arm to stiff attention.

'Did you say Frode?'

I nodded. 'Can you lead me to him?'

'Esruoc fo!'

We set off between the houses and soon came to a little market square with a big well in the middle. The Eight and Nine of Hearts were busy pulling a bucket of water up from the well. Their blood-red dresses stood out brightly in the square.

All four Kings were now standing in front of the well in a ring, with their arms over each other's shoulders. Perhaps they were deliberating over an important command. I remember thinking it must be impractical to have four Kings. They had the same colour clothing as the Jacks, they were just grander, and each of them had his own splendid gold crown.

The four Queens were also on the square. They flitted back and forth between the houses, constantly taking out a little mirror, which they looked into. It appeared as though they forgot who they were and what they looked like so quickly and so often that they had to keep checking their mirrors. The Queens were also wearing crowns, but they were slightly taller and narrower than the Kings' crowns.

Over on the far side of the square I spotted an old man with white hair and a long white beard. He was sitting on a large stone, smoking a pipe. What made the old man even more interesting was his size – he was as big as me. However, there was something else which distinguished him from the dwarfs. The old man was wearing a grey cloth shirt and a pair of wide-legged brown trousers. His clothes had a poor, homemade quality about them, which contrasted sharply with the colourful uniforms of the dwarfs.

The Jack walked straight over and presented me to him.

'Master,' he said, 'a new Joker has arrived.'

He was unable to say more than that before he sank into a heap on the square and fell asleep. Undoubtedly it was because he had drunk from the little bottle.

The old man jumped up from the stone he was sitting on and looked me up and down without saying a word. Then he started to touch me. He ran his hand over my cheek, carefully pulled my hair, and felt the material of my sailor's uniform. It was as though he had to make sure I was a real human being made of flesh and blood.

'This is . . . the worst thing I have seen,' he said in the end.

'Frode, I presume,' I said, and shook his hand.

He squeezed my hand tightly and for a long time. Then he suddenly seemed to be in a hurry, as though he had remembered something unpleasant.

'We must leave the village immediately,' he said.

I thought he seemed as confused as all the others. However, his response was not as uninterested. It was enough to give me at least some hope.

The old man hurried out of the village, though his legs were so weak that he almost fell over a couple of times.

Again I saw the log cabin completely alone above the village on a hill in the distance. We were soon standing in front of it but we didn't go inside. The old man offered me a seat on a little bench.

Just as I sat down, the head of a strange figure appeared from round a corner of the cabin. It was a funny character in a violet suit, wearing a red-and-green hat with donkey ears. Small bells, which jingled crazily every time he moved, were attached to his hat and his violet suit.

He ran right up to me. First he pinched my ear; then he gave me a little pat on my stomach.

'Go down to the village, Joker!' ordered the old man.

'Now, now!' chided the little fellow with a roguish smile. 'One eventually gets a visitor from the homeland, and then it pleases the master to disown old friends. Dangerous conduct,' said the Joker. 'Mark my words.'

The old one sighed in despair.

'Don't you have quite a bit to think about for the big party?' he asked.

The frisky figure did a couple of athletic donkey kicks with his little body. 'It cannot be denied, that's true. One mustn't take anything for granted.'

He bounced back a couple of paces.

'Well, we won't say any more for now,' he said. 'But I'll see you soon!'

With that he disappeared down the hill to the village.

The old man sat beside me. From the bench we could watch all the colourful little people moving around between the brown wooden cabins.

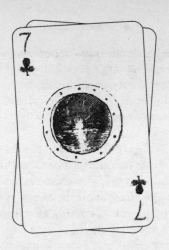

SEVEN OF CLUBS

*... that enamel and ivory
grew in my mouth ...*

I read the sticky-bun book late into the night. When I awoke early the next morning, I shot up in bed. The light was still on above the bedside table. I realized I must have fallen asleep with the magnifying glass and the book in my hands.

I was relieved to see that Dad was still asleep. The magnifying glass lay on my pillow, but I couldn't find the sticky-bun book. I eventually discovered it under the bed and hurriedly hid it in my pocket.

Having removed all the evidence, I climbed out of bed.

Everything I had read before I fell asleep was so disturbing I felt nervous and restless.

I parted the curtains and stood between them and the window. There was water as far as the eye could see. I didn't see any other ships, apart from a few small fishing boats. It was just before sunrise, and dawn lay in a thin glowing strip between the sea and sky.

How could the mystery of all the dwarfs on the magic island make sense? Of course, I couldn't be sure that what I read was true, but everything I had read about Ludwig and Albert in Dorf had seemed so real.

The Rainbow Fizz and all the goldfish had definitely come from the island Baker Hans had landed on ... and I had seen a goldfish in a bowl with my own eyes in the little bakery in Dorf. I hadn't tasted any Rainbow Fizz, but the old baker who gave me a fizzy drink that tasted of pears had said something about a drink which was much better ...

Of course, everything could be made up. I had no exact proof that there was any such thing as Rainbow Fizz, because everything written in the sticky-bun book could be pure fantasy. It wasn't that strange that the baker in Dorf brightened up his window with a goldfish either ... but it couldn't be denied that it *was* a bit strange that he baked a little book inside a sticky bun which he put in a bag and gave to a random traveller. Whatever the case, it was quite an achievement to write a whole book with such tiny lettering; and another thing – which I couldn't get out of my head either – was that, just before this, I had been given a magnifying glass by a mysterious dwarf.

Yet this morning it was not these technical details that bothered me the most. My mind was in turmoil for a totally different reason. I had suddenly realised people living on earth were just as oblivious to things as all the drowsy dwarfs on the magic island.

Our lives are part of a unique adventure, I thought to myself. Nevertheless, most of us think the world is 'normal' and are constantly hunting for something abnormal – like angels or Martians. But that is just because we don't realise the world is a mystery. As for myself, I felt completely different. I saw the world as an amazing dream. I was hunting for some kind of explanation of how everything fitted together.

While I watched the sky grow redder and redder and then lighter and lighter, I felt something all over my body which I had never felt before, and have never lost since.

I stood in front of the window, feeling like a magical creation bursting with life, yet at the same time knowing almost nothing about myself. I realised I was a living being on a planet in the Milky Way. I had probably always known this, because it was not so easy to ignore that sort of thing when you had had an upbringing like mine, but it was the first time I'd felt it myself. Something had taken over every single cell in my body.

I felt as though my body was something odd and unknown to me. How could I stand here in the cabin and think all these strange thoughts? How could I grow skin, hair, and nails? Not to mention teeth! I couldn't grasp the fact that enamel and ivory grew in my mouth, that these hard things *were* me. But most people don't normally think about that sort of thing until they have to go to the dentist.

It was a mystery to me how people on earth could simply roam around the world without asking questions, over and over again, about who they were and where they came from. How could life on this planet be something you either turned your back on or took for granted?

I was brimming with all these thoughts and feelings, which made me feel happy and sad at the same time. They made me feel lonely, too, but this kind of loneliness was good.

I was pleased, however, when Dad suddenly let out one of his gravelly lion roars. Before he got out of bed, it struck me that it was certainly important to keep your eyes open, but nothing mattered more than being with a person you loved.

'You up already?' Dad said, sticking his head under the curtain just as the sun rose above the expansive sea.

'So is the sun,' I replied.

That's how the day we would spend at sea began.

EIGHT OF CLUBS

*... if our brain was simple enough
for us to understand it ...*

T here was quite a bit of philosophical chat during breakfast. Dad jokingly suggested we hijack the ship and interrogate all the passengers to find out if any of them knew anything that might throw light on the mystery of life.

'We have a unique opportunity here,' he said. 'This boat is like human society in miniature. There are more than a thousand passengers, who come from all corners of the world. But we are all on board the same ship. We're all being carried along on the same keel ...'

He pointed around the dining room, then continued. 'There has to be someone who knows something we don't. With such a good hand, there ought to be at least one joker!'

'There are two,' I said, and looked at him. I could tell by his smile that Dad knew what I meant.

'We really ought to round up all the passengers,' he said, 'and ask each of them if they can tell us why they are living. Those who cannot answer we simply throw overboard.'

'What about the children?' I asked.

'They pass the test with flying colours.'

I decided to carry out some philosophical inquiries that morning. After swimming for a long time in the pool while Dad read a German newspaper, I sat on deck watching all the people.

Some of them rubbed greasy suntan lotion all over their bodies; some read French, English, Japanese, or Italian paperbacks. Others sat talking intensely while they drank beer or red drinks filled with ice cubes. There were also some children: the older ones sat in the sun like the adults; the slightly younger ones ran back and forth on deck, tripping over bags and walking sticks; the smallest ones sat on laps whining – and a little baby was being breast-fed by its mother. The mother and baby were as comfortable as if they were sitting in the kitchen at home, in France or Germany.

Who were all these people? Where had they come from? And above all, was there anyone apart from Dad and me who asked these sorts of questions at all?

I sat looking at every one of them to see if anything gave them away. For example, if there was a god who decided what everyone should say and do, then an intensive study of these functions might give some kind of result.

I also had one important advantage. If I found a particularly interesting guinea pig, that person wouldn't be able to escape until we arrived in Patras. In a way, it was easier to study people on board a boat than hyperactive insects or lively cockroaches.

People stretched their arms, some got up from their deckchairs and stretched their legs. An old man managed to put his glasses on and take them off four or five times in the course of one minute.

It was obvious the people on the boat were not aware of everything they did. Every little movement was not consciously made. In a way they were more alive than they were conscious.

I thought it was even more exciting to watch people move their eyelids. Of course, they all blinked, but they didn't all blink at the same rate. It was strange to see how the small folds of skin over their eyes went up and down quite by themselves. I'd once watched a bird blink. It had looked as though there was a built-in mechanism regulating the blinking. I now thought the people on the boat blinked in a similar mechanical fashion.

Some Germans with huge stomachs reminded me of walruses. They lay on deckchairs with white caps pulled down over their foreheads, and the only thing they *did* all morning, apart from dozing in the sunshine, was rub themselves with suntan lotion. Dad called them 'Bratwurst Germans'. At first I thought they came from a place in Germany called Bratwurst, but then Dad explained he called them that because they ate so many fat sausages called bratwurst.

I wondered what a 'Bratwurst German' thought about while he lay in the sun. I decided he thought of bratwurst. At any rate, there was nothing to suggest he thought about anything else.

I continued my philosophical investigations all morning. Dad and I had agreed not to follow each other around all day, so I was given permission to move freely about the boat. The only thing I had to promise was not to jump overboard.

I borrowed Dad's binoculars and spied on some of the passengers a couple of times. This was exciting, because naturally I had to avoid being discovered.

The worst thing I did was follow an American lady who was so crazy I thought she might bring me closer to understanding what a human being is.

I caught her standing in a corner of the lounge, glancing behind her to make sure nobody was watching her. I was spying from behind a sofa, being careful not to be discovered. I had butterflies in my stomach, but I wasn't frightened for myself. I was actually nervous for her sake. What was she up to?

I finally saw her pull out a green makeup bag from her handbag. Inside, she had a little pocket mirror. At first she stared at herself from all angles, then she began to smear on lipstick.

I immediately understood that what I was observing might be of relevance to a philosopher, but there was more. When she had finished putting on her makeup, she started to smile at herself. It didn't stop there either. Just before she stuffed the mirror back into her bag, she raised one of her hands and waved to herself in the mirror. At the same time, she winked and smiled broadly.

When she disappeared out of the lounge, I lay in my hideout completely exhausted.

Why on earth did she wave to herself? After some philosophical deliberation, I decided this lady was a rare bird – maybe even a lady joker. She must have been aware of the fact she existed when she waved to herself. In a way she was two people: she was the lady who stood in the lounge and smeared on the lipstick, and also the lady who waved to herself in the mirror.

I knew it wasn't really legal to carry out human experiments, so I stopped with this one. However, when I spotted the lady again, later that afternoon at a bridge party, I walked straight over to the table and asked, in English, if I could have the joker.

'No problem,' said the lady, and handed me the joker.

When I walked away, I raised one of my hands and waved at her. At the same time I gave her a wink. She almost fell off her chair. She may have wondered whether I knew her little secret. If she did, then she is probably sitting somewhere in America, still suffering from a guilty conscience.

This was the first time I had ever bummed a joker all on my own.

Dad and I had agreed to meet in the cabin before dinner. Without giving everything away, I told him I'd made some important observations, and we had an interesting conversation over dinner about what a human being is.

I said it was strange that we human beings are so clever in so many ways – we explore space and the composition of atoms –

but we don't have a better understanding of what we are. Then Dad said something so brilliant, I can remember it word for word.

'If our brain was simple enough for us to understand it, we would be so stupid we wouldn't be able to understand it after all.'

I sat thinking about this for quite a long time. In the end, I decided it said just about everything that could be said about my question.

'There are brains which are much simpler than ours,' Dad continued. 'For example, we understand how an earthworm's brain functions – at least most of it. Yet the earthworm doesn't understand it itself, its brain is too simple.'

'Maybe there's a God who understands *us*,' I piped up.

Dad jumped in his seat. I think he was rather impressed that I could come up with such an intelligent idea.

'That might be true, yes,' he said. 'But then he would be so hideously complicated, he would hardly understand himself.'

He now waved to the waiter and ordered a bottle of beer with his meal. He sat philosophising until the beer was served.

'If there's one thing I don't understand, it's why Anita left us,' he said as the waiter poured the beer into his glass.

I was surprised when he suddenly used her name. He usually just said Mama, like I did.

I didn't like it when Dad talked about Mama so often. I missed her just as much as he did, but I thought it was better for us to miss her separately, rather than going around missing her *together*.

'I think I know more about the makeup of outer space,' he said, 'than why that woman simply left without giving a proper reason *why* she was disappearing.'

'Maybe she didn't know herself,' I replied.

No more was said during the rest of the meal. I suspect that both Dad and I were wondering whether we really would find her in Athens.

After dinner we walked about the boat. Dad pointed out all the officers and crew we saw and explained what their different stripes and marks meant. I couldn't help thinking about the cards in a pack of cards.

Later on that evening, Dad confessed he had been thinking of making a little trip to the bar. I decided not to make a big deal out of it, but said I would rather go to the cabin and read comics.

I think he thought it was okay to be alone for a while, and as for me, I was eager to find out what Frode would tell Baker Hans while they sat looking down over the village of the dwarfs.

Needless to say, I wasn't going to read comics in the cabin. Maybe I was growing out of comics that summer.

Anyway, one thing this day had taught me was that Dad wasn't the only philosopher. I had started to be a tiny bit of one on my own.

NINE OF CLUBS

. . . a sweet juice which glitters
and tastes mildly sparkling
or fizzy . . .

'It was just as well we left!' began the old man with the long white beard.

He stared fixedly at me for a long time.

'I was afraid you were going to say something,' he added.

Eventually he looked away and pointed down towards the village. Then he slumped back in his seat again.

'You haven't said anything, have you?'

'I'm afraid I don't exactly know what you mean,' I replied.

'No, that's true. I did probably begin at the wrong end.'

I nodded sympathetically. 'If there *is* another end,' I said, 'then it is probably wise to start there.'

'*Aber natürlich!*' he exclaimed. 'But first of all, you must answer an important question. Do you know what the date is?'

'I'm not quite sure,' I had to admit. 'It must be around the beginning of October ...'

'I didn't mean the exact day. Do you know what year it is?'

'Eighteen forty-two,' I replied – and now I began to understand.

The old man nodded.

'Then exactly fifty-two years have passed, my boy.'

'Have you lived on the island that long?'

He nodded again. 'Yes, that long.'

A tear formed in the corner of his eye. It trickled down his cheek, and he made no attempt to wipe it away.

'In October 1790 we set out from Mexico,' he continued. 'After a few days at sea, the brig I was sailing on was shipwrecked. The rest of the crew went down with the ship, but I clung to some solid timbers floating among the debris of the wreck. Eventually I managed to paddle my way to shore ...'

He sat deep in thought.

I told him I had also come to the island following a shipwreck. He nodded sadly, and added: 'You said "island" and I have said the same myself. But can we be sure this really is an island? I have lived here for more than fifty years, my boy – and I have wandered far and wide – but I have never found my way back to the sea.'

'So it's a big island,' I said.

'Which isn't drawn on any map?'

He looked up at me.

'Of course, we might be stranded somewhere on the American continent,' I said. 'Or in Africa, for that matter. It isn't easy to say how long we were prey to the ocean currents before we were washed ashore.'

The old man shook his head in despair. 'In both America and Africa you find *people*, young friend.'

'But if it isn't an island – and not one of the large continents either – what on earth can it be?'

'Something quite different ...' he mumbled.

Once again he sat deep in thought.

'The dwarfs ...' I began, 'is that what you're thinking about?'

He didn't reply. Instead, he said, 'Are you sure you come from the world outside? You're not from here as well, are you?'

Me as well? So he was thinking of the dwarfs after all.

'I signed on in Hamburg,' I replied.

'Is that so? I come from Lübeck myself . . .'

'But so do I. I signed onto a Norwegian ship in Hamburg, but my home town is Lübeck.'

'Really? Now, before you go any further, you must tell me what has happened in Europe these past fifty years, while I have been away.'

I told him what I knew. There was a lot about Napoleon and all the wars. I told him Lübeck was plundered by the French in 1806.

'In 1812, the year after I was born, Napoleon led a military campaign in Russia,' I concluded, 'but he had to withdraw with great losses. In 1813 he was beaten in a great battle at Leipzig. Napoleon then took the island of Elba as his own little empire. However, he returned a few years later and re-established his French empire. He was then defeated at Waterloo, and his last years were spent on the island of Saint Helena, off the west coast of Africa.'

The old man listened intently. 'At least he could see the sea,' he muttered.

It was as though he was putting together everything I told him.

'It sounds like an adventure story,' he said after a while. 'So this is how history has run since I left Europe – but it could have been a lot different.'

I had to agree with him. History is like a long fairy tale. The only difference is that history is true.

The sun was just about to disappear behind the mountains in the west. The little village was already in the shade. Down below, the little people milled around like coloured splotches between the houses.

I pointed towards them. 'Are you going to tell me about them?' I asked.

'Of course,' he said. 'I'm going to tell you about everything. But you have to promise me that nothing I tell you will reach their ears.'

I nodded in anticipation, and Frode began his story.

'I was a sailor on a Spanish brig on its way from Veracruz in Mexico to Cádiz in Spain. We were sailing with a large cargo of silver. The weather was both clear and calm, nevertheless the ship was shipwrecked only a few days after leaving port. We must have drifted, due to the lack of wind, somewhere between Puerto Rico and Bermuda. We had heard of strange things happening in these waters, oh yes, but we shrugged them off as being nothing more than old sea yarns. But then suddenly one morning the ship was lifted up from a perfectly calm sea. It was as though a giant hand had turned the brig around like a corkscrew. It lasted only a few seconds – then we were thrown down again. We lay battered in the sea, and then the cargo shifted and we started to take in water.

'I have only a few hazy memories of the little beach which finally saved me from the sea. That's because I immediately started to wander deeper into the island. After several weeks of roaming I settled down here, and this has been my home ever since.

'I managed fine. Potatoes and corn grow here, as do apples and bananas. And there are also other fruits and plants which I had neither seen nor heard of before. Kurberries, ringroots, and gramines are an important part of my diet. I had to name all the strange plants on the island myself.

'After a few years I managed to tame the six-legged moluks. Not only did they produce a sweet and nutritious milk, I also used them as work animals. Now and then I would kill one and eat the lean and tender meat. It reminded me of the wild boar's meat we used to have at Christmas back home in Germany.

'As the years passed, I developed medicines from the plants on the island, to treat the different illnesses I suffered from. I also concocted different drinks to help my mood swings. As you will soon see, I often drink something called tuff. It is a slightly bitter drink which I boil from the roots of the tufa palm tree. Tuff wakes me up when I am tired and want to stay awake – and makes me tired when I am awake and want to sleep. It is a tasty and completely harmless drink.

'However, I also made something called Rainbow Fizz. It is a drink which is wonderfully good for your whole body, but at the same time so treacherous and dangerous that I am glad you can't buy it over the counter at home in Germany. I brewed it from the nectar of the purpur-rose flower. The purpur is a small bush with tiny crimson flowers, and it grows all over the island. I didn't have to pick the roses or tap the flower nectar myself. That job is done by the big bees; yes, they are bigger than the birds at home in Germany. They make hives in hollow trees, and there they collect their supplies of purpur nectar. All I had to do was help myself.

'When I mixed the flower nectar with water from the Rainbow River, where I also get the goldfish, I got a sweet juice which glitters and tastes mildly sparkling or fizzy. That was why I called it "fizz".

'What was so enticing about Rainbow Fizz was that it didn't give just one taste sensation. Oh no, the red drink attacked every sensory organ with as many tastes as a person can experience. And even more than that: you couldn't just taste Rainbow Fizz in your mouth and throat, you could taste it in every single cell of your body. But it's not healthy to consume the whole world in one gulp, my boy – it's much better to take it in small doses.

'As soon as I had developed Rainbow Fizz, I started to drink it every day. It cheered me up a little, but that was only in the beginning. After a while, I started to lose track of time and space. I might suddenly "wake up" somewhere on the island, unable to remember how I had got there. I would roam around for days and weeks without finding my way home. I would forget who I was and where I came from. It was as though everything around me *was* me. It started with a prickling sensation in my arms and legs, then it would spread to my head – and in the end, the drink started to eat away at my soul. Oh yes – I am glad I managed to stop before it was too late. Today Rainbow Fizz is drunk only by the others who live here on the island. Why this is so I will tell you soon enough.'

We looked down over the little village while he talked. It started to get dark and the dwarfs lit the oil lamps between the houses.

'It's getting a bit chilly,' said Frode.

He got up and opened the cabin door, and we stepped into a little room where the furnishings made it clear that Frode had made everything he needed from things he had found on the island.

Nothing was made of metal; everything was made out of clay, wood, or stone. Only one material gave evidence of civilisation – there were cups, mugs, lamps, and dishes all made out of glass. Around the room there were also a few large glass bowls with gold-fish inside. And the peepholes around the cabin had windows made of glass.

'My father was a master glassblower,' the old man explained – as though he had read my thoughts. 'I had taught myself that skill before I went to sea, and it was useful here on the island. After a while I started to mix different sorts of sand. I was soon able to melt a first-rate glass in ovens which I made from a fireproof stone. I called this stone dorfite, because I found it in a mountain just outside the village.'

'I have already visited the glassworks,' I said.

The old man turned round and looked at me seriously. 'You didn't say anything, did you?'

I wasn't sure whether I understood what he meant by his constant references to 'saying anything' to the dwarfs.

'I just asked the way to the village,' I replied.

'Good! Now let's drink a glass of tuff.'

We each sat on a stool in front of a table, which was made from a dark wood I had never seen before. Frode poured a brown drink from a large glass jug into a couple of round glasses, then he lit an oil lamp which hung from the ceiling.

I took a cautious sip of the brown drink. It tasted like a cross between coconut and lemon. For a long time after I had swallowed it, a bitter aftertaste remained in my mouth.

'What do you think?' the old man asked expectantly. 'It's the first time I've served tuff to a true European.'

I said the drink was refreshing and tasty, which it was.

'Good!' he said. 'Now I must tell you about my little helpers on the island. No doubt they're the ones you're sitting thinking about, my boy.'

I nodded, so the old man continued his story.

TEN OF CLUBS

*. . . I couldn't understand how
something could just grow out of
nothing . . .*

I put the sticky-bun book down on the bedside table and
started to wander about the cabin, thinking about what I
had just read.

Frode had lived on the strange island for fifty-two long years,
and then one day he had met the drowsy dwarfs. Or had the
dwarfs suddenly arrived on the island long after Frode had landed there?

In any case, Frode must have taught the diamonds the art of
glassblowing. No doubt he'd also taught the clubs to till the land,
the hearts to bake bread, and the spades to carpenter. But who
were these extraordinary little people?

I knew I would probably get the answer to that question if I
only read more, but I wasn't sure if I dared to read on when I was
alone in the cabin.

I pushed the curtains away from the window, and suddenly I was staring into a little face outside. *It was the dwarf!* He was standing on the walkway outside, gaping at me.

The whole thing lasted only a few seconds; then he ran away as soon as he realised he had been discovered.

I was frozen with horror. My first reaction was to draw the curtains. After a while I threw myself onto my bed and started to cry.

It never occurred to me that I could simply have walked out of the cabin and found Dad in the bar. I was so scared I didn't dare do anything but hide my head under the pillow, and I hardly dared do that either.

I don't know how long I lay on the bed crying. Dad must have heard some wild howling out in the corridor, because the door swung open and he came charging in.

'What is the matter with you, Hans Thomas?'

He turned me over on the bed and tried to open my eyes.

'The dwarf . . .' I sobbed. 'I saw the dwarf at the window . . . He was standing there . . . staring at me.'

Dad probably thought something a lot worse had happened, because he suddenly let go of me and started to wander round the cabin.

'That's a load of nonsense, Hans Thomas. There's no dwarf on board this boat.'

'I *saw* him,' I insisted.

'All you saw was a little man,' said Dad.

In the end, Dad just about managed to convince me I'd made a mistake. At least he calmed me down. However, I set one condition for not talking about the matter any more. Dad had to promise he would ask the ship's crew before we landed at Patras if there had been a dwarf on board.

'Do you think we're philosophising a bit too much?' he asked, while I continued to give a little snuffle at regular intervals.

I shook my head.

'First we'll find Mama in Athens,' he said. 'Then we'll wait a bit before we solve life's mysteries. Besides, there's no big hurry. Nobody is going to come and steal our project in the meantime.'

He looked down at me again.

'Being interested in who people are and where the world comes from is such an enormously rare hobby, we are virtually the only ones doing it. Those of us who do this sort of thing live so far apart we've never even thought of forming our own society.'

When I had stopped crying, Dad sloshed a little of his whisky into a glass. There was no more than a centimetre. He mixed it with water and handed me the glass.

'Drink this, Hans Thomas. Then you'll sleep well tonight.'

I drank a couple of mouthfuls. I thought the stuff tasted so horrible I couldn't understand why Dad went around quaffing it all the time.

When Dad was ready for bed, I pulled out the joker I had bummed from the American lady.

'This is for you,' I said.

He held it in his hand and studied it closely. I don't think it was an unusual one, but it was the first time *I* had provided him with a joker.

He thanked me for the gift by showing me a card trick. He placed the joker in a pack of cards which he'd had in his bag. Then he laid the pack on the bedside table. The next minute he plucked the same joker from thin air.

I watched carefully and could have sworn he had put the joker into the pack. Maybe he had the card up his sleeve. But how did it get there?

I couldn't understand how something could just grow out of nothing.

Dad kept his promise to ask the crew about the dwarf, but they maintained there had been no small people on board the boat. It must be as I feared: the dwarf was a stowaway.

JACK OF CLUBS

*... if the world is
a magic trick, then there must be
a great magician, too ...*

We agreed not to bother with breakfast on board the boat and to wait until we went ashore at Patras. We had set the alarm clock for seven, an hour before arrival, but I was already awake at six.

The first thing I noticed was the magnifying glass and the sticky-bun book on the bedside table. I had completely forgotten to put them away when the cunning face had appeared at the window. It was pure luck Dad hadn't seen them.

The boss was still asleep, and from the moment I opened my eyes I wondered what Frode would say about the dwarfs on the island. I now read quite a bit further before Dad started to thrash around in bed, something he usually did just before he woke up.

*

'We would play cards a lot when we were at sea. I always had a pack of cards stuck in my breast pocket, and a pack of French cards was the only thing I had on me when I landed on the island after the shipwreck.

'During the first years, I often played solitaire when I was lonely. The cards were the only pictures I had to look at. I didn't just play the solitaire games I had learned in Germany and at sea. With fifty-two different cards – and moreover an ocean of time – I soon discovered there were no limits to how many games of solitaire and other tricks I could come up with.

'After a while, I started to give the individual cards different characteristics. I began to look on them as individuals from four different families. The clubs had brown skin, a stocky build, and thick curly hair. The diamonds were thinner, more delicate and graceful. They had almost translucent complexions and straight, silvery hair. Then there were the hearts – they were simply heartier than the others. They were rounder in build, had rosy cheeks and thick blonde manes of hair. Finally there were the spades – oh me, oh my! They had firm, upright bodies, pale skin, a slightly strict and serious expression, piercingly dark eyes, and thin black hair.

'I could soon picture the figures when I played solitaire. With every card I laid down, it was as though I let a spirit out of a magic bottle. A spirit, yes – because it wasn't only the appearance of the figures that varied from family to family. They also had their own distinct temperaments. The clubs were slightly more sluggish and stiffer in personality than the vague and sensitive diamonds. The hearts were kinder and cheerier than the fierce and hotheaded spades. But there were also great differences within each family. All the diamonds were easily hurt, but the Three of Diamonds cried most frequently. All the spades tended to be a bit quick-tempered, most of all the Ten of Spades.

'So through the course of time I created fifty-two invisible individuals who sort of lived with me on the island. In the end there were fifty-three, because the joker also came to play an important part.'

'But how . . .'

'I don't know if you can imagine how lonely I felt. The stillness was never-ending here. I was always coming across different animals, and owls or moluks were always waking me at night, but I never had anyone to talk to. After a few days I started talking to myself. After a few months I'd started talking to the cards as well. I would lay them in a big circle around me and pretend they were real people made of flesh and blood like myself. Sometimes I would pick up a single card – and hold a long conversation with it.

'Gradually the whole pack became so worn the cards started to disintegrate. The sun had bleached the colours, and I could hardly make out the pictures on the cards. I put the remains in a little wooden box which I have looked after to this very day, but the figures lived on in my mind. I could now play solitaire in my head. I didn't need the physical cards any more. It was like when you can suddenly calculate numbers without using an abacus. Six plus seven is thirteen even if you don't use counters to show it.

'I continued to talk to my invisible friends, and then they seemed to answer me – even though it was only in my head. They were most vivid when I slept, because the figures from the pack of cards nearly always appeared in my dreams. We were like a little society. In my dreams the figures could say and do things quite by themselves. In this way the nights were always a little less lonely than the long days. The cards took on their own personalities. They ran around in my subconscious like proper kings and queens and people made of flesh and blood.

'I had a more intimate relationship with some of the figures than others. In the early days, I was forever having long conversations with the Jack of Clubs. I could joke around for hours with the Ten of Spades – when he managed to control his temper.

'I was secretly in love with the Ace of Hearts for a while. I was so lonely I was able to be in love with my own brainchild. I felt as though I saw her in front of me. She had a yellow dress, long blonde hair, and green eyes. I missed a woman so badly on the island. At home in Germany I'd been engaged to a girl called Stine. Alas, her sweetheart was lost at sea.'

The old man stroked his beard; then he sat for a long time without saying anything.

'It's late, my boy,' he said eventually. 'And you must be exhausted after the shipwreck. Perhaps you'd like me to continue tomorrow?'

'No, no,' I protested. 'I want to hear everything.'

'Yes, of course. You have to know everything before we go to the Joker Banquet.'

'The Joker Banquet?'

'Yes, the Joker Banquet!'

He got up and walked across the floor. 'But you must be hungry,' he said.

I couldn't deny that. The old man went into a little pantry and brought out some food which he put on beautiful glass plates. He set the food on the table between us.

I had imagined the food on the island to be rather simple and modest. However, Frode first put a dish with loaves of bread and rolls on the table; then he returned with different cheeses and pâtés. He also brought a jug of lovely white milk that I realised was moluk's milk. Dessert arrived last. It was a large bowl of ten or fifteen different fruits. I recognised the apples, oranges, and bananas. The others were specialities of the island.

We ate for a while before Frode continued with his story. The bread and cheese tasted a little different from what I was used to. So did the milk; it was much sweeter than cow's milk. The greatest taste shock, however, came with the fruit bowl. Some of the fruits tasted so different from any other fruit I knew that now and again I would exclaim in astonishment.

'I have never had to go wanting for food,' the old man said.

He cut a slice from a round fruit the size of a pumpkin. The fruit was soft and yellow inside, like a banana.

'Then one morning it happened,' he continued. 'I had been dreaming extra vividly that night. When I left the cabin early in the morning, the dew was still lying on the grass and the sun was rising over the mountains. Suddenly two silhouettes came walking towards me from a ridge of hills in the east. I thought I finally had some visitors on the island and started to walk towards them. My heart turned somersaults in my chest when I got closer and recognised them. It was the Jack of Clubs and the King of Hearts.

'At first I thought I must still be lying in the cabin asleep and the meeting was just another dream. Yet I was absolutely positive that I was wide awake. But this had happened to me many times when I had been asleep, so I wasn't completely sure.

'The two of them greeted me as though we were old friends. Which we were in a way!

' "It's a lovely morning, Frode," said the King of Hearts.

'They were the very first words which were spoken on the island by someone other than myself.

' "Today we're going to do something useful," continued the Jack.

' "I order that we build a new cabin," said the King.

'And that was exactly what we did. They slept in the cabin with me here for the first two nights. Then after a couple of days they were able to move into a brand-new cabin just below mine.

'They were my equals – with one important difference. They never realised they hadn't lived on the island for as long as I had. There was something inside them which didn't allow them to see that in reality they were my own brainchildren. Of course, it's the same with all our thoughts. Nothing of what we create in our minds is aware of itself. But these particular brainchildren were not exactly like other conceptions. They had followed the inexplicable path from the creative space in my own brain to the created space outside beneath the heavens.'

'That . . . that is impossible!' I gasped.

But Frode just continued his story.

'Other figures gradually appeared. The oddest thing was that the old ones never made a scene when the new ones arrived. It was like when two people suddenly meet each other in the garden – neither of them makes a fuss.

'The dwarfs talked as though they had known each other for a long time, which in a way was true, too. They had been together on the island for many long years, because I had dreamed and day-dreamed about them holding conversations.

'One afternoon I was chopping wood in the forest just down the hill when I met the Ace of Hearts for the first time. I think she lay somewhere in the middle of the pack. I mean, she was neither the first nor the last to be dealt out.

'She didn't see me at first. She was walking around by herself humming a beautiful tune. I stopped what I was doing, and I had tears in my eyes. It was because I was thinking of Stine.

'I gathered my courage and called to her. "Ace of Hearts," I whispered.

'She looked up and walked towards me. She threw herself round my neck and said, "Thank you for finding me, Frode. What would I have done without you?"

'That was a justifiable question. Without me she wouldn't have done anything. But she didn't know this, and she must never find out either.

'Her mouth was so soft and red, I wanted to kiss her, but there was something which stopped me.

'As the newcomers gradually populated the island, we built new houses for them. A whole village grew up around me. I no longer felt lonely. We soon created a society where everyone had his own special job to take care of.

'The solitaire was complete as early as thirty or forty years ago – with fifty-two figures. There was only one exception. Joker was an addition who first showed up on the island sixteen or seventeen years ago. He was a troublemaker who interrupted the idyll just when we had all grown used to our new existence. But this can wait until later. There is another day tomorrow, Hans. If there is one thing life on the island has taught me, it is that there are always new days ahead.'

What Frode told me was so incredible I remember every word to this day.

How could fifty-three dream pictures manage to jump out into reality as living people made of flesh and blood?

'It's . . . it's impossible,' I said again.

Frode nodded and said, 'During the course of a few years all the playing cards had managed to creep out of my mind onto the island, where I was living. Or had I gone the other way? That is a possibility I have constantly had to think about.

'Although I have lived with these friends around me for many, many years, although we have built the village together, worked the land together, prepared and eaten food together, I have never stopped asking myself whether the figures around me are real.

'Had I entered an eternal world of fantasy? Was I lost – not only on the great island but in my own imagination? And if that was the case, would I ever find my way back to reality?

'Only when the Jack of Diamonds brought you along to the water pump could I be sure the life I was living was real. Because *you're* not a new Joker in the pack of cards, are you, Hans? I haven't dreamed you up as well?'

The old man looked up at me imploringly.

'No,' I replied quickly. 'You haven't dreamed me. But you'll have to excuse me if I turn the question around: if you're not the one sleeping, then it could be me. Then I am the one dreaming this fantasy which you are telling.'

Dad suddenly turned over in bed. I jumped out onto the floor, pulled on my jeans, and shoved the sticky-bun book safely into one of the pockets.

He didn't wake up properly right away. I went to the window and stood behind the curtains. I could now see that land was in sight, but I didn't dwell on that very much. My thoughts were elsewhere entirely – and in an entirely different time, too.

If what Frode had told Baker Hans was really true, I had read about the world's greatest card trick ever. To conjure up a whole pack of cards would be pretty impressive in itself, but to turn all fifty-two playing cards into real people bursting with life was magic on a totally different level. It had taken many years to do.

I have been sceptical about everything in the sticky-bun book many times since then. At the same time, from that day on I have regarded the whole world – and all the people who live in it – as one great big magic trick.

But if the world is a magic trick, then there must be a great magician, too. I hope one day I'll be able to expose him or her, but it isn't easy to reveal a trick when the magician never shows up on stage.

Dad went into a complete spin when he popped his head under the curtains and saw the strip of land we were nearing.

'We'll soon be in the homeland of the philosophers,' he declared.

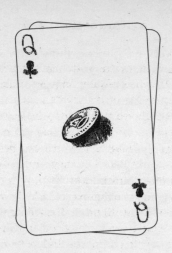

QUEEN OF CLUBS

*. . . could at least have
signed the masterpiece before He
took off . . .*

The first thing Dad did when we drove on land in the Peloponnese was buy an issue of the woman's magazine his aunt had bought in Crete.

We sat down at an outdoor restaurant in the busy port and ordered breakfast. While we waited for the coffee and juice and the dry bread with a dab of watered-down jam, Dad started to flick through the magazine.

'Well, I'll be damned!' he suddenly exclaimed.

He turned the magazine towards me and showed me a whole page spread of Mama. She was not quite as skimpily dressed as the ladies in the pack of cards Dad had bought in Verona, but she wasn't far from it. Her flimsy attire could at least be excused here – it was obvious she was advertising swimwear.

'Maybe we'll meet her in Athens,' Dad said. 'But it won't be easy to get her home.'

Something was written at the bottom of the page, but it was in Greek, and even Dad had certain language difficulties there. It wasn't only the meaning of the words which was a problem; Greece still hadn't bothered to change to the Roman alphabet.

Breakfast was put on the table, but Dad did not even lift his coffee cup. Taking the magazine with him, he started to ask people sitting at nearby tables if they understood English or German. He eventually struck lucky with some teenagers. Dad then unfolded the picture of Mama and asked them to translate what was written in the small print. The teenagers glanced over at me. The whole business was totally embarrassing. I just hoped Dad wouldn't start arguing about the theft of Norwegian women or anything like that.

When Dad returned, he had written down the name of an advertising agency in Athens.

'We're getting warm,' he said.

Of course, there were pictures of lots of other women in the magazine as well, but Dad was interested only in the picture of Mama. He carefully tore it out and threw the rest of the magazine in a waste paper basket – in much the same way as he would chuck a brand-new pack of cards after nabbing the joker.

The fastest route to Athens went south of the Bay of Corinth and across the famous Corinth Canal. However, Dad had never been one to take the fastest route if there was an interesting detour to be made.

The truth was, he wanted to ask the Delphic Oracle something. That meant we had to cross the Bay of Corinth by ferry and then drive through Delphi on the north side of the bay.

The ferry trip took no longer than half an hour. When we had driven twenty miles or so, we came to a little town called Naupaktos. We stopped there and drank coffee and a fizzy drink in a square with a view over a Venetian fortress.

Of course, I thought about what would happen when we met

Mama in Athens, but I was just as interested in everything I had read in the sticky-bun book. I tried to work out how I could talk to Dad about some of the things on my mind without giving myself away.

Dad waved to the waiter and asked for the bill, and then I said, 'Dad, do you believe in God?'

He jumped. 'Don't you think it's a bit early in the day?' he asked.

I could agree with him there, but Dad had no idea where I had been in the early hours of the morning while he was in dreamland. If only he knew. He sat turning some clever thoughts over in his mind; now and again he might do a card trick, too, but I had seen how a pack of cards could flit around in broad daylight like living people made of flesh and blood.

'If God really exists,' I went on, 'then He's clever at playing hide-and-seek with His creations.'

Dad laughed out loud, but I knew he completely agreed with me.

'Maybe He was frightened when He saw what He'd created,' he said. 'So He ran away from everything. You know, it's not easy to tell who got the biggest fright; Adam or the Lord. I think such an act of creation terrifies both parties. Mind you, I agree He could at least have signed His masterpiece before He took off.'

'Signed it?'

'He could easily have carved His name into a canyon or something.'

'So you believe in God, then?'

'I haven't said that. Actually what I did say was, God is sitting in heaven laughing at us because we don't believe in Him.'

That's right, I thought to myself. That was what he'd been going on about in Hamburg.

'Even though He didn't leave his calling card behind, He did leave the world. I think that's fair enough,' Dad said.

He sat for a while deep in thought before he went on: 'A Russian cosmonaut and a Russian brain surgeon were once discussing Christianity. The brain surgeon was Christian, but the cosmonaut wasn't. "I have been in outer space many times," bragged the cosmonaut, "but I have never seen any angels." The brain surgeon stared in amazement, but then he said, "And I have operated on many intelligent brains, but I have never seen a single thought."'

Now it was my turn to be amazed.

'Is that something you've just made up?' I asked.

He shook his head. 'It's one of the corny jokes from my philosophy teacher in Arendal.'

The only thing Dad had done to get a piece of paper showing he was a philosopher was take the Introduction to Philosophy course at the Open University. He had already read all the books, but last autumn he went to lectures on the history of philosophy at the School of Nursing in Arendal.

Of course, Dad didn't think it was enough just to sit and listen to what 'the professor' said. He brought him home to Hisøy as well. 'I couldn't just let the guy sit alone at the Central Hotel,' Dad said. So I, too, got to know him. The guy talked nineteen to the dozen all the time. He was as hooked on the boundless truths as Dad. The difference was that 'the professor' was a halfway educated bluffer, whereas Dad was just a bluffer.

Dad sat staring down at the Venetian fortress.

'No, God is dead, Hans Thomas. And we're the ones who have murdered Him.'

I thought this comment was so incomprehensible and so upsetting I let it go unanswered.

When we had put the Bay of Corinth behind us and started the climb up to Delphi, we passed endless groves of olive trees. We could have driven to Athens that day, but Dad insisted that we couldn't just speed past Delphi without paying the old sanctuary a proper visit.

When we reached Delphi around midday, we checked into a hotel above the town with a beautiful view over the Bay of

Corinth. There were lots of other hotels, but Dad picked the one with the best view over the sea.

We walked from the hotel through the old town to the famous temple site a couple of kilometres further east. As we got closer to the excavation, Dad started to spout like a waterfall.

'People came to consult the oracle of Apollo here throughout ancient times. They asked about everything – whom they should marry, where they should travel, when they would go to war against other states, and which calendar system they should use.'

'But what's the oracle?' I had to ask.

Dad told me that the god Zeus had sent two eagles to fly from different ends of the earth across its surface. When they met in Delphi, the Greeks declared it the middle of the world. Then Apollo came. Before he could settle in Delphi, he had to kill the dangerous dragon Python – that's why his priestess was called Pythia. When the dragon was killed, it transformed itself into a snake, which Apollo carried around with him at all times.

I had to admit I didn't understand everything Dad said, and he still hadn't told me what an oracle was, but we'd just about reached the entrance to the temple site. It was situated in a ravine at the foot of Mount Parnassus. The Muses, who gave people creative powers, had lived on that mountain.

Before we went in, Dad insisted we drink from one of the holy springs just below the entrance. He claimed that everyone had to wash before going into the holy site. He also said that you got wisdom and poetic powers when you drank from this spring.

When we went into the site of the temple, Dad bought a map showing how it had looked two thousand years ago. We definitely needed the map, because all that was left was a load of chaotic ruins.

At first we walked around the remains of the old city's treasury. In order to ask the oracle's advice, you had to bring exquisite presents to Apollo, and they were kept in a special house which the different states had to build.

When we reached the great Temple of Apollo, Dad gave a better explanation of what the oracle was.

'What you see here are the remains of the great Temple of Apollo,' he began. 'Inside the temple was an engraved stone called the "nave", because the Greeks believed this temple was the navel of the world. They also believed that Apollo lived inside the temple – at least at certain times of the year – and he was the one they asked for advice. He spoke through his priestess Pythia, who sat on a three-legged stool across a crevice in the ground. Hypnotic vapours rose from this crevice which put Pythia in a trance. This enabled her to be Apollo's mouthpiece. When you came to Delphi, you presented your question to the priests, who passed it on to Pythia. Her answer would be so obscure and ambiguous that the priests had to interpret it. In this way, the Greeks made use of Apollo's wisdom, because Apollo knew everything – about the past and the future.'

'What are we going to ask?'

'We'll ask if we're going to meet Anita in Athens,' Dad said. 'You can be the priest who asks, and I'll be Pythia, who brings the god's reply.'

With that he sat down in front of the ruins of the famous Temple of Apollo and started to shake his head and wave his arms around like a madman. Some French and German tourists stepped back in horror.

I asked solemnly, 'Will we meet Anita in Athens?'

It was clear that Dad was waiting for the powers of Apollo to work within him. Then he said, 'Young man from land far away . . . meets beautiful woman . . . near the old temple.'

He soon returned to his old self and nodded with satisfaction.

'That'll do,' he said. 'Pythia's answers were never any clearer than that.'

I wasn't satisfied, however. Who was the young man, who was the beautiful woman, and where was the great temple?

'Let's flip a coin to see if we'll meet her,' I said. 'If Apollo can control your tongue, then he's bound to be able to control a coin, too.'

Dad went along with the suggestion. He took out a 20 drachma piece, and we agreed that if it was tails we would meet Mama in Athens. I flipped the coin into the air and stared excitedly at the ground.

It was tails! Tails it was. The coin lay on the ground as though it had been there for thousands of years, waiting for us to come along and discover it.

KING OF CLUBS

*... he thought it was
downright annoying that he didn't know
more about life and the world ...*

After the oracle had assured us we would meet Mama in Athens, we walked further up through the temple site and found an old theatre, which had room for five thousand spectators. From the top of the theatre we looked out over the temple site and right down to the bottom of the valley.

On the way down Dad said, 'There is still something I haven't told you about the Delphic Oracle, Hans Thomas. You know, this place is of great interest to philosophers like us.'

We sat down on some temple remains. It was strange to think they were a couple of thousand years old.

'Do you remember Socrates?' he began.

'Not really,' I had to admit. 'But he was a Greek philosopher.'

'That's right. And first of all I'm going to tell you what the word "philosopher" means ...'

I knew this was the beginning of a mini-lecture, and honestly I thought it was a bit much, because the sweat was pouring off my face under the burning sun.

' "Philosopher" means one who seeks wisdom. This does not mean a philosopher *is* particularly wise, however. Do you understand the difference?'

I nodded.

'The first person to live up to this was Socrates. He walked around the market square in Athens talking to people, but he never instructed them. On the contrary – he spoke to people he met in order to learn something himself. Because "the trees in the country cannot teach me anything," he said. But he was rather disappointed to discover that the people who liked to say they knew a lot really knew nothing at all. They might be able to tell him the day's price of wine and olive oil, but they didn't know anything considerable about *life*. Socrates readily said himself that he knew only one thing – and that was that he knew nothing.'

'He wasn't very wise, then,' I objected.

'Don't be so hasty,' Dad said sternly. 'If two people haven't a clue about something but one of them gives the impression of knowing a lot, who do you think is the wisest?'

I had to say that the wisest one was the one who didn't give the impression of knowing more than he did.

'So you've got the point. This is exactly what made Socrates a philosopher. He thought it was downright *annoying* that he didn't know more about life and the world. He felt completely out of it.'

I nodded again.

'And then an Athenian went to the Delphic Oracle and asked Apollo who the wisest man in Athens was. The oracle's answer was Socrates. When Socrates heard this, he was, to put it mildly, rather surprised, because he really thought he didn't know much at all. But after he visited those who were supposed to be wiser than he and asked them a few intelligent questions, he found that the oracle was right. The difference between Socrates and all the others was that the others were satisfied with the little they knew, although they didn't know any more than Socrates. And people who are satisfied with what they know can never be philosophers.'

I thought the story had a point, but Dad didn't stop there. He gestured towards all the tourists swarming out of the tour buses far below and crawling like a fat trail of ants up through the temple site.

'If there is one person among all those who regularly experiences the world as something full of adventure and mystery . . .'

He now took a deep breath before he continued.

'You can see thousands of people down there, Hans Thomas. I mean, if just one of them experiences life as a crazy adventure – and I mean that he, or she, experiences this every single day . . .'

'What about it?' I asked now, because again he had stopped in the middle of a sentence.

'Then he or she is a joker in a pack of cards.'

'Do you think there's a joker like that here?'

A look of despair now crossed his face. 'Nope!' he said. 'Of course I can't be sure, because there are only a few jokers, but the chance is infinitesimal.'

'What about yourself? Do you experience life as a *fairy tale* every single day?'

'Yes, I do!'

He was so forthright with his answer I didn't dare argue with him.

'Every single morning I wake with a bang,' he said. 'It's as though the fact that I am alive is injected into me; I am a character in a fairy tale, bursting with life. For who are we, Hans Thomas? Can you tell me that? We are thrown together with a sprinkling of stardust. But what's that? Where the hell does this world come from?'

'Haven't a clue,' I replied, and at that moment I felt just as much out of it as Socrates had.

'Then it sometimes pops up in the evening,' he continued. 'I am a person living right now, I think to myself. And I'll never return.'

'You live a tough life, then,' I said.

'Tough, yes, but incredibly exciting. I don't need to visit cold castles to go on a ghost hunt. I am a ghost myself.'

'And you worry when your son sees a little ghost outside the cabin window.'

I don't know why I mentioned that, but I thought I had to remind him of what he'd said on the boat the night before.

He just laughed. 'You can handle it,' he replied.

The last thing Dad said about the oracle was that the old Greeks had engraved an inscription into the temple here. It said: 'Know thyself.'

'But that's easier said than done,' he added, mostly to himself.

We sauntered back down to the entrance. Dad wanted to visit a museum just beside it, to study the famous 'navel of the world' which had been inside the Temple of Apollo. I humbly asked if I could be excused from joining him inside, and in the end I was allowed to sit in the shade of a tree and wait for him. The museum could not have contained anything essential to a child's upbringing.

'You can sit under that strawberry tree,' he said.

He dragged me along and showed me a tree I had never seen the like of before. I could have sworn it was impossible, but the tree was bulging with red strawberries.

Of course, I had an ulterior motive for not going inside the museum: the magnifying glass and the sticky-bun book had been burning in my pocket all morning. From then on, I didn't allow any opportunity to pass without reading more from the sticky-bun book. I would have preferred not to look up from the little book until I had completely finished it, but I had to show a little consideration to Dad, too.

I had started to wonder whether the little book was like an oracle which would eventually give me the answers to all the questions I asked. I got a chill down my spine when I read about the Joker on the magic island, especially when there had just been so much talk about jokers.

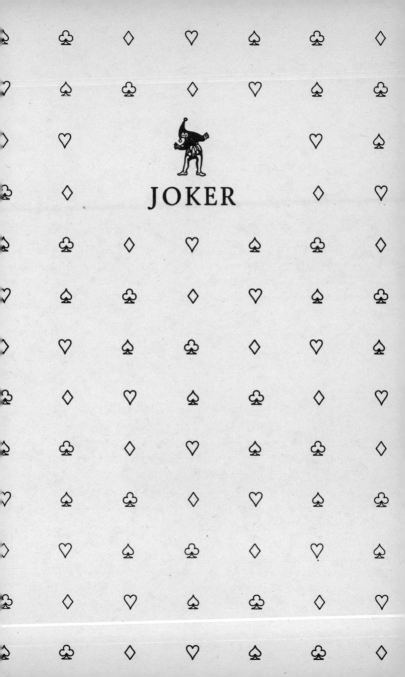

JOKER

JOKER

... He stole into the
village like a poisonous snake ...

The old man got up and walked across the room. He opened the front door and peered out into the black night. I followed him.

'I have a starry sky above me and a starry sky below me,' he said softly.

I understood what he meant. Above us sparkled the clearest star-filled sky I had ever seen. But that was only one of the starry skies. Down in the valley a faint light shone from the cabins in the village. It was as though some stardust had come loose from the sky and had fallen down to earth.

'These starry skies are equally unfathomable,' he added.

He pointed down to the village. 'Who are they? Where do they come from?'

'No doubt they ask themselves the same question.'

The old man turned to me suddenly. 'No, no,' he exclaimed.

'That's something they must never ask.'

'But . . .'

'They wouldn't be able to live side by side with the person who created them. Don't you understand that?'

We went back inside the cabin, closed the door behind us, and sat down on either side of the table.

'These fifty-two figures were all different,' the old man resumed, 'yet there was one thing they all had in common: none asked any questions about who they were or where they came from. In this way, they were one with nature. They just *existed* in the lush garden – as bold and carefree as the animals . . . but then the Joker arrived. He stole into the village like a poisonous snake.'

I whistled.

'Several years had passed since the assembly of cards had been completed, and I never expected a Joker to come to the island, even though there had been such a card in the pack. I think I thought that I was the Joker. One day, however, the little fool came strolling into the village. The Jack of Diamonds spotted him first, and for the first time in the island's history there was a bit of a commotion over a newcomer. Not only did he have funny clothes with jingling bells, but he didn't belong to any of the four families either. Above all, he could provoke the dwarfs by asking them questions they were unable to answer. After a while he kept more and more to himself. He had a separate cabin on the outskirts of the village.'

'Did he understand more than the others?'

The old man breathed deeply and sighed. 'One morning when I was sitting on the front steps he jumped out from round the corner of the house. He turned a frisky somersault, bounced up to me with his bells jingling, cocked his little head, and said 'Master, there's something I don't understand . . .'

'I was surprised that he called me "master", because the other dwarfs had never called me anything but Frode. They didn't normally begin a conversation by saying they didn't understand anything, either. When you realise there is something you don't understand, then you're generally on the right path to understanding all kinds of things.

'The sprightly Joker cleared his throat a couple of times; then he said, "There are four families in the village, with four Kings, Queens, Jacks, Aces, and Twos to Tens."

' "That's right."

' "So there are four of each kind, but there are also thirteen of each kind, because they are all either diamonds, hearts, clubs, or spades."

'It was the first time one of the dwarfs had given such a precise description of the order they were all a part of.

' "Who could possibly have structured everything so wisely?" he went on.

' "It is probably sheer coincidence," I lied. "When you throw some sticks into the air, they will always land in a way which is open to interpretation."

' "I don't agree," said the little jester.

'It was the first time anyone on the island had ever challenged me. I was no longer dealing with a piece of cardboard – this was a person, and in a way I was pleased about that. The Joker might prove to be a creditable conversationalist. However, I was also worried – what would happen if the dwarfs suddenly understood who they were and where they came from?

' "What do you think?" I asked him.

'He stared at me intently, and although his body was as still as a statue, one of his hands trembled, making his bells jingle.

' "Everything seems so planned," he said, trying hard not to look worried. "So organised and thought-out. I think we're standing with our backs to something which will choose either to turn us picture-side-up – or to leave us as we are."

'The dwarfs often used words and expressions taken from card games; in this way, they could express exactly what they meant. When it was appropriate I would answer them in the same way.

'The little jester now flipped over a couple of times, making his bells ring crazily.

' "I am the *Joker*!" he exclaimed. "Don't forget that, dear master.

I'm not as clear-cut as all the others, you see. I am neither King nor Jack, nor am I diamond, club, heart, or spade."

'I had cold feet now, but I knew I couldn't put the cards on the table.

' "Who am I?" he pressed. "Why am I the Joker? Where do I come from, and where am I going?"

'I decided to take a chance.

' "You have seen everything I have made from the island's plants," I began. ' "What would you say if I told you I had created you and all the other dwarfs in the village, too?"

'He stared at me fixedly, and I saw how his little body shook, his bells jingling nervously.

'With trembling lips he said, "Then I would have no other choice, dear master – I would have to try to kill you, to regain my pride."

'I forced a laugh.

' "Of course," I replied. "But fortunately it isn't so."

'He stood looking at me suspiciously for a second or two; then he dashed around the corner of the cabin. Within seconds he was standing in front of me again, and this time he had a little bottle of Rainbow Fizz in his hand. I had kept it in the back of a cupboard for many, many years.

' "Cheers!" he said. "Yum, yum, says the Joker!" and with that he put the bottle to his mouth.

'I was stunned. I wasn't frightened for myself, I was afraid everything I had created on the island would fall apart and disappear as quickly as it had once come.'

'But that didn't happen?'

'I realised the Joker had drunk from the bottle, and the remarkable drink had suddenly made him very astute.'

'Didn't you say Rainbow Fizz dulls your senses and disorients you?'

'Of course, but not right away. At first the drink makes you brilliantly clever, because all your senses are stimulated at the same time. Then the drowsiness gradually takes over. This is what makes the drink so dangerous.'

'What happened to the Joker?'

' "We'll say no more for now!" he cried. "But I'll be seeing you!"

'He ran down to the village, and there he let the bottle go round among the dwarfs, and ever since that day everyone in the village has drunk Rainbow Fizz. The clubs go out several times a week to fetch purpur nectar from the hollow tree trunks, and the hearts brew the red drink, which the diamonds bottle.'

'Did all the dwarfs become as clever as the Joker?'

'No, not quite. Some days they were so sharp-witted I was afraid they would see through me, but then they became even vaguer than before. What you have seen here today are only the remains of something that once was.'

I thought about all the colourful costumes and uniforms, and I suddenly pictured the Ace of Hearts in her yellow dress.

'Still, the remains are beautiful,' I said.

'Oh yes, they are beautiful, but oblivious to everything. They *are* part of the lush natural world, they just don't know it. They see the sun and the moon, they taste all the produce here, but it doesn't register. When they made the big leap, they were proper people, but when they started to drink Rainbow Fizz, they became more and more distant. It was as though they withdrew into themselves. Of course, they can hold a conversation, but they forget what they have said almost as soon as they've said it. The Joker is the only one who still has some of the old spark left in him, and possibly the Ace of Hearts. She is always saying she's trying to find herself.'

'There's something I don't understand,' I interrupted.

'Yes?'

'You said the first dwarfs came to the island only a few years after you landed here yourself – but they all look so young; it is difficult to believe that some of them are almost fifty years old.'

An enigmatic smile crept over the old man's face. 'They don't get old.'

'But –'

'When I was alone on the island, the images in my dreams grew stronger and stronger. Then they slipped out of my thoughts and threw themselves into existence here. But they are still fantasy – and fantasy has the wonderful ability to keep what was once created, young and full of life for ever.'

'That's unbelievable . . .'

'Have you heard of Rapunzel, my boy?'

I shook my head.

'But you've heard of Little Red Riding Hood? Or Snow White? Or Hansel and Gretel?'

I nodded.

'How old do you think they are? A hundred? A thousand maybe? They are both very young and very old. That's because they have leapt from people's imagination. No, I hadn't thought the dwarfs on the island would become old and grey-haired. Even the clothes they wear haven't got so much as a tear in them. It is different for us mortals. We are the ones who become old and grey. We are the ones who become worn at the seams and disappear. But not our dreams. They can live on in other people even after we have gone.'

He stroked his white hair and pointed to his threadbare jacket.

'The big question for me,' he continued, 'was not whether the figures would be ravaged by time but whether they really *were* in the garden and whether they could be seen by other people if someone ever visited the island.'

'And they were!' I said. 'First I met the Two and Three of Clubs, then I met the diamonds in the glassworks . .'

'Mmm . . .'

The old man was in a world of his own, as though he wasn't listening to a word I said.

'The other big question,' he said eventually, 'is whether they will remain here after I am gone.'

'What do you think?'

'I don't have an answer to that question, and I never will. Because when I'm not here, then I won't know whether my figures are here or not either.'

Once again he sat for a long while without saying anything. I found myself wondering whether everything was a dream. Maybe I wasn't sitting in front of Frode's cabin. Maybe I was somewhere else completely – and everything else was something inside me.

'I will tell you more tomorrow, my boy. I must tell you about the calendar – and about the great Joker Game.'

'The Joker Game?'

'Tomorrow, son. We both need to sleep now.'

He led me to a bed made of skins and woven blankets, and gave me a nightshirt made of wool. It was good to change out of my dirty sailor's uniform.

That evening Dad and I sat on the balcony looking down over the town and further out across the Bay of Corinth. Dad was so full of impressions that he didn't say very much. Maybe he was wondering whether he could trust the oracle's prediction that we would meet Mama.

Later that night a full moon rose above the horizon in the east. It lit up the whole of the dark valley and made the stars in the sky seem pale.

It was like sitting in front of Frode's cabin, spying down over the village of dwarfs.

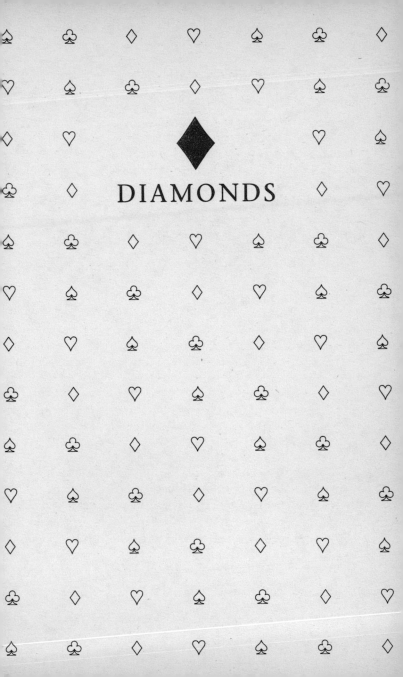

DIAMONDS

ACE OF DIAMONDS

... a fair man who
wanted all the cards on the table ...

As usual I got up before Dad, but it wasn't long before his muscles began to twitch.

I decided to see whether it was true that he woke up every single morning with a bang, as he had claimed the day before.

I concluded that he was right, because when he opened his eyes, he really did look pretty startled. He could just as well have woken up in a totally different place – in India, for example, or on a little planet in another galaxy.

'You are a living person,' I said. 'At this moment you are in Delphi. It is a place on earth, which is a living planet at present orbiting a star in the Milky Way. It takes 365 days for this planet to circle this star.'

He stared at me intently, as though his eyes had to adjust to the change from dreamland to the bright reality outside.

'Thanks for the clarification,' he said. 'I normally have to work all that out for myself before I climb out of bed.'

He got up and walked across the room.

'Maybe you should whisper some words of truth like that in my ear every morning, Hans Thomas. It would certainly get me into the bathroom more quickly.'

It didn't take us long to pack, eat breakfast, and get back on the road.

'It's incredible to think how gullible they were,' Dad said as we drove past the old temple site.

'You mean believing in the oracle?'

He didn't reply right away; I was worried that he had started to doubt the oracle's word that we would meet Mama in Athens, but then he said, 'Well, that, too, but think about all the gods: Apollo, Asclepias, Athena, Zeus, Poseidon and Dionysus. For years and years people built costly marble temples to these gods, which normally meant dragging heavy blocks of marble across huge distances.'

I didn't know a great deal about what he was describing; nevertheless, I said, 'How can you be so sure that these gods didn't exist? They might not be here now – or they've found some other gullible people – but once upon a time they walked around on this earth.'

Dad glanced at me in the rear view mirror. 'Do you believe that, Hans Thomas?'

'I'm not quite sure. But in a way they *were* in the world, as long as people believed in them. People see what they believe – the gods didn't grow old or frayed at the edges until people started to doubt.'

'Well said,' Dad exclaimed. 'That was damn well put, Hans Thomas. Maybe you'll be a philosopher one day, too.'

For once I felt I had said something so profound that even Dad had to think about it. At any rate, he didn't say anything for a long time.

I'd actually fooled him a little, because I would never have said anything like that if I hadn't read the sticky-bun book. I wasn't really thinking of the Greek gods, I was thinking of Frode's playing cards.

It was quiet in the car for such a long time that I carefully tried to sneak out the magnifying glass and the sticky-bun book. Just as I was about to start reading, however, Dad braked sharply and pulled off the road. He jumped out of the Fiat, lit a cigarette, and stood poring over a road atlas.

'Here! Yes, it must be here,' he exclaimed.

I said nothing. To our left was a narrow valley; otherwise I didn't see anything that might explain this sudden outburst.

'Have a seat,' Dad said.

I could tell a mini-lecture was on its way, but this time it didn't bother me. I knew I was really very lucky.

'That's where Oedipus killed his father,' he said, pointing down to the valley.

'Well, of course that was pretty dumb of him,' I remarked, 'but what on earth are you talking about?'

'Destiny, Hans Thomas. I'm talking about destiny, or the family curse, if you prefer. It's something which should particularly concern us – seeing as we've come to this country to find a lost wife and mother.'

'And you believe in destiny?' I had to ask. Dad stood next to me, with his foot on the stone I was sitting on and a cigarette in his hand.

He shook his head. 'But the Greeks did, and if you rebelled against your destiny, you paid for it.'

I was already starting to feel guilty.

'In an old town called Thebes, which we will soon be passing, lived King Laius and his wife, Jocasta. Laius had been told by the Delphic Oracle that he must never have any children, because if he had a son that boy would kill his father and marry his mother, so when Jocasta gave birth to a son, Laius decided to abandon the child to starve to death or be torn apart by wild animals.'

'That's barbaric,' I exclaimed.

'Of course, but wait until you hear the rest. King Laius ordered a shepherd to get rid of the child, and to be safe the King slashed the boy's Achilles tendons, so there would be no way he could move around in the mountains and find his way back to Thebes. The shepherd did as the King had commanded, but on his way up into the mountains he met a shepherd from Corinth. The King of Corinth also had pastures in these parts. The shepherd from Corinth felt sorry for the little boy, who was going to be left either to starve to death or be eaten alive by wild animals. He asked the shepherd from Thebes if he could take the boy back with him to the King in Corinth. And so it came to be that the boy was raised as a prince in Corinth, since the King and Queen had no other children. They called him Oedipus, which means "swollen foot", as the little boy's feet were very badly swollen after the unpleasant treatment he had received in Thebes. Oedipus grew up to be a very handsome man whom everybody liked, but nobody told him that he wasn't the royal couple's true son. However, one day at a royal party a guest showed up and started to gossip about Oedipus not being the King and Queen's real son –'

'But he wasn't.'

'Exactly. But when Oedipus asked the Queen about it, she wouldn't give him a proper answer, so he decided to consult the Delphic Oracle. Oedipus asked Pythia whether he was the rightful heir to the Corinth estate, and she said, 'Leave your father, because if you meet him again, you will kill him. Afterwards, you will marry your mother and beget children with her.'

I whistled loudly. It was the same prophecy the King of Thebes had received.

'On hearing this,' Dad continued, 'Oedipus didn't dare return to Corinth, because he still believed the King and Queen there were his real parents. Instead, he took the road to Thebes. When he reached this exact spot, he met a noble gentleman who was being driven in a stately carriage drawn by four horses. He had several guards with him, and one of them struck Oedipus to make him stand aside. Oedipus – who had been brought up as the heir to the throne of Corinth – didn't care for this treatment, and after a great deal of pushing and shoving, the whole unfortunate meeting ended with Oedipus killing the rich man.'

'And this really was his true father?'

'Yes. The guards were also killed, but the coachman finally managed to escape. He drove back to Thebes and told the people that King Laius had been killed by a robber. The Queen and the people of Thebes were overcome with grief, but there was also another thing worrying the city's inhabitants.'

'What was that?'

'There was a Sphinx, a monstrous beast with a lion's body and a woman's head. It guarded the road to Thebes and tore apart any passerby who couldn't solve the riddle it posed. The people of Thebes promised that whoever could solve the Sphinx's riddle would be able to marry Queen Jocasta and become the King of Thebes after King Laius.'

I whistled again.

'Oedipus, who quickly forgot that he'd been forced to use his sword on the long journey, soon arrived at the Sphinx's mountain, and the Sphinx now demanded that he solve the following riddle: what walks on four legs in the morning, two legs in day time, and three legs in the evening?'

Dad looked at me to see whether I could solve this difficult riddle. I just shook my head.

'"*Human beings* do, during the three stages of life," replied Oedipus. "In infancy they crawl on all fours, for most of their life they walk upright on two legs – and in old age they hobble on three because they have to use a stick." Oedipus had given the correct answer, and the Sphinx didn't survive this; it tumbled down the mountainside to its death. Oedipus was greeted as a hero in Thebes. He received the promised reward and married Jocasta, who was in fact his own mother, and in time they had two sons and two daughters.'

'Well, I'll be damned,' I exclaimed. I hadn't taken my eyes off

Dad for a second, but now I just had to glance down at the place where Oedipus had killed his father.

'But that's not the end of the story,' Dad continued. 'A terrible plague broke out in the city. In those times the Greeks believed such misfortunes were due to the wrath of Apollo and that there must be a reason for his anger. They asked the Delphic Oracle why Apollo had sent this terrible plague. Pythia's answer was that the city had to find King Laius' murderer, otherwise the whole city would be destroyed.'

'No way!'

'King Oedipus took it upon himself to do everything he could to find the previous King's murderer. He had never linked the fight on the road to the murder of King Laius. Without knowing it, Oedipus became the murderer who had to solve his own crime. The first thing he did was ask a clairvoyant about who might have murdered King Laius, but the man refused to answer, simply because the truth was too harsh. However, Oedipus – who was prepared to do everything in his power to help his people – managed to squeeze the truth out of him. The clairvoyant confided to Oedipus that the King himself was guilty. Even though Oedipus gradually remembered what had happened that day on the road and realised that he had murdered the King, he still had no proof that he was King Laius's son. However, Oedipus was a fair man who wanted all the cards on the table. He finally managed to confront the old shepherd from Thebes and the shepherd from Corinth, and they confirmed that he had killed his own father and married his mother. When the truth eventually became clear to Oedipus, he tore out both his eyes. In a way he had been blind all along.'

I sighed heavily. I thought the old story was deeply tragic and terribly unfair.

'That's what you call a real family curse,' I murmured.

'But on several occasions King Laius and Oedipus tried to escape their destiny. According to the Greeks, this was totally impossible.'

As we passed Thebes there was silence in the car. I think Dad sat mulling over his own family curse; at least he didn't utter a word.

After having thought over the tragedy of King Oedipus from all angles, I reached for the magnifying glass and the sticky-bun book.

TWO OF DIAMONDS

*... Old master receives important
message from the homeland ...*

I was woken up early the next morning by the sound of a cock crowing. For a moment I thought I was at home in Lübeck, but then I remembered the shipwreck. I recalled pushing the lifeboat up the beach by the little lagoon encircled by palm trees. Then I had wandered further inland and fallen asleep beside a large lake, after swimming in a multitude of goldfish.

Was this where I was now? Had I dreamed of an old seaman who had lived on the island for more than fifty years – and who moreover had created the island's population of fifty-three lively dwarfs?

I tried to answer this question before I opened my eyes.

It couldn't just be a dream! I had gone to bed in Frode's cabin above the little village ...

I opened my eyes. The morning sun threw golden rays into a dark wooden cabin, and I understood that what I had experienced was as real as the sun and the moon.

I scrambled out of bed. Where was Frode, I wondered. At the same time I noticed a little wooden box on a shelf above the door.

I took it down and looked inside – it was empty. This must have been the box that had contained the old playing cards before the big transformation.

I put the box back in its place and went outside. Frode was standing with his hands behind his back, surveying the village. I went and stood beside him; neither of us said a word.

The dwarfs were already busy at work. The village and the surrounding hills were bathed in sunshine.

'Joker Day . . .' the old man said finally. A worried expression swept across his face.

'Joker Day?' I asked.

'We'll eat breakfast outside, my boy. Now just sit yourself here and I'll be back in a minute with some food.'

He pointed to a short bench set up against the cabin wall, in front of a little table. When we sat down, the view was wonderful. Some of the dwarfs were on their way out of the village, pulling a cart behind them. They were probably the clubs off to work in the fields. From the big workshop I could hear the clatter of materials.

Frode returned with bread, cheese, moluk's milk, and hot tuff. He sat beside me, and after a while he started to tell me more about his first days on the island.

'I often think of this time as my Solitaire Period,' he said. 'I was as lonely as anyone can be. Maybe that's why it wasn't so surprising that fifty-three playing cards gradually turned into the same number of fantasy figures. But that was only part of it. The cards also came to play an important part in the calendar we follow here on the island.'

'The calendar?'

'Yes. The year has fifty-two weeks, so each week is represented by one of the cards in the pack.'

I started to work it out.

'Seven multiplied by fifty-two,' I said aloud, 'is 364.'

'Exactly. But the year has 365 days. The day which is left over we call Joker Day. It belongs to no month and no week either. It is an extra day, a day when anything can happen. Every four years we have *two* such Joker Days.'

'That's clever . . .'

'The fifty-two weeks – or "the cards," as I call them – are also divided into thirteen months, each of twenty-eight days, because thirteen multiplied by twenty-eight is also 364. The first month is Ace, and the last month is King. Then there is an interval of four years between every two Joker Days. It begins with the year of the diamonds, followed by the year of the clubs, then hearts and finally spades. In this way all the cards have their own week and month.'

The old man glanced at me quickly. It was as though he felt embarrassed about his ingenious calendar, but proud of it, too.

'At first it sounds a bit complicated,' I said, 'but it is extremely clever!'

Frode nodded.

'I had to use my head for something. The year is also divided into four seasons – diamonds during the spring, clubs in the summer, hearts in the autumn, and spades in the winter. The first week of the year is the Ace of Diamonds, and all the rest of the diamonds follow. The summer begins with the Ace of Clubs and the autumn with the Ace of Hearts. The winter commences with the Ace of Spades, and the last week in the year is the King of Spades.'

'Which week are we in now?'

'Yesterday was the last day in the King of Spades's week, but it was also the last day in the King of Spades's month.'

'And today –'

'. . . today is Joker Day – or the first of two Joker Days. It will be celebrated with a big banquet.'

'How odd . . .'

'Yes, dear countryman. It is odd that you came to the island just as we were about to play the joker card – and about to start a new year and a whole four-year period. But there's even more . . .'

The old sailor now sat deep in thought.

'Yes?'

'The cards formed what can be regarded as an "era" on the island.'

'I don't follow you.'

'You see, every card was given its own week and month, so I could keep track of the days of the year. Every single *year* has been in one of the cards' signs. My first year on the island was given the name the Ace of Diamonds. Then it was the Two of Diamonds – and thereafter all the other cards followed in order like the fifty-two weeks. But I told you I had lived on the island exactly fifty-two years . . .'

'Yes . . .'

'We have just laid the King of Spades behind us, sailor, and further than that I have not thought, because to live more than fifty-two years on the island –'

'Was something you hadn't counted on?'

'No, I hadn't. Today Joker will declare the beginning of the year of the Joker. The great celebration will be launched this afternoon. The spades and hearts are busy turning the big carpentry workshop into a banquet hall. The clubs are collecting fruits and berries, and the diamonds are setting out the glasses.'

'Will . . . will I be going to the banquet?'

'You'll be the guest of honour. But before we go down to the village, there's something else you should know. We still have a couple of hours, sailor, so we must make the most of that time . . .'

He poured some of the brown drink into a glass from the glass factory. I sipped it carefully, and the old man went on: 'The Joker Banquet is celebrated at the end of each year – or at the beginning of a new year, if you like. But solitaire is played only every four years . . .'

'Solitaire?'

'Yes, every four years. The Joker Game is performed.'

'I'm afraid you're going to have to explain.'

He cleared his throat twice. 'As I have already told you, I had to have something to fill my time when I lived alone on the island. I would flick through the cards and pretend they "said" their own sentence. It became a sort of game to try to remember all the sentences. When I eventually learned what all the cards said, the second part of the game began. I tried to shuffle the cards around so the sentences would join together and form a continuous unit. I would often end up with a kind of story – made up of the sentences the cards had "come up with", completely independently of one another.'

'Was that the Joker Game?'

'Mmm, yes – it was a kind of solitaire to play when I was lonely, but it was also the beginning of the great Joker Game, which is now performed every fourth year on Joker Day.'

'Go on.'

'During the four years that pass between each period, every one of the fifty-two dwarfs has to come up with one sentence. It might not sound that impressive, but you have to remember they think very slowly. The sentence also has to be remembered, and to go from day to day remembering a whole sentence is not a simple task for dwarfs whose heads are practically empty.'

'And they all say their sentences at the Joker Banquet?'

'Right. But that's only the first part of the game. Then it's the Joker's turn. He hasn't thought of any sentence himself, but when all the sentences are being spoken he sits on a throne and makes notes. During the Joker Banquet he shuffles the order of the cards so that the characters' sentences make a coherent whole. He positions the dwarfs in the right order, and then they repeat their sentences, but now every single sentence is a tiny piece of a big fairy tale.'

'That's clever.'

'Yes, clever indeed, but it can also be pretty amazing.'

'What do you mean?'

'You might think that the Joker – with all his talent – attempts to create an entirety out of something which began as pure chaos. After all, the figures have devised their own sentences quite independently of each other.'

'Yes?'

'But sometimes it seems as though the entirety – that is the fairy tale or story – has existed before.'

'Is that possible?'

'I don't know, but if it is the case, then the fifty-two dwarfs are really something quite different – and something far more than just fifty-two individuals. An invisible thread is tying them together, because I still haven't told you everything.'

'Go on!'

'When I sat and played with the cards during the first days on the island, I also tried to *read* the future in the cards. Of course, it was just a game, but I thought it might be true, as I had heard so often among the company of sailors in the many ports I had visited that a pack of cards could reveal the future. And sure enough, in the days prior to the Jack of Clubs and the King of Hearts appearing as the very first figures on the island, these exact cards took prominent positions on several occasions in the many games of solitaire I played.'

'How odd.'

'I did not give it a lot of thought when we started the Joker Game, once all the figures were in position – but do you know what the very last sentence in the tale at the last Joker Banquet was? I mean, four years ago?'

'No, how could I?'

'Well, wait until you hear this: "Young sailor comes to the village on the last day in King of Spades. The sailor guesses riddles with Jack of glass. Old master receives important message from the homeland."'

'That ... that was bizarre.'

'I haven't thought of these words for four years, but when you showed up in the village last night – which was the last day in the week, month, and year of the King of Spades – yes, then the old prediction came flooding back to me. In a way you were foreseen, sailor ...'

Something suddenly hit me.

'Old master receives important message from the homeland,' I repeated.

'Yes?'

The old man's eyes burned into mine.

'Didn't you say she was called Stine?'

The old man nodded.

'From Lübeck?'

He nodded again.

'My father's name is Otto. He grew up without a father, but his mother was called Stine too. She died only a few years ago.'

'It is a very common name in Germany.'

'Of course ... Father was an "illegitimate child", as they say, because Grandmother never married. She ... she was engaged to a sailor who was lost at sea. Neither of them knew she was pregnant when they last saw each other ... There was so much gossip. There was talk of a fleeting relationship with a casual sailor who had run away from his responsibilities.'

'Hmm ... and when was your father born, boy?'

'I ...'

'Tell me! When was your father born, boy?'

'He was born in Lübeck on May 8, 1791, about fifty-one years ago.'

'And this "sailor" – was he the son of a master glassblower?'

'I don't know. Grandmother didn't talk about him very much. Possibly because of all the gossip. The only thing she told us children was that he had once climbed up high into the rigging of a sailing ship to wave goodbye to her as he sailed out of Lübeck. Then he had fallen down and hurt one of his arms. She used to smile when she told us that. The whole display had sort of been in honour of her.'

The old man now sat for a long time staring out over the village.

'That arm,' he finally spoke, 'is nearer to you than you realise.'

With that he rolled up the sleeve of his jacket and showed me an old scar under his arm.

'Grandfather!' I shouted. I threw my arms around him and hugged him tightly.

'Son,' he said, and started to sob into the crook of my neck. 'Son, son ...'

THREE OF DIAMONDS

... She was drawn here
by her own reflection ...

A kind of family curse had appeared in the sticky-bun book, too, and I thought the plot was thickening in more ways than one.

We stopped for lunch at a country taverna, where we sat at a long table under a couple of massive trees. An abundance of orange trees grew around the taverna in large plantations.

We ate meat on skewers and Greek salad with goat's cheese, and when the dessert arrived, I started to tell Dad about the calendar on the magic island. Of course, I couldn't tell him where I'd got it from, so I was forced to say it was something I had made up while I had been sitting in the back seat.

Dad was dumbfounded. He worked it out with a pen on a napkin.

'Fifty-two cards are fifty-two weeks. That really would be 364 days, and then there were thirteen months of twenty-eight days –

that is also 364. In both cases there is an extra day ...'

'And that is Joker Day,' I said.

'Well, I'll be blowed!'

He sat for a long time gazing into the orange groves.

'And when were you born, Hans Thomas?'

I didn't know what he meant.

'February 29, 1972,' I replied.

'But what kind of day was that?'

It suddenly dawned on me: indeed, I had been born in a leap year. According to the calendar from the magic island, it was a sort of Joker Day. How come I hadn't thought of that when I was reading?

'Joker Day,' I said.

'Exactly!'

'Do you think it's because I am the son of a joker – or do you think it's because I am a joker myself?' I asked.

Dad looked at me seriously and said, 'Both, of course. When I *get* a son, it's on a Joker Day, and when *you* are born, that also happens on a Joker Day. It makes sense, you know.'

I wasn't quite sure if he just liked the idea that I was born on a Joker Day, but there was also something in his voice which made me wonder whether he'd started to get scared that I might take over his trade as a joker.

At any rate, he was quick to turn the conversation back to the calendar.

'Did you think of that just now?' he asked me yet again. 'Hah! Every week has its own card, every month has its own number from ace to king, and every season has one of the four suits. You should take out a patent for that, Hans Thomas. As far as I know, to this day a proper bridge-calendar hasn't been invented.'

He sat chuckling over his coffee cup. Then he added, 'At first we used the Julian calendar, then we went over to the Gregorian – maybe it's about time we changed again.'

He was clearly more taken with this calendar business than I. He did some hectic calculations on his napkin, and soon he glanced up with a cunning joker's look in his eye and said, 'And there's more ...'

I looked at him.

'If you add all the symbols in a suit together,' he continued, 'you get ninety-one. Ace is one, king is thirteen, queen is twelve – and so on. Yes, you definitely get ninety-one.'

'Ninety-one?' I said. I didn't quite follow.

He put his pen down on the napkin and looked deeply into my eyes.

'What is ninety-one multiplied by four?'

'Nine fours are thirty-six ...' I said. 'It's 364! Well, I'll be damned!'

'Exactly! There are 364 symbols in a pack of cards – plus the joker. But then there are some years which have two Joker Days. Maybe that's why there are two jokers in a pack, Hans Thomas. This can't be coincidence.'

'Do you think a pack of cards is made with this in mind?' I asked. 'Do you think it is deliberate that there are the same number of markings on a pack of cards as there are days in a year?'

'No, I can't believe that, but I do think this is an example of the way in which people are unable to interpret the signs that are right in front of their noses. Nobody has bothered to literally put two and two together, even though there are many millions of playing cards.'

He sat pondering things over in his mind. Then a dark shadow crept over his face.

'But I see a serious problem. It'll no longer be so easy to bum jokers off people if they have a place in a calendar,' he said, and laughed out loud like a horse. Obviously it wasn't that serious after all.

He continued to chuckle to himself when we were back in the car. He was undoubtedly still thinking of the calendar.

As we neared Athens, I noticed a large road sign. I had already seen the same sign several times before, but now my heart jumped for joy.

'Stop!' I cried. 'Stop the car!'

Dad was scared out of his wits. He pulled over, braking sharply.

'Whatever's the matter now?' he asked, turning to face me.

'Out!' I ordered. 'We must get out of the car!'

Dad opened the car door and jumped out. 'Are you going to be sick?' he asked.

I pointed to the road sign only a few metres away.

'You see that sign there?'

Dad was so confused I really should have taken pity on him, but I could only think about the sign.

'And what about that sign?' Dad asked. He must have thought I'd totally flipped.

'Read it,' I instructed.

'ATHINAI,' Dad read, only starting to calm down. 'It is Greek and means Athens.'

'Is *that* all you see? What does it sound like backward?'

'IANIHTA,' he now read aloud.

I didn't say anything else, I just looked at him seriously and nodded.

'Yes, it does sound a lot like Anita,' he admitted, and lit a cigarette.

He was taking it so calmly, I started to get irritated.

'Funny? Is that all you have to say? I mean, she's here, you realise that, don't you? I mean, she came here. She was drawn here by her own reflection. It was *her* destiny. You have to see the connection now!'

For one reason or another I had managed to get Dad angry.

'Now just try to calm down, Hans Thomas.'

It was obvious he didn't like the bit about destiny and her reflection.

We got back in the car.

'Sometimes you can go a bit far with all this ... this inventiveness of yours,' he said.

He wasn't just thinking about the sign, no doubt he meant the dwarfs and the strange calendar as well. If this was so, then I thought he was being unfair. I don't think he was the right person to criticise other people's 'inventiveness'. After all, I wasn't the one who had started talking about a family curse.

On the road to Athens I sneaked open the sticky-bun book and read about the preparations for the Joker Banquet on the magic island.

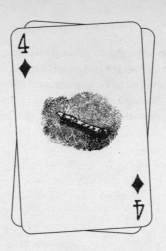

FOUR OF DIAMONDS

... Her little hand was
as cold as the morning dew ...

I had met my very own grandfather on the magic island, because I was the son of the unborn child he had left behind in Germany when he had set off across the Atlantic Ocean before the fateful shipwreck.

Which was stranger: the fact that a little seed could grow and eventually become a living person? Or that a living person could have such vivid fantasies that these fantasies eventually start to spurt out into the world? But weren't human beings lively, living fantasies like these as well? Who let *us* out into the world?

Frode had lived alone on the big island for half a century – would we ever be able to travel back to Germany together? Would I be able to walk into my father's bakery one day, at home in Lübeck, and introduce the old man with me and say, 'Here I am, Dad, I have returned from foreign lands. I've brought Frode with me – he is your father.'

Thousands of thoughts about the world, history, and all the generations filled my head while I embraced Frode tightly. I wasn't able
to think for very long, however, as a bunch of dwarfs dressed in red
were hurrying up the hill from the village.

'Look!' I whispered to the old man. 'We've got visitors!'

'It's the hearts,' he said in a broken voice. 'They always come and
fetch me for the Joker Banquet.'

'I am looking forward to it.'

'So am I, son. Did I tell you that it was the Jack of Spades who
conveyed the sentence about the important message from the
homeland?'

'No ... what about it?'

'Spades always bring bad luck. I learned that in the harbour bars
long before the shipwreck, and it has also been true here on the
island. Every time I stumble across a spade down in the village, I can
be sure there will be an accident.'

He wasn't able to say more than that now, because all the hearts
from Two to Ten were dancing around in front of the cabin. They
all had long fair hair and red dresses with hearts on. Next to
Frode's brown clothes and my own threadbare sailor's uniform,
their red dresses shone with an intensity so bright I had to rub my
eyes.

We walked toward them, and they now formed a tight ring
around us.

'Happy Joker!' they shouted, and laughed.

They then started to walk round us in a circle, singing and swinging their skirts.

'Okay! That's enough,' the old man said.

He talked to them as you would normally talk to pet animals.

With that, the girls started to nudge us down the hillside. The Five
of Hearts held my hand and dragged me along behind her. Her little
hand was as cold as the morning dew.

It was quiet in the village streets and square, but yelling and
screeching could be heard coming from some of the houses. The
hearts disappeared inside one of the cabins.

Lit oil lamps hung around the outside of the carpentry workshop, even though the sun was still high in the sky.

'Here it is,' Frode announced, and we stepped inside the banqueting hall.

None of the dwarfs had arrived yet, but four large tables were set with glass plates and tall dishes piled high with fruit. There were also many bottles and decanters filled with the sparking drink. Thirteen chairs were placed around each table.

The walls were constructed of a light-coloured wood, and oil lamps of coloured glass hung from the beams in the ceiling. Four windows were carved out of a wall along the far side of the room, and on the windowsills and tables there were glass bowls filled with red, yellow, and blue fish. Soft blankets of sunlight drifted in through the windows, hitting the bottles and goldfish bowls, sending tiny rainbow flickers across the floor and along the walls. Three tall chairs were positioned next to each other on the opposite side of the room. They reminded me of the bench in a courtroom.

Before I'd had the chance to look at everything, the door burst open and the Joker bounced into the banqueting hall from the street outside.

'Greetings!' he said, grinning from ear to ear.

Every time he made the slightest movement, the bells on his violet costume rang zealously, and if he nodded just a touch, his red-and-green hat with the donkey ears jangled.

He suddenly bounded towards me, hopped up, and pulled my ear. The noise he made sounded like bells on a sleigh pulled by a fearsome horse.

'Now,' he said, 'are you pleased to be invited to the great banquet?'

'Thank you for the invitation,' I replied. I was almost scared of the little gnome.

'Really – so you have learned the art of gratitude? Not bad,' said the Joker.

'Why don't you try to calm down a little, you fool,' Frode said sternly.

But the little Joker just looked suspiciously at the old sailor.

'No doubt you have cold feet before the great occasion, but Joker says it's too late for regrets, for today all the cards will be turned picture-side-up – and the truth lies in the cards. Let's say no more! Enough!'

The little clown ran back outside and Frode was left slowly shaking his head.

'Who is the real figure of authority on the island here?' I asked. 'Is it you, or is it that fool?'

'Until now it has been me,' he replied perplexedly.

After a little while, the Joker came back in. He sat down on one of the tall chairs along the wall and solemnly signalled to me and Frode to take our seats next to him. Frode sat in the middle, with the Joker to his right and me to his left.

'Silence!' ordered the Joker when we had sat down, even though neither of us had uttered a word.

Some beautiful flute music grew louder and louder, and now all the diamonds came scampering in through the door. The pint-sized King led the way, followed by the Queen, the Jack, and then all the other diamonds, with the Ace bringing up the rear. Everyone except the royal family was playing her own little glass flute. They played a wonderful waltz, and the notes from the glass flutes were so delicate and pure, they sounded like the notes from the very smallest pipes on a church organ. The diamonds were all dressed in pink and had silvery hair and twinkling blue eyes, and apart from the King and the Jack, they were all female.

'Bravo!' exclaimed the Joker, clapping his hands, and seeing Frode do the same, I joined in, too.

The diamonds stood in one corner of the room, forming a quarter circle, and now the clubs, dressed in their dark blue uniforms, entered. The Queen and the Ace had the same colour dresses, and all the clubs had brown curly hair, dark skin, and brown eyes. They were slightly chubbier than the diamonds in build, and this time the Queen and the Ace were the only females.

The clubs joined the diamonds, and together they formed a half circle. The hearts came next, wearing their blood-red dresses. The King and the Jack were the only males, and both wore deep red uniforms. The hearts had blonde hair, warm complexions, and green eyes. Only the Ace of Hearts stood out from the others. She was wearing the same yellow dress she had worn the day I had met her in the woods. She walked over to the King of Clubs and stood beside him. The dwarfs had now formed three-quarters of a circle.

The spades entered last. They had wiry black hair, black eyes, and black uniforms. They were more broad-shouldered than the other dwarfs, and their expressions were as grim and sombre as their uniforms. The Queen and the Ace were the only women, and they wore purple dresses.

The Ace of Spades joined the King of Hearts, and the fifty-two dwarfs now formed a full circle.

'Amazing,' I whispered.

'The Joker Banquet begins like that every year,' Frode whispered back to me. 'They form the fifty-two weeks of the year.'

'Why is the Ace of Hearts wearing a yellow dress?'

'She is the sun at its height in midsummer.'

There was a little space betwen the King of Spades and the Ace of Diamonds. The Joker now climbed down from his chair and stood between them. With that, the circle was complete. The Ace of Hearts stood directly opposite the Joker.

The dwarfs held hands and cheered: 'Merry Joker and a happy New Year!'

The little jester opened his arms wide, making his bells jingle, and announced in a loud voice: 'Not only has one year passed, but we've also come to the end of a whole pack of fifty-two years! The future now stands with the Joker. Happy birthday, Brother Joker! Let's say no more! Enough!'

He shook his own hand as though he was congratulating himself, and all the other dwarfs clapped, although none of them appeared to have understood the Joker's speech. Each of the four families then gathered around its own table.

Frode put his hand on my shoulder. 'They don't really understand what they are part of,' he whispered. 'They just repeat year in and year out what I once did myself when I laid the cards in a circle every new year.'

'But –'

'Have you seen horses and dogs run around a circus ring, my boy? It's the same with these dwarfs; they are like trained animals. It's just that the Joker . . .'

'Yes?'

'I have never seen him so arrogant and sure of himself.'

FIVE OF DIAMONDS

*... the unfortunate thing was
that the drink I was given actually tasted
sweet and good ...*

D ad interrupted my reading to tell me we were coming into Athens, so I felt it didn't really do to be elsewhere on the planet.

With the help of a map and some perseverance, the boss managed to find a tourist information office. I sat in the car watching the Greeks while Dad was in the tourist office trying to find a suitable hotel.

When he returned, he was smiling from ear to ear.

'Hotel Titania,' he said when he got back into the car. 'They have parking facilities and vacancies – of course that is important – but I also told them that if I was going to spend some days in Athens, then I wanted to *see* the Acropolis. So we found this hotel with a roof terrace and a panoramic view over Athens.'

He wasn't exaggerating – our room was on the twelfth floor,

and even the view from there matched its description. Nevertheless, the first thing we did was take the lift up to the roof and then
we could see right across to the Acropolis.

Dad stood staring at the ancient temples, speechless.

'It's amazing, Hans Thomas,' he said, breaking his silence. 'It is
truly amazing.'

He paced back and forth. When at last he had calmed down, he
ordered himself a beer. We sat closest to the railing at the end of
the terrace facing the Acropolis. Soon the floodlights around the
old temples were switched on, and Dad almost flipped with
excitement.

When he had stopped gazing at everything around him, he
said, 'You and I will go there tomorrow, Hans Thomas, and
we'll also visit the old market square. I'll show you where the
great philosophers walked about discussing many important
questions which unfortunately the Europe of today has
forgotten.'

He now began a longer lecture on the philosophers in Athens,
but after a while I just had to interrupt him: 'I thought we'd
come here to look for Mama – you haven't forgotten that, have
you?'

He had ordered his second or third beer.

'Of course not,' he replied. 'But if we haven't seen the Acropolis
first, we might not have anything to talk to her about, and that
would be a damn shame after all these years. Don't you think,
Hans Thomas?'

As we were nearing our goal, I understood for the first time that
Dad was actually dreading meeting her. This was such a painful
realisation that I thought it made an adult out of me.

Up until now I had taken it for granted that when we got to
Athens we would meet Mama, and when we met her, all our
problems would be solved. I now understood that this wasn't the
case.

It wasn't Dad's fault that I had been so slow to understand this;
on several occasions he had said it was not certain that she'd

come home with us. However, that had been like water off a
duck's back to me. I had failed to see that despite all our efforts,
such a thing could be possible.

I knew now that I had been very childish, and I suddenly felt
terribly sorry for Dad. Naturally I felt sorry for myself, too. I think
this must have played a part in what happened next.

After making some flippant remarks about Mama and the
ancient Greeks, Dad turned to me and said, 'Would you like to try
a glass of wine, Hans Thomas? I'm going to have one, but it's a bit
dull drinking on my own.'

'Well, first of all I don't like wine,' I said. 'And second, I'm not
an adult.'

'I'll order something you'll like,' he said confidently. 'And
you're not that far from being an adult either.'

He caught the waiter's attention and ordered a glass of Martini
Rosso for me and a glass of Metaxa for himself.

The waiter looked at me and then Dad in astonishment. 'Really?' he asked.

Dad nodded, and so it came to be.

Unfortunately, the drink I was given actually tasted sweet and
good. Moreover, it was very refreshing with all the ice cubes in it.
So I ended up having two or three of these drinks before the great
blunder became obvious.

My face turned deathly white and I almost collapsed onto the
terrace floor.

'Oh, son,' Dad groaned apologetically.

He took me down to the room, and I don't remember much
more before waking up the next morning, but I do know I felt
pretty awful as I slept. I think Dad did, too.

SIX OF DIAMONDS

*. . . now and then they climbed
down to mingle with the people . . .*

When I woke up the next morning, the first thing I thought about was how sick and tired I was of all this boozing.

I had a father who was possibly the brightest person north of the Alps, and this person was slowly being dulled by bottled madness. I decided we had to sort this out once and for all before we met Mama.

When Dad leaped out of bed and started talking about the Acropolis, I realized that it was better to wait until breakfast.

When we had finished eating, Dad asked the waiter for another cup of coffee, lit a second cigarette, and unfolded a large map of Athens.

'Don't you think it's beginning to go too far?' I asked.

He turned towards me.

'You know what I mean,' I pressed on. 'We've talked about this constant drinking before, but when you want your son to be part of it as well, then I think you're crossing the line.'

'I'm sorry, Hans Thomas,' he admitted at once. 'I suppose those drinks were slightly too strong for you.'

'Maybe. But you might slow your tempo a little, too. It would be a terrible shame if the only joker in Arendal ended up a good-for-nothing like all the others.'

He reeked of a guilty conscience, and for a moment I felt sorry for him, but I couldn't always rub him the right way.

'I'll think about it,' he replied.

'Then I think you should think about it fast. I doubt whether Mama is particularly fond of sloppy philosophers who are always on the bottle, either.'

He squirmed in his seat. It must have been quite a blow for him to be put in his place like that by his son, so I wasn't that surprised when he said, 'Actually, I have been thinking the same thing, Hans Thomas.'

His reply was so assertive that it would do for now. There was something else which struck me, however. I don't know why, but I suddenly got the feeling that I hadn't heard all the reasons why Mama left us.

'How do we get to the Acropolis, then ?' I asked, pointing to the map.

We were back in business.

To save time we took a taxi to the entrance, and from there we walked through an avenue of trees along the side of the mountain before we began the ascent to the temple site itself.

When at last we reached the largest temple, which was called the Parthenon, Dad started to pace back and forth.

'Wonderful . . . It is truly wonderful,' he declared.

We wandered around for quite a while, until we stood peering down at two ancient theatres which lay directly below a sheer mountain drop. The tragic tale of Oedipus had been one of the dramas performed in the oldest theatre.

Dad finally pointed to a large rock and said, 'Sit here,' and so the long lecture on the Athenians began.

When the lecture was over and the sun was so high in the sky that there were hardly any shadows, we examined every single temple. Dad pointed here and there and taught me the difference between Doric and Ionic columns and showed me how the Parthenon didn't have a single straight line. The enormous building had been empty except for a twelve-metre-high statue of Athena, the goddess of Athens.

I learned how the Greek gods had lived on Mount Olympus in the north of Greece, and how now and then they climbed down to mingle with the people. Dad said they were like huge jokers in a pack of cards made of human beings.

There was a small museum here, too, but once again I begged for mercy. I was excused, and we agreed on where I could sit and wait.

I definitely would have gone into the museum with him, because he was such a interesting guide, but something in my pocket prevented me from doing so.

I had listened to everything Dad told me about the ancient temples, but I had also been wondering what would happen at the great Joker Banquet. The fifty-two dwarfs on the magic island had all made a big ring in the banqueting hall, and now each of them was about to recite a line.

SEVEN OF DIAMONDS

. . . a big party where the guests had been told to turn up as playing cards . . .

The dwarfs all sat chatting away, but the Joker soon clapped his hands and shouted across the gathering: 'Has everyone thought of a sentence for the Joker Game?'

'Yes,' the dwarfs replied in harmony, so that it resounded around the hall.

'Then let the sentences begin!' declared the Joker.

With that, the dwarfs immediately recited their sentences. Fifty-two voices droned together for a few seconds, and then a hush fell on the hall, as though the whole performance was over.

'It happens every single time,' whispered Frode. 'Of course, nobody hears anything except their own voice.'

'Thank you for your attention,' said the Joker. 'From now on, let us concentrate on one sentence at a time. We'll begin with the Ace of Diamonds.'

The little princess stood up, brushed her hair away from her forehead, and said, '*Destiny is a cauliflower head which grows equally in all directions.*'

She sat back down, her pale cheeks blushing furiously.

'A cauliflower head, I see ...' The Joker scratched his head. 'Those were ... wise words.'

The Two suddenly jumped up and said, '*The magnifying glass matches chip in goldfish bowl.*'

'You don't say?' commented the Joker. 'It would have been even more helpful if you had told us which magnifying glass matches which goldfish bowl. But all in good time, all in good time! The whole truth cannot be squeezed into two diamonds. Next!'

It was now the Three of Diamonds's turn: '*Father and son search for the beautiful woman who can't find herself.*' She sniffed, and began to cry.

I remembered that I had seen her cry on a previous occasion, and while the King of Diamonds comforted her, the Joker said, 'And why can't she find herself? We won't know that until all the cards are turned picture-side-up. Next!'

The rest of the diamonds followed in turn.

'*The truth is that the master glassblower's son has made fun of his own fantasies,*' said the Seven. She had said exactly the same thing to me at the glassworks.

'*The figures are shaken out of the magician's sleeve and appear out of thin air bursting with life,*' stated the Nine assertively. She was the one who had said she would really like to think a thought which was so difficult she wasn't able to think it. I thought she had learned that art pretty well.

The last to speak was the King of Diamonds: '*The solitaire is a family curse.*'

'Very interesting,' exclaimed the Joker. 'Even after the first quarter, many important pieces have fallen into place. Do we understand the depths of this?'

There was a rush of whispers and hushed discussions, and then the Joker continued: 'We still have three-quarters of the wheel of fortune left. Next – clubs!'

'Destiny is a snake which is so hungry it devours itself', said the Ace of Clubs.

'The goldfish does not reveal the island's secret, but the sticky bun does,' continued the Two. I realised that he must have gone around with this sentence on the tip of his tongue for a long time, and had spat it out just before he had fallen asleep in the field because he was afraid he might forget it.

All the other dwarfs now followed in turn – the rest of the clubs, the hearts and finally the spades.

'The inner box unpacks the outer box at the same time as the outer box unpacks the inner,' recited the Ace of Hearts – exactly as she had done when I had met her in the woods.

'One beautiful morning King and Jack climb out of the prison of consciousness.'

'The breast pocket hides a pack of cards which is placed in the sun to dry.'

The rest of the fifty-two dwarfs stood up in running order and contributed a sentence each more absurd than the previous one. Some delivered their sentences in a whisper, some with a laugh, some boldly, and some with a sniffle or a tear. The general impression – if you could use such a term for something so confused and disordered as these speeches – was void of any kind of meaning or coherence. Nevertheless, the Joker strove to make a note of all the statements and the order in which they were delivered.

The King of Spades was the last to speak, and with a piercing glance at the Joker he concluded: *'The one who sees through destiny must also live through it.'*

I remember thinking that this last sentence was the wisest thing to have been said. The Joker obviously thought so too, because he started to clap so wildly that his bells jangled and he sounded like a one-man band. Frode shook his head in despair.

We got up and climbed down to join the dwarfs, who were milling around between the tables.

I got a sudden flashback to my earlier notion that this island must be a sanctuary for the incurably mentally ill. Perhaps Frode was the medical orderly, who had promptly become deranged himself. If so, a doctor's visit to the island some time next month wouldn't help.

Everything he had told me about the shipwreck and the playing cards – or the fantasy figures who had suddenly burst into life – could be the confused ramblings of a man who had lost his mind. I had only one piece of solid evidence to suggest otherwise: my grandmother's name really was Stine – and Mother and Father *had* spoken of a grandfather who had fallen from the rigging and injured his arm.

Perhaps Frode really had lived on the island for fifty years. I had heard tales of others who had survived a shipwreck just as long. He could well have had a pack of cards on him, too, but I could not believe that the dwarfs were figments of Frode's imagination.

I knew there was another possible explanation – all this absurdity could be going on inside my head, I could be the one who had suddenly gone mad. For example, what had been in the berries I had eaten by the lake with all the goldfish? Well, it was too late to think about that now . . .

My thoughts were interrupted by what I assumed was the sound of ship's bells and by somebody tugging at my uniform. It was the Joker and the ship's bells were the bells on his costume.

'What do you make of the cards' convention?' he asked, and stood gazing up at me with a knowing look. I didn't reply.

'Tell me,' the little fool continued, 'wouldn't you think it rather strange if something which somebody *thought* suddenly started to jump around in the space outside the head which had thought it?'

'Yes, absolutely,' I said. 'Of course, it . . . it is totally impossible.'

'Yes, it is impossible,' he agreed. 'Yet at the same time it seems to be true.'

'What do you mean?'

'As I said, we're standing here looking at each other beneath the sky, so to speak . . . bursting with life. How does one manage to "climb out of the prison of consciousness"? What kind of ladder does one use to do that?'

'Maybe we've been here all the time,' I said in an attempt to shake him off.

'Indeed, but the question still remains unanswered. Who are we, sailor? Where do we come from?'

I didn't like the way he was involving me in his philosophical contemplation, and I had to admit I had no answers to any of his questions.

'We were shaken out of the magician's sleeve and appeared out of thin air, bursting with life,' he exclaimed. 'Bizarre, says the Joker! What does the sailor think?'

It was at this point that I realised Frode had gone.

'Where is Frode?' I asked.

'One should really answer the question in hand before asking a new question of one's own,' he said, rippling with laughter.

'What happened to Frode?' I repeated.

'He had to go out for some air. He always has to do that at this point in the Joker Game. Sometimes he worries so much about what is said, he pees his pants, and then Joker thinks it is far better he go outside.'

I felt terribly vulnerable when I was suddenly left alone with all the dwarfs in the large banqueting hall. Most of them had left the tables, and the colourful figures were running around us like children at an over-large birthday party. There was no need to invite the whole village, I thought to myself.

As I watched them, I understood that this was not a normal birthday party. It was more like a large fancy-dress party where the guests had been told to turn up as playing cards, and then everybody had been given a drink at the door to make them shrink so there would be enough room for all the guests. I had turned up for the party just slightly too late to taste the secret aperitif.

'Would you like to taste the sparkling drink?' the Joker said, smiling broadly.

He held out a tiny bottle, and in my confusion I put it to my lips and swallowed a mouthful. A little taste could hardly do any harm.

However, although the mouthful had been ever so little, it completely overpowered me. All the flavours I had tasted in my short life – and many more – charged through my body, washing through me like a tidal wave of desire. There was a relentless taste of strawberry in one of my toes, and peach or banana in a lock of my hair. In my left elbow bubbled a taste of pear juice, and in my nose there steamed a mix of heavenly scents.

It was so good that I was motionless for several minutes. When I now looked at the swarm of dwarfs in their colourful costumes, it was as if they were figments of my own imagination. At once I felt as though I was lost inside my own head, and then the next moment I thought the figments of my imagination had stormed out of my head in protest at being held back by the limitations of my own thoughts.

I continued to think many more weird and wonderful thoughts; it was as though something was tickling the inside of my head. I decided I would never part with this bottle and I would refill it as soon as it was empty. Nothing in the world was more important than having plenty of this sparkling drink.

'Did it taste . . . good or bad?' asked the Joker, grinning from ear to ear.

It was the first time I had seen his teeth, and when he smiled there was a faint tinkle from the bells on his costume. It was as though each tiny tooth was somehow connected to each little bell.

'I'll have another sip,' I said.

At that moment Frode came rushing in from the street. He tripped over the Ten and the King of Spades before he snatched the bottle out of the Joker's hands.

'You lout!' he roared.

The figures in the hall looked up for a moment, but then returned to their festive pleasures.

I suddenly noticed smoke rising from the sticky-bun book and felt a burning sensation on one of my fingers. I threw down the book and the magnifying glass and the people around me stared as if I had just been bitten by a poisonous snake.

'No problem!' I shouted, picking up the magnifying glass and the sticky-bun book again.

The magnifying glass had acted as a burning-glass, and as I now thumbed through the book, I found a large scorch mark on the last page I had read.

Something else had begun to burn, too, only it had a slow-burning fuse: it wouldn't be long before I realised that a great deal of what was written in the sticky-bun book was a reflection of things *I* experienced.

I sat whispering to myself some of the sentences the dwarfs on the island had said.

'Father and son search for the beautiful woman who can't find herself . . . The magnifying glass matches chip in goldfish bowl . . . The goldfish does not give away the island's secret, but the sticky-bun does . . . The solitaire game is a family curse . . .'

There could be no doubt about it: there *was* a mysterious connection between my life and the sticky-bun book. I didn't have the faintest idea how it was possible, but Frode's island wasn't the only magic thing, the little book was a magical piece of work in itself.

For a moment I wondered whether the book wrote itself as I experienced the world around me, but when I leafed through further, I saw that it was already complete.

Even though it was still very hot, I felt a shiver down my spine.

When Dad finally appeared, I jumped down from the rock I was sitting on and asked him three or four questions about the Acropolis and the Greeks. I had to have something else to think about.

EIGHT OF DIAMONDS

*... We are conjured up
and tricked away ...*

Once again we strolled through the grand entrance of the
Acropolis, and Dad stood for a long time looking down
over the town.

He pointed to a hill called Areopagus. The apostle Paul had
once delivered a great speech to the Athenians there about an
unknown God who didn't live in a temple built by human
hands.

The ancient market square of Athens was situated below
Areopagus and was called the agora. The great philosophers had
walked and meditated along the colonnades, but now ruins lay
where magnificent temples, official buildings, and courtrooms
had once stood. The only thing left standing on a small hill is the
ancient marble temple of Hephaestus, the god of fire and
metalworkers.

'We'd better make our way down, Hans Thomas,' Dad said. 'For me this is what it must be like for a Muslim to arrive in Mecca. The only difference is that my Mecca lies in ruins.'

I think he was afraid the agora would be a big disappointment, but when we hustled into the ancient market square and started to clamber among the blocks of marble, he soon managed to revive the culture of the old city. He was helped along by a couple of good books about Athens.

There were hardly any people here. There had been thousands of people milling around up at the Acropolis, but here there were only a couple of jokers who showed up now and again.

I remember thinking that if it were true, as some people claimed, that you have several lifetimes, then Dad would have been walking around this square a thousand years ago. When he spoke about life in ancient Athens, it was as if he 'remembered' how everything had been.

My suspicions were confirmed when he suddenly stopped, pointed across the ruins, and said, 'A young child sits building sandcastles in a sandbox. It constantly builds something new, something which it treasures for only a moment before it knocks it all down again. In the same way Time has been given a planet to play with. This is where the history of the world is written, this is where the events are engraved – and smoothed over again. This is where life bubbles like in a witch's cauldron. One day we'll be modelled here, too – from the same brittle material as our ancestors. The wind of Time blows through us, carries us and *is* us – then drops us again. We are conjured up and tricked away. There is always something lying and brewing in anticipation of taking our place. Because we're not standing on solid ground, we're not even standing on sand – we *are* sand.'

His words frightened me, not only his choice of words but also the powerful way in which he said them.

He went on: 'You cannot hide from Time. You can hide from kings and emperors, and possibly from God, but you can't hide from Time. Time follows our every move, because everything around us is immersed in this transient element.'

I nodded seriously, but Dad had only just begun his long lecture on the ravages of time.

'Time doesn't pass, Hans Thomas, and Time doesn't tick. We are the ones who pass, and our watches tick. Time eats its way through history as silently and relentlessly as the sun rises in the east and sets in the west. It topples great civilisations, gnaws at ancient monuments, and wolfs down generation after generation. That's why we speak of the "ravages of time." Time chews and chomps – and *we* are the ones between its jaws.'

'Is that what the old philosophers talked about?' I asked.

He nodded and continued: 'For a fleeting moment, we are part of a furious swarm. We run around on earth as though *it* was the most obvious thing of all. You saw how the ants crawled and crept up at the Acropolis! But everything will disappear. It will disappear and be replaced with new multitudes, because people are always standing in line. Shapes and masks come and go, and new ideas are always popping up. Themes are never repeated, and a composition never shows up twice ... There is nothing as complicated and precious as a person, my boy – but we are treated like trash.'

I thought this lecture was so pessimistic that at last I dared to make a little comment. 'Are things really so bleak?'

'Wait,' he interrupted, before I'd had a chance to finish what I was going to say. 'We skip around on earth like characters in a fairy tale. We nod and smile at each other as if to say, "Hi there, we're living at the same time! We're in the same reality – or the same fairy tale ..." Isn't that incredible, Hans Thomas? We live on a planet in the universe, but soon we'll be swept out of orbit again. Abracadabra – and we're gone.'

I sat looking at him. There was nobody I knew better, and nobody I loved more, but something strange had come over him while he stood here surveying the marble blocks in the old square in Athens. It wasn't Dad speaking; I thought he had been possessed by Apollo or some kind of demon.

'If we had lived in another century,' he went on, 'we would

have shared our lives with different people. Today we can easily nod and smile and say hello to thousands of our contemporaries: "Hi, there! How strange we should be living at exactly the same time." Or perhaps I bump into someone and open a door and shout: "Hi, soul!"'

He demonstrated with both hands how he could open the door to his soul.

'We're alive, you know, but we live this only once. We open our arms and declare that we exist, but then we are swept aside and thrust into the depths of history. Because we are *disposable*. We are part of an eternal masquerade where the masks come and go. But we deserve more, Hans Thomas. You and I deserve to have our names engraved into something eternal, something that won't be washed away in the great sandbox.'

He sat on a block of marble catching his breath. Only now did I understand that Dad had spent a long time preparing the speech he would give here in the ancient square in Athens. In this way he had also taken part in the ancient philosophers' discussions.

He wasn't really talking to me; everything was directed at the great Greek philosophers. Dad's speech was addressed to a distant past.

I still wasn't a fully fledged philosopher, but I thought I was entitled to give my opinion all the same.

'Don't you think there might be something which isn't washed away in the great sandbox?'

He turned around, and for the first time he spoke to *me*. I think I woke him from a deep trance.

'*Here*,' he said, and pointed to his head. 'There's something in here which can't be washed away.'

For a moment I was worried he'd become a megalomaniac, but he wasn't really just pointing to his own head.

'Thoughts don't flow, Hans Thomas. You see, I have sung only the first verse. The philosophers in Athens believed that there was also something which didn't run. Plato called this the "world of ideas". The sandcastle isn't the most important thing. What is most important is the *image* of a sandcastle which the child had pictured *before* it started to build. Why do you think the child knocks the castle down as soon as it is finished?'

I had to admit I understood the first verse better than the second, but then he said, 'Have you ever wanted to draw or make something but you just haven't been able to get it right? You try over and over again, without giving up. It is because the image you have in your head is always more complete than the representations you try to form with your hands. It's the same with everything we see around us. We think everything could be *better*, and do you know why we do that, Hans Thomas?'

I just shook my head. By now he was so excited that he started to whisper. 'It's because all the images inside our heads have come from the world of ideas. That's where we really belong, you know – not down here in the sandbox, where time snaps at everything we love.'

'So there is another world, then?'

Dad nodded secretively. 'It was our soul before it lodged itself in a body, and it will return there when the body succumbs to the ravages of time.'

'Is that true?' I said, looking up at him in awe.

'Well, that's what Plato thought. Our bodies have the same fate as the sandcastles in the sandbox, nothing can be done about it. But we do have something which time can't gnaw through. That's because it doesn't really belong here. We need to look up from everything flowing around us and see what it is all a representation of.'

I hadn't understood everything Dad had said, but I did understand that philosophy was an enormous thing and Dad was an enormous philosopher. I also felt as though I had made closer contact with the ancient Greeks. I realised that what I had seen today was more or less all that was left of the Greeks' worldly goods, but that their thoughts were as resilient as ever.

To conclude, Dad pointed to the place where Socrates had been imprisoned. He had been charged with leading young people astray, and died after being made to drink a vial of deadly poison. Of course, in truth he was the only joker in Athens at that time.

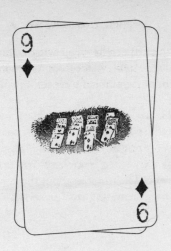

NINE OF DIAMONDS

. . . we are all part of the same family . . .

When we had left the ancient square and the Acropolis behind us, we walked along some shopping streets to Syntagma Square in front of the large parliament building.

Dad bought an interesting pack of cards on the way. He immediately ripped it open, pulled out the joker, and handed me the rest.

We ate dinner at one of the many tavernas on the plaza, and after Dad had gulped down a cup of coffee, he said he was going to make some enquiries to track Mama down. My feet were tired after all that walking in the footsteps of the ancient Greeks, so we agreed I could wait at the café while he made a few telephone calls and visited a model agency nearby.

After Dad had gone, I was left sitting alone in the large square, which was swarming with Greek people. The first thing I did was spread out all the cards on the table. I tried to give each of them a short sentence and make a story out of them. But it was too confusing without a pencil and a piece of paper, so I soon gave up.

Instead, I took out the magnifying glass and the sticky-bun book and read more about the magic island. I was sure I was nearing a decisive point in the story. The Joker was about to put together all the disjointed sentences which the dwarfs had invented, and I might learn more about the connection between myself and all the fascinating stuff Baker Hans had told Albert long, long ago.

The contents of the tiny bottle stimulated my whole body so much that the ground seemed to sway beneath my feet. It was like being at sea again.

I heard Frode say, 'How could you think of offering him the bottle?'

And I heard the Joker reply, 'Well, he did sort of ask for a taste.'

I am not really sure if these were his exact words, because the next minute I fell fast asleep. I was woken by somebody gently kicking me in the side. When I opened my eyes, I saw Frode's face before me.

'You must wake up now!' he said. 'The Joker is about to solve the great riddle.'

I sat bolt upright. 'What riddle?'

'The Joker Game, remember? He's going to put all the sentences together to form a story.'

As I clambered to my feet, I saw the Joker instructing the dwarfs to stand in a particular order. They were arranged in a circle as before, only now the different colours were mixed up and I quickly noticed that the same numbered dwarfs were standing next to each other.

The Joker climbed back onto his throne, and Frode and I did the same.

'Jacks!' shouted the Joker. 'Stand between the Kings and the Tens. The Queens shall stand between the Kings and the aces.'

He scratched his head a couple of times. Then he continued: 'Nine of Clubs and Nine of Diamonds, change places!'

A chubby Nine of Clubs padded across the floor and stood beside a nimble Nine of Diamonds, who skipped across the floor and took the club's place.

The Joker made a few more alterations before he was satisfied.

'This is called a spread,' Frode whispered. 'First, all the cards get a meaning; then they are shuffled together and redealt.'

I could hardly follow what he was saying; a sharp tang of lemon was biting into one of my legs and a blissful scent of lilac was tickling my left ear.

'Everyone has his own sentence,' the Joker began, 'but only when the sections are joined together does the solitaire make sense. For we are all part of the same family.'

A breathless silence fell upon the room. Then the King of Spades spoke: 'Which one of us starts?'

'He is just as impatient each time,' Frode whispered.

The Joker opened his arms wide and declared, 'Naturally the beginning of the story sets the course for everything to follow, and our story begins with the Jack of Diamonds. Off you go, glass Jack, the floor is yours.'

'*Silver brig drowns in foaming sea*', announced the Jack of Diamonds.

The King of Spades stood to the right of him and followed with: '*The one who sees through destiny must also live through it.*'

'No, no!' interrupted the Joker in frustration. 'This play follows the sun. The King of Spades comes at the very end.'

Frode's face was tense and serious. 'It's as I feared,' he mumbled.

'What is?'

'The King of Spades is last.'

I was unable to reply, as an overwhelming taste of eggnog was flowing like a waterfall through my head, and that wasn't something we had every day back home in Lübeck.

'Let's start from the very beginning,' said the Joker. 'First the Jacks then all the Tens and then everyone else in the direction of the sun.

Take it away, Jacks!'

Each of the Jacks now reeled off his sentence.

'*Silver brig drowns in foaming sea. Sailor is washed ashore on island which grows and grows. The breast pocket hides a pack of cards which is placed in the sun to dry. Fifty-three pictures are company for the master glassblower's son for many long years.*'

'That's better,' said the Joker. 'That's how our story begins. Perhaps not such an unusual beginning, but a beginning nevertheless. Okay, Tens!'

And the Tens continued: '*Before the colours fade, fifty-three dwarfs are cast in the lonely sailor's imagination. Peculiar figures dance in the master's mind. When the master sleeps, the dwarfs live their own lives. One beautiful morning King and Jack climb out of the prison of consciousness.*'

'Bravo! It couldn't be better put. Nines!'

'*The images jump out of the creative space into the created space. The figures are shaken out of the magician's sleeve and appear out of thin air bursting with life. The fantasies are beautiful in appearance, but all except one have lost their minds. Only a lonesome Joker sees through the delusion.*'

'That's true! Because truth is a lonely thing. Eights!'

'*Sparkling drink paralyses Joker's senses. Joker spits out the sparkling drink. Without the lie-nectar the little fool thinks more clearly. After fifty-two years the shipwrecked grandson comes to the village.*'

The Joker gave me a look of acknowledgment.

'Sevens!' he commanded.

'*The truth lies in the cards. The truth is that the master glassblower's son has made fun of his own fantasies. The fantasies lead a fantastic rebellion against the master. Soon the master is dead; the dwarfs have murdered him.*'

'Oh dear! Sixes!'

'*Sun princess finds her way to the ocean. The magic island crumbles from within. The dwarfs become cards again. The baker's son escapes the fairy tale before it is folded up.*'

'That was better. Fives, it's your turn now. You must speak clearly and loudly. The slightest error in pronunciation can have dramatic consequences.'

I was so confused by what he said about dramatic consequences that I missed the first sentence.

'*The baker's son escapes over the mountains and settles in remote village. The baker conceals the treasures from the magic island. The future lies in the cards.*'

The Joker now began to applaud eagerly.

'Everyone gets raked over the coals here,' he said. 'The good thing about this play is that not only does it reflect what *has* happened; it also brings promise of what *will* happen – and we're only halfway through the solitaire.'

I turned to Frode, who put his arm around my shoulder and whispered almost inaudibly. 'He's right, my boy.'

'What do you mean?'

'I don't have long to live.'

'Nonsense!' I replied agitatedly. 'You mustn't take such a silly party game so seriously.'

'It's not just a game, son.'

'You're not allowed to die!' I shouted so loudly that several of the figures in the ring turned and looked up at us.

'All old people have to be allowed to die, my boy, but it's good to know that there is someone to pick up where the old leave off.'

'I'll probably die on this island, too.'

With a gentle voice he replied, 'But weren't you listening? "*The baker's son escapes over the mountains and settles in remote village.*" Aren't you the baker's son?'

The Joker clapped his hands once more, and the whole room was filled with the sound of jingling bells.

'Silence!' he ordered. 'Carry on, Fours!'

I was now so afraid that Frode might die, I heard only the Four of Clubs and the Four of Diamonds.

'*The village shelters neglected boy whose mother has passed away. The baker gives him the sparkling drink and shows him the beautiful fish.*'

'And now it's the Threes' turn. Off you go!'

I heard only two of the Threes.

'The sailor marries beautiful woman who gives birth to a baby boy before she travels to land in the south to find herself. Father and son search for the beautiful woman who can't find herself.'

When the Threes had recited their sentences, the Joker interrupted again.

'That was a sure winner!' he said. 'Now we sail into the land of tomorrow.'

I turned to Frode and saw he had tears in his eyes.

'I don't understand any of this,' I said despondently.

'Hssh!' whispered Frode. 'You must listen to history, son.'

'History?'

'Or the future, my boy, but it is also part of history. This game takes us many, many generations into the future. That's what the Joker meant by the "land of tomorrow". We don't understand everything that lies in the cards, but people will come after us.'

'Twos!' cried the Joker.

I tried to remember everything that was said, but I heard only three of the sentences.

'The dwarf with cold hands points the way to remote village and gives the boy from the land in the north a magnifying glass on his journey. The magnifying glass matches chip in goldfish bowl. The goldfish does not reveal the island's secret, but the sticky bun does.'

'Elegant!' declared the Joker. 'I knew that the magnifying glass and the goldfish bowl were the key to the whole story ... And now it's the Aces' turn. Take it away, princesses!'

I managed to hear three of the sentences.

'Destiny is a snake which is so hungry it devours itself. The inner box unpacks the outer box at the same time as the outer box unpacks the inner. Destiny is a cauliflower head which grows equally in all directions.'

'Queens!'

I was so groggy I caught only two sentences.

'*The sticky-bun man shouts down a magic funnel, so his voice carries hundreds of miles. The sailor spits out strong drink.*'

'Now the Kings will conclude the solitaire with some wise words,' announced the Joker. 'Come on, Kings. We're all ears.'

I heard everyone except for the King of Clubs.

'*The solitaire is a family curse. There is always a Joker to see through the delusion. The one who sees through destiny must also live through it.*'

It was the third time the King of Spades had said this about living through destiny. The Joker now clapped his hands, and all the other figures joined in.

'Bravo!' cried the Joker. 'We can all be proud of this solitaire, because everyone has done his bit.'

The dwarfs applauded once more, and now the Joker beat his chest.

'Praise be Joker on Joker Day,' he said. 'For the future belongs to him!'

TEN OF DIAMONDS

... a little figure peeping
out from behind a newspaper stand ...

When I looked up from the sticky-bun book, a fierce storm of thoughts raged through my head.

As I sat in the great Syntagma Square – with all the Greeks hurrying past with their newspapers and briefcases – it was even clearer to me that the sticky-bun book was an oracle linking my journey to something which had happened on the magic island 150 years ago.

I sat thumbing back and forth through the pages I had just read.

Even though Baker Hans hadn't heard the whole of the old prophecy, there was a clear relationship between a lot of the sentences.

'*The baker's son escapes over the mountains and settles in remote village. The baker conceals the treasures from the magic island. The future lies in the cards. The village shelters neglected boy whose mother*

has passed away. The baker gives him the sparkling drink and shows
him the beautiful fish . . .'

The baker's son was obviously Baker Hans. Frode had already
understood that much. The remote village had to be Dorf, and
the boy whose mother had died – it couldn't be anyone but
Albert.

Then Baker Hans had missed two of the Threes, but if I read the
sentences of the other Threes together with the Twos' sentences,
there was another clear relationship.

'The sailor marries beautiful woman who gives birth to a baby boy
before she travels to land in the south to find herself. Father and son
search for the beautiful woman who can't find herself. The dwarf with
cold hands points the way to remote village and gives the boy from the
land in the north a magnifying glass on his journey. The magnifying
glass matches chip in goldfish bowl. The goldfish does not give away
the island's secret, but the sticky bun does . . .'

This was all pretty clear, yet there were some sentences I didn't
understand.

'The inner box unpacks the outer box at the same time as the outer
box unpacks the inner . . .' 'The sticky-bun man shouts down a magic
funnel, so his voice carries hundreds of miles . . .' 'The sailor spits out
strong drink . . .'

If the last sentence meant that Dad would stop drinking every
single night, I would be greatly impressed with him and the old
prophecy.

The problem was that Baker Hans had heard only forty-two of
the cards' sentences. He had found it particularly difficult to concentrate towards the end, which wasn't surprising, because the
more the Joker Game progressed, the more distant it was from his
own time. All this must have been veiled speech for Frode and
Baker Hans, and that is always more difficult to remember than
clear speech.

The old prophecy would be veiled speech for most people
today, too. I was the only one who knew who the dwarf with
the cold fingers was, I was the only one who had access to the

magnifying glass, and nobody else would understand what was meant by the sticky bun giving away the island's secrets.

Still, I was annoyed that Baker Hans hadn't heard all the sentences, because now, due to his lack of concentration, a great deal of the prophecy would remain a hidden treasure for ever, and it was that exact part which concerned me and Dad. I was sure that one of the dwarfs had said something about us meeting Mama, and her wanting to return home to Norway with us ...

While I sat flicking through the sticky-bun book, out of the corner of my eye I saw a little figure peeping out from behind a newspaper stand. At first I thought it was a child who was having fun spying on me because I was sitting on my own, but then I realized that it was the little man from the garage. He appeared only for a moment and then he was gone.

I was stiff with fear for a few seconds, but then I started to think: why was I so frightened of the dwarf? It was obvious he was following me, but there had been no indication that he wanted to harm me.

Maybe he knew about the secret of the magic island, too. Yes, maybe he had given me the magnifying glass and sent me to Dorf just so I could read about it. In which case it wasn't so odd that he wanted to see how I was doing. Literature like that wasn't easy to find.

I remembered that Dad had jokingly said that the dwarf was an artificial person who had been made by a Jewish sorcerer hundreds of years ago. Of course, he had only been joking, but if it was true, then maybe he had known Albert and Baker Hans.

I wasn't able to think or read any further, because Dad came running across the plaza toward me. He was a good head taller than everyone else. I hurriedly hid the sticky-bun book in my pocket.

'Was I long?' he asked breathlessly.

I shook my head.

I had already decided to keep quiet about the dwarf. The fact that a little man was shuffling around Europe like us was nothing compared to what I had read in the sticky-bun book.

'What have you been up to?' Dad continued.

I showed him the cards and told him I had been playing solitaire.

At this point the waiter appeared and wanted his money for the last fizzy drink I had ordered.

'That's very small!' he said.

Dad shook his head in confusion.

Of course, I knew the waiter was referring to the sticky-bun book, and I was afraid I'd be exposed. Therefore, I pulled out the magnifying glass, held it up in front of the waiter, and said, 'It's very clever.'

'Yes, yes!' he said. In this way I managed to avoid an embarrassing situation.

When we left the café, I explained: 'I was examining the playing cards to see whether there was more on them than the naked eye could see.'

'And what was the result?' Dad asked.

'Wouldn't you like to know,' I said secretively.

JACK OF DIAMONDS

... any vanity Dad had
was associated with being a joker ...

When we got back to the hotel room, I asked Dad if he had come any closer to finding Mama.

'I visited an agent who makes a living by running some kind of liaison business for models. He insisted that there was no model working in Athens called Anita Tørå. He was quite sure and claimed that he knew all the models here – at any rate, all the foreign ones.'

I must have looked like a grey winter's afternoon, and on this particular day it was raining. I felt the tears press against my eyelids. Dad quickly added, 'I showed him the picture from the fashion magazine, and suddenly there was a lot more life in the Greek. He told me she was called Sunny Beach, and no doubt this was her modelling name. He said she has been one of the most-sought-after models in Athens for several years.'

'So?' I said, staring searchingly into Dad's eyes.

He threw his hands in the air and said, 'I have to call tomorrow after lunch.'

'And that was all?'

'Yes! We'll just have to wait and see, Hans Thomas. We'll go up to the roof terrace this evening, and tomorrow we'll drive to Piraeus. There's bound to be a telephone there as well.'

When he mentioned the roof terrace, I remembered something. I gathered my courage and said, 'There's just one more thing.'

Dad looked at me with a puzzled expression on his face, but maybe he already knew what I was going to say.

'There was something you were going to think about, and we agreed that you should think about it quickly.'

He tried a manly laugh, but it didn't quite work.

'Oh that!' he said. 'Like I said, Hans Thomas – I'll think about it, but today there have just been so many other things to think about.'

I had a good idea – I dashed over to his travel bag and dug out a half bottle of whisky that was stuffed between his socks and T-shirts. Within a couple of seconds I was in the bathroom pouring it down the toilet.

When Dad followed me into the bathroom and realised what I had done, he stood staring into the toilet bowl. Maybe he was debating whether he could bend down and lap up the remains before I flushed the toilet. But he hadn't sunk that low. He turned towards me again, and couldn't decide whether he should rage like a tiger or wag his tail like a puppy dog.

'Okay, Hans Thomas. You win!' he said in the end.

We went back into the bedroom and sat down on a couple of chairs by the window. I looked at Dad, who was staring at the Acropolis.

'*Sparkling drink paralyses Joker's senses,*' I muttered.

Dad looked at me in astonishment.

'What are you babbling about, Hans Thomas? Is it the Martini Rosso from yesterday?'

'Nope! I Just meant that a true joker doesn't drink alcohol, because he thinks better without it.'

'You really *are* crazy, but it's probably hereditary.'

I knew that I had attacked his weakest point, because any vanity Dad had was associated with being a joker.

However, when I thought he might still be thinking about what was down the toilet, I said, 'Now let's go up to the roof terrace and sample every kind of soft drink that they have on the menu. You can have cola or Seven-Up, orange juice, tomato juice, or a fizzy drink with a pear flavour – or maybe you'd like to try all these at once? You can fill your glass with freezing ice cubes and stir them with a long spoon –'

'Okay, thank you, that'll do,' he interrupted.

'But we have a deal?'

'Yes, sir, and an old sailor always keeps his word.'

'Great! In return I'll tell you a wild story.'

We hurried up to the roof and sat at the same table as the night before; it wasn't long before the same waiter appeared.

In English I asked what kind of soft drinks he had. We ended up ordering two glasses and four different bottles. The waiter shook his head and mumbled something about father and son wanting wine one day and then drinking themselves silly on fizzy drinks the next. Dad replied that it kept the balance and there was justice in everything.

When the waiter had disappeared, Dad turned to me and said, 'It's quite incredible, Hans Thomas. We're sitting in a city with millions of people, and there's just one ant we want to find in this enormous anthill.'

'And it is the queen herself.'

I thought this was a pretty smart comment, and Dad obviously did too; he unleashed a wide grin.

'But this anthill is so well organised you really can find ant number 3,238,905,' he said. He sat philosophising for a moment before he continued: 'Athens is really just a smaller chamber in a much bigger anthill which is home to over five billion ants. Yet you can nearly always contact one particular ant among those five billion. You just have to plug a telephone into a wall and dial a number, and you know this planet has billions of telephones, Hans Thomas. You find them high up in the Alps, in the deepest African jungle, in Alaska and Tibet – and you can reach all of them from the telephone in your front room.'

Something suddenly made me jump in my seat.

'*The sticky-bun man shouts down a magic funnel, so his voice carries hundreds of miles,*' I whispered excitedly, and in a flash I understood what the sentence from the Joker Game meant.

Dad sighed wearily. 'What is it now?' he asked.

I didn't know how to explain, but I had to say something.

'When you mentioned the Alps, I was reminded of the baker who gave me the sticky buns and the fizzy drink in the little village we visited. I remember he had a telephone, too, and with that he can contact people all over the world. He just needs to ring the operator and he can get the number for anybody on the whole planet.'

He clearly wasn't satisfied with my answer, and sat for a long time staring at the Acropolis.

'So it's not that you can't tolerate philosophising, then?'

I shook my head. The truth was, I was bursting with everything I had read in the sticky-bun book and was having difficulty keeping it to myself.

As darkness started to creep over the town and the floodlights on the Acropolis were switched on, I said, 'I promised to tell you a story.'

'Go on, then,' said Dad.

So I began. I retold a great deal of what I had read in the sticky-bun book – all about Albert, Baker Hans, Frode, and the magic island. I didn't think I was breaking my promise to the old baker in Dorf, because I presented the whole thing as though I had just made it up on the spot. I did have to make a bit up myself, and I tried not to mention the sticky-bun book.

Dad was clearly impressed.

'You have a damn good imagination, Hans Thomas,' he said. 'Maybe you shouldn't be a philosopher after all, maybe you should try your hand at being a writer first.'

Once again I was being praised for something I didn't really have anything to do with.

When we went to bed later that evening, I was the first to fall asleep. I lay awake for quite a while before I dozed off, but Dad stayed awake for even longer. The last thing I remember was him getting out of bed and standing by the window.

When I woke up the next morning, Dad was still fast asleep. I thought he looked like a bear who had just begun his long winter hibernation.

I found the magnifying glass and the sticky-bun book and read more about what happened on the magic island after the great Joker Banquet.

QUEEN OF DIAMONDS

*... And then the little clown
broke down and cried ...*

The large circle broke up as soon as the Joker had beaten his chest and said a few formal words in praise of himself, and then the festivities were under way again. Some of the dwarfs helped themselves to fruit and others poured themselves some of the sparkling drink. It wasn't long before they started to call out all the names of all the flavours in the strange drink:

'Honey!'

'Lavender!'

'Kurberry!'

'Ringroot!'

'Gramines!'

Frode sat watching me. Even though he was an old man with white hair and wrinkles, his eyes still shone like polished emeralds. I thought what I had so often heard was true: that the eyes are the mirrors of the soul.

The Joker clapped his hand again.

'Do we fathom the depths of the Joker Game?' he shouted across the hall.

When he received no answer, he started to wave his arms around impatiently.

'Don't you see, Frode was the sailor with the pack of cards, and we are those playing cards. Or are you as pigheaded as he is?'

It was obvious that the dwarfs in the hall didn't know what the little fool was talking about. They didn't seem very interested in finding out, either.

'Ugh, what a troublemaker,' exclaimed the Queen of Diamonds.

'Yes, he is absolutely unbearable,' another dwarf blurted out.

The little Joker sat for a few seconds looking thoroughly miserable.

'Does anybody understand?' he tried again. He was so tense his bells tinkled, although he was trying to sit completely still.

'No!' a choir of dwarfs sang in harmony.

'Don't you realise that Frode has fooled us all and I am the fool?'

Some of the dwarfs now put their hands over their eyes and ears, while others hurried to gulp down as much Rainbow Fizz as possible. It was as though they were doing their utmost not to understand the Joker.

The King of Spades walked over to one of the tables and fetched a bottle of the sparkling drink. He held it up in front of the Joker and said, 'Have we come here to solve riddles or have we come here to drink Rainbow Fizz?'

'We have come to hear the truth,' replied the Joker.

Frode grabbed my arm and whispered into my ear, 'I wouldn't like to say how much of what I've created on the island will be left by the time this is over.'

'Shall I try to stop him?' I asked.

Frode shook his head. 'No, no. This game of solitaire must follow its own set of rules.'

The next moment the Jack of Spades had run up to the Joker and pulled him off his throne. The other Jacks joined in. Three of them held the little fool down while the Jack of Clubs tried to force a bottle into the Joker's mouth.

The Joker tried to keep his mouth shut as tightly as possible at the same time, he spat out what they were trying to pour into him, so that it spurted across the hall.

'*Joker spits out the sparkling drink,*' he said, wiping his mouth. '*Without the lie-nectar the little fool thinks more clearly.*'

With that, he jumped up and wrenched the bottle out of the Jack of Clubs's hands, before throwing it to the floor. Then he ran to each of the four tables and started to smash bottles and decanters, so that the whole hall tinkled with the sound of breaking glass. Even though glass shards rained down on the dwarfs, none of them was cut. Only Frode was cut slightly. I watched a drop of blood trickle across one of his hands.

The sparkling liquid ran across the floor and gathered in big, sticky puddles. Some of the Twos and Threes lay down on the floor and began to lap up the Rainbow Fizz among all the shards of glass. Several of them got splinters of glass in their mouths, but they just spat them out again unharmed. Scandalised, the other dwarfs just stared.

The first to speak was the King of Spades.

'Jacks!' he said. 'I order you to chop off that fool's head at once!'

He needed to say no more; the four Jacks drew their swords and marched over to the Joker.

I couldn't just sit and watch, but as I was about to intervene, I felt a firm hand hold me back.

The Joker's little face crumpled with dejection.

'Only Joker,' he mumbled. 'No . . . nobody else . . .'

And then the little clown broke down and cried.

The Jacks stumbled backwards; even the ones who had been covering their eyes and ears looked up in confusion. No doubt over the years they had witnessed many kinds of pranks from the mischievous clown, but this must have been the first time they had seen him cry.

Frode's eyes were shiny, and I understood then that there was no figure he cared for more than the little troublemaker. He tried to put his arm around the Joker's shoulders.

'There, there . . .' he said comfortingly, but the Joker just shrugged his arm away.

The King of Hearts now joined those gathered around the Joker and said, 'I must remind you that you are not allowed to chop off a head which is crying.'

'Bother!' exclaimed the Jack of Spades.

The King of Hearts continued: 'Another very old rule says that you are not permitted to chop off a head before it has finished talking, and seeing as not all the cards have been put on the table, I command that the Joker be put on the table before we do away with his head.'

'Thank you, dear King,' sniffed the Joker. 'You are the only one in this whole solitaire with thirteen good hearts.'

With that, the four Jacks picked the Joker up and placed him on one of the tables. He lay back, resting his head in his hands. He bent one of his legs over the other, and in this position he delivered a long speech. The dwarfs in the great hall flocked around him.

'I was the very last one to come to this village,' he began, 'and everyone knows I am different from you all. That's why I have kept mostly to myself.'

Something suddenly made all the dwarfs *listen* to what the Joker had to say. No doubt they had often wondered why he was so different.

'I don't belong anywhere,' he went on. 'I am neither a heart, a diamond, a club, nor a spade. I am neither a King, a Jack, an Eight, nor an Ace. As I am here – I am merely the Joker, and who that is I have had to find out for myself. Every time I toss my head, the jingling bells remind me that I have no family. I have no number – and no trade either. I cannot share the diamonds' art of glassblowing, or the hearts' ability to bake. I haven't got green fingers like the clubs or muscle power like the spades. I have gone around observing your activities from the outside. Because of this I have also been able to see things to which you have been blind.'

The Joker lay on the table wagging his leg as he spoke, his bells tinkling softly.

'Every morning you have gone to work, but you have never been fully awake. Of course, you have seen the sun and the moon, the stars in the sky, and everything that moves, but you haven't really seen it at all. It is different for the Joker, because he was put into this world with a flaw: he sees too deeply and too much.'

At this point the Queen of Diamonds broke in: 'Spit it out, then, you fool! If you have seen something we haven't then you must tell us at once.'

'*I have seen myself.*' declared the Joker. 'I have seen how I crawl in between the bushes and trees in the large garden.'

'Can you see yourself from the air?' piped the Two of Hearts. 'Have your eyes got wings to fly like the birds?'

'In a way, yes. You see, it's no good gazing at yourself in a tiny mirror you pull out of your pocket – like the four Queens in the village always do. They are so preoccupied with how they look, they don't even realise that they are living.'

'I have never heard anything so cheeky,' the Queen of Diamonds blurted out. 'How long is this fool going to be allowed to rant and rave?'

'These aren't just words,' continued the Joker. 'I feel it deep inside. I feel I am a shape bursting ... bursting with life ... a remarkable being ... with skin, hair, nails, and everything ... a wideawake living puppet ... graspable like rubber ... Joker asks, Where does this rubber man come from?'

'Are we just going to let him go on?' the King of Spades interrupted. The King of Hearts nodded his assent.

'We're alive!' the Joker now announced, and threw out his arms so his bells jangled wildly. 'We are living in a mystical fairy tale beneath the heavens. Odd, says Joker, and is forever pinching himself to make sure it is true.'

'Does it hurt?' the Three of Hearts twittered.

'Every single time a bell rings I realise that I exist – and that happens every time I make the slightest movement.'

He lifted his arm and shook it violently, and several of the dwarfs stepped back in fright.

The King of Hearts cleared his throat and said, 'Do you know where the rubber man comes from?'

'You have guessed that riddle for yourselves, but only tiny pieces have been understood. Because you have only a tiny grain of sense, you have to stick your heads together to think the very simplest of thoughts. The reason for this is that you have drunk too much Rainbow Fizz. Joker says he is a mysterious puppet – and you are just as mysterious as he, only you don't see it. You don't feel it either, because when you drink Rainbow Fizz, you can taste only honey, lavender, kurberry, ringroot, and gramine. You have become one with the garden without realising you exist, for the one who has the whole world in his mouth forgets that he has a mouth. And he who has all the flavours of the world in his arms and legs forgets he is a mysterious puppet. Joker has always tried to tell the truth, but you have had no ears to listen to him. Indeed, you have had folds of skin on the sides of your faces, but the passages have been blocked with apples, pears, strawberries, and bananas. The same goes for your vision. Naturally you have eyes to see, but what good are they when you are constantly searching for more to drink? Joker says this is so, because only the Joker knows the truth.'

The dwarfs in the hall looked at each other.

'Where does the rubber man come from?' the King of Hearts reiterated.

'We are figments of Frode's imagination,' said the Joker, flinging out his arms again. 'But one day the images were so vivid they started to spurt out of his head. Impossible! cries the Joker, as impossible as the sun and the moon, he says – but the sun and the moon are also true.'

The dwarfs stared at Frode in amazement, and the old man gripped my wrist tightly.

'But there is even more,' the Joker went on, 'for who is Frode? He, too, is an odd puppet full of life. He was the only one on the island, but in reality he belongs to another pack. Nobody knows how many cards there are in that pack, or knows who is dealing them out. The Joker knows only one thing: Frode also is a puppet who appeared out of thin air one morning, bursting with life. Which forehead did he spring from, the Joker wants to know, and he will ask and ask – until one day he finally gets an answer.'

Now it was as though the dwarfs started to stir from a long hibernation. The Two and Three of Hearts each found a broom and began sweeping the floor.

The four Kings huddled together in a tight circle, with their arms around each other. They stood like this, talking in hushed voices, until the King of Hearts turned towards the Joker and announced: 'It is with great sorrow that the village Kings have agreed the little fool is speaking the truth.'

'And why is the fact he is speaking the truth so sorrowful?' the Joker asked. He was still lying on the table, but now he rolled onto his side, and leaning on his arm, he looked up at the King of Hearts.

This time the King of Diamonds spoke: 'It is terribly sad that the Joker has told us the truth, because it means the master must die.'

'And why must the master die?' the Joker enquired. 'One should always refer to a rule before striking.'

The King of Clubs replied, 'If Frode walks around the village, he will constantly remind us that we are artificial. Therefore, he must die under the swords of the Jacks.'

The Joker now climbed down from the table. He pointed at Frode and then turned to the Kings and said, 'It is never a very good idea that master and creation live too close to one another, because they very easily get on each other's nerves. However, Frode can hardly be blamed for having such a vivid imagination that in the end his fantasies start to spurt out of his head.'

The King of Clubs straightened his miniature crown and said, 'Everyone is free to fantasise about what he likes, but it is also his duty to make his fantasies aware of the fact that they are just fantasy. Otherwise, he is making fun of them, and then they are entitled to kill him.'

The sun disappeared behind a large cloud, and the hall immediately became much darker.

'Did you hear what we said, Jacks?' the King of Spades barked. 'Off with the master's head!'

I jumped from my chair, but at the same time the Jack of Spades said, 'It isn't necessary, Your Highness, the master is already dead.'

I spun around and saw Frode lying lifeless on the floor. It was not the first time I had seen a dead person and I knew that Frode would never look at me with his sparkling eyes again.

I felt as lost and forlorn as anyone can be. All at once I was alone on the island. A living pack of cards surrounded me, but not one of them was a person like me.

The dwarfs crowded around Frode. Their faces were empty of expression – even more so than when I had arrived in the village the day before.

I saw the Ace of Hearts whisper something to the King of Hearts, and then she ran to the door and was gone.

'Now we can stand on our own feet,' the Joker finally declared. 'Frode is dead, and his creations have murdered him.'

I was so sad and also so angry that I strode over to the Joker, picked him up, and shook him in the air so that his bells jangled noisily.

'You were the one who murdered him,' I cried. 'You were the one who stole the Rainbow Fizz from Frode's cabin, and you were the one who gave away the knowledge of Frode's playing cards.'

I let go of him, and the King of Spades now declared, 'Our guest is correct, therefore we have the right to chop off the little fool's head. We'll never be rid of the one who made fools of us until we have done away with his fool. Jacks! Off with that cuckoo's head at once!'

The Joker dashed across the floor, and by simply shoving a few Sevens and Eights out of the way he disappeared out of the door, just as the Ace of Hearts had done only a few moments before. I understood that my visit was over, too, and followed him outside. A golden carpet of evening sunshine still lay between the corners of the houses, but neither the Joker nor the Ace of Hearts was to be seen.

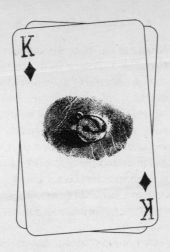

KING OF DIAMONDS

. . . we had to wear a bell
around our necks . . .

D ad started to stir long before I had read about Frode's
death, but I was so absorbed in the sticky-bun book I
couldn't put it down. Only when Dad started to grunt
did I hurriedly smuggle it into my pocket.

'Did you sleep well?' I asked as soon as he sat up in bed.

'Wonderfully,' he said, opening his eyes wide. 'And I dreamed
about some weird stuff.'

'Like what?' I asked.

He stayed in bed as though he was afraid he would lose his
dream if he got up.

'I dreamed about the dwarf-sized people you told me about on
the roof terrace, but although they were alive, you and I were the
only ones who were surprised that we were living. There was an
old doctor who suddenly discovered that all the dwarfs had a
little mark under their big-toe nail. But you had to use a magnify-

ing glass or a microscope to see it. The mark was made up of a playing card symbol and a number from one to several million. One had a heart and the number 728964, one had the symbol of a club and the number 60143 – and another had a diamond symbol and the number 2659. After a kind of census was held, it turned out that nobody had the same number. The people were like one big game of solitaire. But then – and now I am coming to the point – it appeared that two of the little people didn't have any symbol at all. And they – yes, they were you and me. When the other dwarfs heard this, they were frightened of us and decided we had to wear a bell around our necks so everybody would know where we were.'

I had to admit it was a crazy dream, but I thought he had just carried on from what I had told him the night before.

Finally, he said, 'It is quite extraordinary the kind of thoughts and ideas we have, but our very deepest thoughts jump out only when we are asleep.'

'At least if we haven't had too much to drink,' I commented.

For once he looked at me and smiled without trying to out-shine me with a smarter answer. It was also unusual that we went to breakfast without him having a cigarette.

The breakfast at Hotel Titania was simple but absolutely first-rate. Some cheap stuff which was included in the room price was automatically placed on the table, but there was also a huge buffet with the most delicious dishes which you could help yourself to if you were rich enough to pay for it.

Dad had never been a particularly big eater, but today he had juice, yogurt, egg, tomato, ham, and asparagus. I stuffed myself, too.

'You were right about the drinking,' he admitted as he opened his egg. 'I had almost forgotten how bright the world could be.'

'But you're not going to stop philosophising, are you?' I asked.

I had always been a little worried that his clever thoughts were linked to his drinking and he would become a different person as soon as he stopped.

He looked up at me, bewildered.

'No, are you absolutely crazy? I'll be a *dangerous* philosopher now.'

I sighed with relief and he was off again. 'Do you know why most people just shuffle around the world without marvelling at everything they see?'

I shook my head.

'It's because the world has become a habit,' he said, sprinkling salt on his egg. 'Nobody would believe in the world if they hadn't spent years getting used to it. We can study this in children. They are so impressed by everything they see around them that they can't believe their eyes. That's why they point here and there and ask about everything they lay their eyes on. It's different with us adults. We have seen everything so many times before that we take reality for granted.'

We sat for a long time eating cheese and ham. When our plates were empty, Dad said, 'Shall we promise each other something, Hans Thomas?'

'It depends,' I replied.

He looked me straight in the eyes. 'Let's promise not to leave this planet before we have found out more about who we are and where we come from.'

'It's a deal,' I said, and shook his hand across the table.

'But first of all we have to find Mama,' I added. 'Because without her I don't think we'll manage it.'

HEARTS

ACE OF HEARTS

*. . . when I turned the card over, I saw
that it was the Ace of Hearts . . .*

D ad was pretty wound up by the time we got in the car to
drive to Piraeus.

I wasn't quite sure if he was wound up because we
were going to Piraeus or because later that morning he would call
the agent who might be able to tell us where we could meet
Mama.

We parked the car in the centre of the large town, on the coast,
and made our way to the international harbour.

'This is where we moored seventeen years ago,' Dad told me,
pointing to a Russian cargo ship and proceeding to tell me how
life goes in full circles.

'When are you supposed to call?' I asked.

'After three o'clock.'

He glanced at his watch, and I did the same. It was only half
past twelve.

'Destiny is a cauliflower head which grows equally in all directions,'
I said.

Dad flapped his arms about in irritation. 'What are you gab-
bling about, Hans Thomas?'

I realised he was nervous about meeting Mama.

'I'm hungry,' I replied.

It wasn't really true, but it wasn't that easy to think of something to do with cauliflower. Anyway, we ended up going to the
famous Microlimano marina for lunch.

On the way there, we strolled past a boat bound for an island
called Santorini. Dad told me that the island had been much
bigger in prehistoric times, but due to a violent volcanic explo-
sion, most of it had sunk into the sea.

We ate moussaka for lunch, and except for Dad's comments on
some fishermen repairing a net just below the restaurant, not a
lot was said during the meal. However, we did look at our
watches three or four times. We both tried to do it without the
other noticing, but neither of us was very good at peeping on the
sly.

Dad finally said he would call – it was quarter to three. Before
he went, he ordered a big bowl of ice cream for me; by the time it
was brought to the table, I had already fished out the magnifying
glass and the sticky-bun book.

This time I hid the little book under the edge of the table and
tried to read it without anybody seeing.

I raced up the hill to Frode's cabin. As I ran I thought I felt a weak
rumbling under my feet, as though the ground was giving way.

When I reached the cabin, I turned round and looked back down
at the village. A lot of the dwarfs had also left the banqueting hall
and were swarming in and around the houses.

One of them cried at the top of his voice: 'Kill him!'

'Kill them both!' shouted another.

I wrenched open the cabin door. It looked terribly empty inside now that I knew Frode would never set foot here again. I collapsed on a bench gasping for breath.

When I stood up again, I found myself gazing at a little goldfish swimming round and round inside a big glass bowl on the table in front of me. At the same time I noticed a white sack over in the corner, possibly sewn from the hide of one of the six-legged animals. I poured the water and the goldfish into an empty bottle standing on a bench by the window and carefully placed the bottle and the gold-fish bowl into the white sack. From the shelf above the door, I took down the empty wooden box which had housed Frode's playing cards during his first days on the island, and I put this in the sack, too. Just as I was picking up a glass statue of a moluk, I heard a jingling sound outside the cabin, and the next moment the Joker came burst-ing through the door.

'We must make our way to the sea at once,' he said, catching his breath.

'We?' I asked, bewildered.

'Yes, both of us. But you must hurry, sailor.'

'Why?'

'*The magic island crumbles from within*,' he said – and then I remembered the Joker Game.

As I tightened the drawstring on the sack, the Joker started to rummage for something inside a cupboard. He soon turned round with a glittering bottle in his hand. It was half filled with Rainbow Fizz.

'And this,' he said.

We went out onto the front steps and met with a terrifying sight. The whole pack of dwarfs was on its way up the hill, some on foot and some riding moluks. The four Jacks were leading the way with their swords drawn.

'This way,' said the Joker. 'Quickly!'

We ran round to the back of the cabin and took a little path which wound its way through a grove of trees above the village. As we dashed into the trees, we saw that the first of the dwarfs had reached the ridge of the hill.

The Joker leaped and sprang like a mountain goat on the path before me. I remember thinking it was a pity that this particular goat had bells, since the sound of his bells certainly made it easier for the rest of the herd to follow.

'The baker's son must find the way to the sea,' he shouted as we ran.

I told him that I had passed a wide plain with large bees and moluks before I had caught sight of the Two and Three of Clubs working in the field.

'Then it is this way,' said the Joker, pointing to a path leading off to the left.

We soon emerged from the woods and stood on a cliff which looked out across the plain where I had met the first of the little men.

Just as the Joker was about to climb down the crag, he tripped and tumbled down over the sharp stones. The sound of the bells on his costume echoed round the mountainside, and I was afraid he had hurt himself badly. He simply jumped up again, however, threw out his arms, and laughed heartily. The little fool hadn't so much as a scratch on him.

I thought I had better take it a little more carefully, though, and as soon as I was down, I felt the ground tremble beneath my feet.

We crossed the plain; it seemed a lot smaller than I remembered. Soon we saw the bees. They were still much larger than the bees at home in Germany, but I thought they didn't seem quite as big as before.

'I think it's that way,' I said, pointing to a high mountain.

'Does one have to climb it?' the Joker asked in despair.

I shook my head. 'I came out through a narrow opening in the mountain.'

'Then one must find that opening, sailor.'

He pointed across the plain – all the dwarfs were charging toward us. Eight to ten moluks with their riders were leading the way, and the six-legged animals were churning up clouds of dust behind them.

Once again I heard a curious sound – like distant thunder, but the

sound wasn't coming from the galloping moluks. At the same time, I
thought the dwarfs had a shorter distance to cross than we had just
had.

When there were only a few metres between the moluks and us, I
spotted the little opening in the mountain.

'Here it is!' I cried.

I squeezed myself through the hole. Once I was inside the grotto
the Joker tried to follow, but even though he was much smaller than
I, I had to haul and drag him by the arms to pull him through. I was
almost soaked through with sweat, but the Joker was as cold as the
mountain.

Now we could hear the moluks pull up in front of the grotto. The
next moment a face appeared in the opening – it was the King of
Spades. He just managed to peer in before the mountain closed
completely. We watched him withdraw his arm at the last minute.

'I think the island is shrinking,' I whispered.

'Or crumbling from the inside,' replied the Joker. 'We must try to
get out of here before it goes completely.'

We ran through the grotto. It was not long before we were outside
in the deep valley. The frogs and lizards were still hopping and crawling around here, but they were no longer the size of rabbits.

We ran up through the valley, and it was as though we leaped a
hundred metres with each step we took; at any rate, it wasn't long
before we were among the yellow rosebushes and the humming
butterflies. The butterflies were as numerous as before, but apart
from the odd giant, they, too, were much smaller. I couldn't hear
them hum either, but that might have been because the Joker's bells
were ringing frantically as he ran.

We soon reached the top of the mountain, where I had watched
the sunrise the morning after the shipwreck. It felt as though we
were floating over the landscape by simply lifting our feet. Down on
the other side we could see the lake where I had swum with the
rainbow-coloured goldfish. The lake seemed much smaller than I
remembered, and now – now we could see the sea. Far, far away a
white foam washed up over the island.

The Joker started to hop and dance around like a child.

'Is that the sea?' he asked excitedly. 'Do you see the sea, sailor?'

But I couldn't answer him, because again the hill thundered and crashed under our feet. There was a grinding sound, like somebody crunching rocks.

'The mountain is eating itself!' the Joker shouted.

We ran down the mountain. Within moments we were by the lake where I had dived, but now it was no bigger than a little pool. The goldfish were still there, packed even more tightly than before. It looked as though a rainbow had fallen from the sky and was boiling in the little puddle.

While the Joker looked around, I untied the white sack I was carrying on my back and carefully lifted out the glass bowl and filled it with goldfish. Just as I was about to pick up the glass bowl, it tipped over. I had hardly touched it – it fell over of its own accord – or the fish in the bowl let it happen. I noticed the bowl was chipped, but now the Joker turned round and said, 'We must hurry, sailor.'

He helped me refill the bowl with the goldfish. I tore off my shirt and wrapped it tightly round the bowl. I slung the sack over my shoulder and hugged the goldfish bowl close to my body.

All at once we heard a sound so loud and horrific it was as if the whole island was about to break apart. We ran between the tall palm trees and soon came out by the lagoon where I had landed only two days before. The first thing I spotted was the little boat. It lay tucked neatly between two palm trees, just as I had left it. When I turned round, I saw that the island was nothing more than a little islet in the great ocean, and I thought I could spy the sea on the other side through a group of palm trees. Only one thing about the little lagoon was different from when I had arrived. The great ocean was as calm as before, but it had begun to froth by the water's edge. I realised the island was sinking into the ocean.

Out of the corner of my eye I saw something yellow flutter under a palm tree. It was the Ace of Hearts. I put the sack and the goldfish bowl in the boat and went over to her while the Joker danced around the boat like a small child.

'Ace of Hearts?' I whispered.

She turned round and looked at me with so much tenderness and longing that I thought she was going to throw herself on my neck.

'I have finally found my way out of the labyrinth,' she said. 'I know now that I belong to a different shore ... Can you hear the waves beat against the shore – which is years and miles away from this one?'

'I don't know what you mean,' I replied.

'A little boy is thinking of me,' she continued. 'I can't find him here ... but maybe he can find me. I am so far away from him, you see. I have crossed oceans and moods, I have struggled over mountains and difficult thoughts, but someone has shuffled the cards ...'

'They're coming!' the Joker screeched suddenly.

I turned around and saw the whole swarm of dwarfs running towards us through the palm trees. Four moluks were ahead of the pack, and now the Kings were riding.

'Get them!' cried the King of Spades. 'Get them back in the pack!'

A loud boom sounded from inside the island – and in an instant something happened which made me stumble in fright. As though by magic the moluks and the dwarfs disappeared like dew before the sun. I turned back to face the Ace of Hearts – but now she had vanished, too. I ran to the palm tree which she had been leaning against, and there – exactly where the Ace of Hearts had stood – I found a playing card lying face down. When I turned the card over, I saw that it was the Ace of Hearts.

I could feel tears begin to well in my eyes, and at the same time a strange fury forced its way through my despair. I dashed over to where the moluks and the dwarfs had come storming through the palm trees, and just as I reached the spot a burst of wind sent a whole swarm of playing cards whirling up into the air. I already had the Ace of Hearts in my hand and now I counted the other fifty-one cards. They were all terribly worn and tattered around the edges, and I could only just make out the different pictures. I put the fifty-two cards in my pocket.

When I looked at the ground again, I saw four white beetles; each of them had six legs. I tried to catch them with my fingers, but they crawled under a stone and were gone.

Another massive boom sounded from within the tiny island, and at the same moment some powerful waves washed up over my legs. I saw that the Joker was sitting in the boat and had already started to row away from the island. I hurriedly waded after him. The water was up to my waist before I reached the boat and could climb aboard.

'So the baker's son wanted to come along after all,' said the Joker. 'Otherwise I had thought to leave here alone.'

He gave me an oar, and while we rowed as hard as our palms could bear, we watched the island sink into the sea. The water bubbled and swirled around the palm trees, and as the last one disappeared beneath the waves I saw a little bird take off from the treetop.

We had to row for our lives so as not to be pulled under by the backwash as the island disappeared into the depths. My hands were torn and bloody by the time it was safe to rest the oars inside the boat. The Joker had also rowed fiercely, but his hands were as clean and white as they had been when we had shaken hands outside Frode's cabin the day before.

The sun soon sank below the horizon, and we drifted with the wind and the elements all night long and all the next day. I made several attempts to talk to my companion, but I didn't get much out of him. Most of the time he sat silently, with a big grin on his face.

Later the next day we were picked up by a schooner from Arendal. We told them we had been on board the *Maria*, which had capsized a few days before, and that we were probably the only survivors from the shipwreck.

The schooner was en route to Marseille, and throughout the long journey to Europe the Joker was as quiet as he had been in the lifeboat. The ship's crew probably thought he was an odd creature, but nobody said anything.

As soon as we moored in Marseille, the little jester ran between some boat sheds and was gone. He ran off without saying a word of goodbye.

Later that year I arrived here in Dorf. Everything I had experienced had been so bizarre, I felt I needed the rest of my life to think about it. In which case Dorf was the perfect place to be. Coincidentally, I came here fifty-two years ago.

When I discovered that they didn't have a baker, I settled down and opened a little bakery. After all, I had been a baker's apprentice back home in Lübeck before I went to sea. This has been my home ever since.

I have never told anybody about what I experienced; nobody would believe me anyway.

Of course, there have been times when I have doubted the story of the magic island myself, but when I stepped ashore in Marseille I was carrying the white sack over my shoulder. I have guarded the sack and its contents all these years.

TWO OF HEARTS

*. . . She is probably standing on a wide
beach looking out over the sea . . .*

I glanced up from the sticky-bun book. It was half-past three, and my ice cream had melted.

For the very first time I was struck by a monstrous thought: Frode had said the dwarfs on the magic island didn't grow old like people. If this was so, then the Joker must still be running around the world today.

I remembered what Dad had said in the old square in Athens about the ravages of time, but time hadn't had any power over the little people on the island. Although they had been as full of life as people and animals, they hadn't been made of flesh and blood like us.

In several places in the sticky-bun book it was suggested that dwarfs could not be wounded. None of them cut themselves when the Joker smashed the bottles and decanters at the Joker Banquet. The Joker hadn't been hurt when he had tumbled down the mountain crag, and *his* hands weren't sore after all the rowing to escape the sinking island. And there was more – Baker Hans had also said that the dwarfs had cold hands . . .

An icy shiver ran up and down my spine.

The dwarf! I thought to myself. He'd also had cold hands!

Could it be possible that the strange little man we met at the garage was the very one who had jumped ashore and disappeared between some fishing huts in Marseille more than 150 years ago? Had the Joker himself given me the magnifying glass and indeed pointed the way to the sticky-bun book for me to read?

Had it been the Joker who had popped up at the fair in Como, on the bridge in Venice, on board the boat to Patras, and in Syntagma Square in Athens?

The thought was so terribly exciting that the melted ice cream on the table in front of me made me feel quite sick.

I looked around – I wouldn't have been surprised if the little man suddenly popped up here in Piraeus, too. Just then Dad came bounding down from the street above the restaurant and tore me from my thoughts.

I could see right away that he hadn't given up hope of finding Mama.

For some reason I remembered the Ace of Hearts looking out across the sea before she had been transformed into a playing card, and how she had said something about a shore which was both years and miles away from the shore she'd been standing on.

'I'll find out where she is this afternoon,' Dad said.

I nodded solemnly. In a way we were nearing the end of the road.

'She's probably standing on a wide beach looking out over the sea,' I said.

Dad sat down opposite me. 'Something very like it, yes. But how could you know that?'

I shrugged my shoulders.

Dad told me that Mama was busy filming on a large point

jutting out into the Aegean Sea. It was called Cape Sounion and lay on the southern peninsula of the Greek mainland, fifty miles south of Athens.

'On the headland cliffs there are some huge ruins of a temple to Poseidon,' he went on. 'Poseidon was the Greek god of the sea. They're going to snap a few pictures of Anita in front of the temple.'

'Young man from land far away meets beautiful woman near the old temple,' I said.

Dad sighed in despair.

'What are you blabbering about?'

'The Delphic Oracle,' I said. 'You were the one who was Pythia!'

'Yeah, of course! But you know, I was really thinking of the Acropolis.'

'*You* were. But not Apollo, for goodness' sake!'

He laughed excitedly. I wasn't sure why.

'Pythia was so woozy she can't remember what she said,' he finally admitted.

A lot of my experiences from the long journey have been difficult to recall, but I will never forget the trip out to Cape Sounion.

Once we had zoomed past all the resort towns which lay south of Athens, we had the chillingly blue Mediterranean Sea constantly on our right-hand side.

Although Dad and I thought of nothing but what it was going to be like to see Mama again, Dad kept the conversation on quite different topics. I think it was to stop me from getting my hopes up too much. At one point he insisted on asking me whether I thought we'd had a good holiday.

'I really should have taken you to Cape Horn or the Cape of Good Hope,' he said, 'but at least you're getting to see Cape Sounion.'

The trip was just long enough for Dad to need a cigarette stop. We stopped and stood on an exposed ledge in a moonlike landscape. The sea foamed at the bottom of a steep crag below, and a couple of water nymphs who looked like seals lay on the bare rocky slopes.

The water was so blue and clear my eyes almost started to water looking at it. I thought it must be twenty metres deep, but Dad claimed it was only about eight or ten metres.

Not a lot more was said after that. It was probably the quietest cigarette stop of the whole trip.

Long before we reached our destination we could see the Temple of Poseidon towering up from a point on our right.

'What do you think?' Dad asked.

'Do you mean, do I think she's there?'

'At all,' he said.

'I know she's there,' I replied. 'And I know she'll come home to Norway with us.'

He laughed boisterously. 'It's not that easy, Hans Thomas. I'm sure you understand. You don't leave your family for eight years just to be hauled back home again.'

'She has no choice,' I said.

I don't think either of us said any more before we parked the car below the great temple fifteen minutes later.

We made our way between a couple of coaches and forty or fifty Italians. Then we had to pretend we were sightseeing and pay a couple of hundred drachmas to get into the temple site. On the way, Dad took out a comb and removed a silly sunhat he had bought in Delphi.

THREE OF HEARTS

... a woman who was all dressed up and wearing a wide-brimmed hat ...

From then on, everything happened so fast I now have problems reshuffling my memories.

Dad saw a couple of photographers and a little group of people who obviously were not ordinary tourists at the far end of the promontory. As we moved closer, we noticed a woman who was all dressed up and wearing a wide-brimmed hat, a pair of dark sunglasses, and a long bright yellow dress. She was clearly the centre of all the attention.

'There she is,' Dad said.

He froze like a statue, but I just walked straight over to her.

'You can take a break from this snapping now,' I announced so loudly that the two Greek photographers spun round, even though they hadn't understood a word I had said.

I remember I was pretty angry. I thought this was going too far. All these people feasting on Mama by taking photos of her from all angles, when *we* hadn't had a glimpse of her for over eight years.

Now it was Mama's turn to freeze like a statue. She removed her sunglasses and looked down at me from a distance of ten to fifteen metres. She glanced at Dad – and then down at me again.

She was so bowled over, I had time for a great many thoughts to pass through my head before anything else happened.

First I thought of how I didn't know her. Yet I was also certain that she was my own Mama. That's something a child always knows. I also thought she was incredibly beautiful.

The rest was like a slow-motion movie. Although Dad was the one Mama had recognised, I was the one she ran to. For a few seconds I felt sorry for Dad, because it might have looked as though Mama cared more about me.

As she ran towards me she threw off her fancy hat, and then she tried to pick me up, but she couldn't – Athens isn't the only place where things change in eight years. Instead, she wrapped her arms round me and squeezed me tightly.

I remember smelling her and feeling happier than I had done for many years. It wasn't the kind of pleasure you have when you eat or drink something – this happiness wasn't just in my mouth, it bubbled through my whole body.

'Hans Thomas, Hans Thomas,' she said breathlessly. After that she didn't say another word. All she could do was cry.

Only when she looked up again did Dad walk onstage. He took a couple of steps towards us and said, 'We have travelled across the whole of Europe to find you.' He didn't have to say any more before Mama threw both her arms round his neck and sobbed there, too.

The photographers were not the only witnesses to this bitter sweet scene. Several tourists stood gaping at us, without the faintest idea that it had taken more than two hundred years to arrange this meeting.

When Mama stopped crying, she suddenly switched to her role

as model. She turned and said something in Greek to the photo-graphers. They shrugged their shoulders and said something which must have made Mama angry, and a heated argument developed between Mama and the photographers before they understood that they had to make themselves scarce. They packed up their things and shuffled off down through the temple site. One of them even picked up the hat Mama had tossed aside as she ran towards me. As they rounded the corner of the entrance, one of them pointed to his watch and shouted some-thing impudent at us in Greek.

Once we were left to ourselves, the three of us were so embar-rassed we didn't know what to say or do. It is relatively easy to meet people you haven't seen for many years, but it always gets more difficult once you've got over the initial shock.

The sun was already so low in the sky that it lay below the gable of the ancient Temple of Poseidon. The columns along the one short wall cast long shadows across the promontory. I wasn't particularly surprised to notice a red heart on the bottom left-hand corner of Mama's dress.

I don't know how many times we walked round the temple, but I understood that Mama and I were not the only ones who needed time to get to know each other again. It wasn't so easy for an old seaman from Arendal to know how to speak to an experi-enced model who spoke fluent Greek and had lived in Greece for many years. It probably wasn't any easier for the model. Never-theless, Mama talked about the sea god's temple and Dad talked about the sea. Many years ago Dad had sailed past Cape Sounion on his way to Istanbul.

As the sun slipped below the horizon and the contours of the ancient temple grew clearer and darker, we started to make our way down to the entrance. I held back for a few minutes because it was up to the two adults to decide whether this was going to be just a short meeting or the end of a long separation.

In any case, Mama had to drive back to Athens with us, as the photographers hadn't waited for her in the carpark. Dad opened the Fiat door as though it were a Rolls-Royce and Mama was a princess.

Before Dad had got as far as putting the car in gear, all three of us were talking at once. Then we sped back to Athens, and after we passed the first village, I was appointed as moderator.

In Athens we parked the car in the hotel garage and walked along the pavement up to the entrance to the lobby. We stood there for a long while without saying anything. The truth was that the chatter had been constant from the moment we'd left the ancient temple, but none of us had raised the topic of what all this really was about.

Eventually I broke the awkward silence. 'It's about time we made some plans for the future.'

Mama put one of her arms round me, and Dad added a few sickening words about everything happening in due course.

After many if and whens, we all three went up to the roof terrace to celebrate the reunion with something cold and refreshing. Dad waved the waiter over and asked for soft drinks for the father and son and the house's finest champagne for the lady.

The waiter scratched his head and sighed. 'First the two gentlemen have a party on their own,' he said. 'Then they restrain themselves. Is it ladies' night tonight?'

When he didn't get an answer, he made note of the order and stumped back to the bar. Mama – who knew nothing about the previous occasions – looked at Dad in confusion. He in turn gave me a very stern joker stare, confusing her all the more.

Once we had talked at random for an hour without getting closer to the question everyone was thinking about, Mama insisted I go and get ready for bed. In a way, it was her contribution to child-rearing after having been away from her son for more than eight years.

Dad gave me a familiar 'do as she says' look, and it suddenly dawned on me that *I* was the reason for the halting conversation. I understood that the grown-ups had to talk together one to one.

After all, they were the ones who had separated. I was just something which had complicated the whole affair.

I gave Mama a hug, and she whispered in my ear that she would take me to the best pastry shop in the city the next day. I was already preparing some secrets to tell her, too.

Once I had undressed in the hotel room, I got out the sticky-bun book right away and read on while I waited for Dad. There weren't many pages of the teeny book left.

FOUR OF HEARTS

*... we don't know who is
dealing the cards either ...*

Baker Hans stared into space. While he was talking about the magic island, his deep blue eyes had possessed a special gleam, but now it was as if the spark had died.

It was late and very dark in the small room. Only a faint glow from the fireplace was left of what earlier that evening had been a roaring fire. Baker Hans got up and started to rake through the embers with a poker. The fire found a second life for a little while, throwing a flickering light over the goldfish bowls and all the other strange objects in the room.

Throughout the long evening I had absorbed every word the old baker had said. From the moment he had started to talk about Frode's playing cards, I had been so captivated that I had hardly been able to breathe. On several occasions I had caught myself sitting with my mouth half open. I had never dared to interrupt him, and although he told me about Frode and the magic island only once, I am sure I remember everything he said.

'And so in a way Frode returned to Europe after all,' he concluded.

I wasn't sure whether he said this to me or to himself. I just know I wasn't quite sure what he meant.

'Are you thinking of the cards?' I asked.

'Yes, them too.'

'Because those were *the* cards lying upstairs in the attic?'

The old man nodded. Then he went into his bedroom. When he returned he had the little card box in his hand.

'These are Frode's playing cards, Albert.'

He placed the cards on the table in front of me. I felt my heart beat faster as I carefully lifted the pile out of the box and put it on the table. On top of the pile lay the Four of Hearts. I carefully thumbed through the other cards and studied each one. The colours were so faded I could hardly make out what they depicted, but some were quite clear – I found the Jack of Diamonds, the King of Spades, the Two of Clubs, and the Ace of Hearts.

'Were these the cards ... which ran around on the island?' I finally managed to ask.

The old man nodded again.

I felt as though every single card I held in my hand was like a living person. When I held the King of Hearts in front of the fire, I remembered what he had said on the strange island. Once upon a time, I thought to myself, once upon a time he was a little man full of life. He had run between the flowers and trees in the big garden. I sat for a long time holding the Ace of Hearts in my hand. I remembered her saying something about not belonging to this solitaire game.

'Only the Joker is missing,' I said, after I had counted all the cards and discovered there were only fifty-two in the pack.

Baker Hans nodded.

'He joined me in the *great* solitaire game. Do you understand that, son? We are also dwarfs gushing with life, and we don't know who is dealing the cards either.'

'Do you think ... that he *is* still in the world?'

'You can be sure of that, son. Nothing in this world can harm the Joker.'

Baker Hans stood with his back to the fire, casting enormous shadows over me. For a moment or two I was quite scared. I was no more than twelve years old at the time. Maybe Father was at home, in a rage because I was at Baker Hans's and still hadn't come home. Ah yes, but only on rare occasions did he wait up for me. He was probably lying somewhere or other in town sleeping off the booze. Baker Hans was the only one I could really depend on.

'Then he must be terribly old,' I protested.

Baker Hans shook his head vigorously. 'Don't you remember? The Joker doesn't grow old like us.'

'Have you seen him since you both came back to Europe?' I asked.

Baker Hans nodded. 'Just once ... and that was only about six months ago. For a second or two I thought I saw the little figure jump out in front of the bakery. But by the time I had run out onto the street, he had disappeared into thin air. That was when you came into this story, Albert. That same afternoon I had the pleasure of beating up some youngsters who were making your life miserable. And that ... that was exactly fifty-two years after Frode's island sank into the ocean. I have worked it out over and over again ... I am almost positive that it must have been a Joker Day ...'

I stared at him in amazement.

'Does the old calendar still hold true?' I asked.

'It looks like it, son. It was on that day that I realised you were the neglected boy whose mother had passed away. Thus I was able to give you the sparkling drink and show you the beautiful fish ...'

I was dumbfounded. Now I realised that the village dwarfs had been talking about me too at the Joker Banquet.

I swallowed hard.

'How ... how did the story continue?' I asked.

'Unfortunately, I didn't catch everything that was said on the magic island, but it is true for us human beings that everything we hear is stored in our minds even if we don't remember it. Then one day it suddenly pops up again. Just now, as I was telling you about what happened on the magic island, I remembered what the Four of Hearts said after the Four of Diamonds spoke about showing the boy the sparkling drink and the beautiful fish.'

'Yes?'

'The boy grows old and his hair turns white, but before he dies, unhappy soldier comes from land in the north.'

I sat staring into the fire before me. I was in awe of life – and I have never lost this feeling. My whole life was framed in one sentence. I knew that Baker Hans would soon die – and I would become the next baker in Dorf. I also understood that I was the one who had to carry the secret of the Rainbow Fizz and the magic island into the future. I would live my life in this cabin here, and one day – one day an unhappy soldier would arrive from the land in the north. I knew that it was a long way off; it would be fifty-two years before the next baker arrived in Dorf.

'The goldfish also form a string of generations which go all the way back to the fish I took from the island,' Baker Hans continued. 'Some of them live only a few months, but many of them live for years. I get just as sad each time one of them stops wriggling around the glass bowl, because they are all different. That is the secret of the goldfish, Albert – even a little fish is an irreplaceable individual. That's probably why I bury them beneath some trees up in the woods. I put a tiny white stone on each silent grave, because I believe every goldfish deserves a little monument made of a more durable material than itself.'

Baker Hans died only two years after he had told me about the magic island. Father had died the previous year and Baker Hans managed to adopt me as his son, so everything he owned was left in my name. The last thing he said – as I leaned over the old man of whom I was infinitely fond – was: *'The soldier doesn't know that shaven girl gives birth to beautiful baby boy.'*

I understood that this must be one of the sentences omitted from the Joker Game, which suddenly rushed through his head just before he died.

*

Around midnight I was lying on the bed deep in thought when Dad knocked on the door.

'Is she going to come home to Arendal with us?' I burst out before he'd even got through the door.

'We'll have to wait and see,' he replied, and I watched a secretive smile flit across his face.

'But Mama and I are going to the pastry shop tomorrow morning,' I said, to assure myself that the fish hadn't got away just as we were about to pull it into the boat.

Dad nodded. 'She'll be in the lobby at eleven o'clock,' he said. 'She has cancelled all other engagements.'

That night Dad and I both lay staring up at the ceiling before we fell asleep. The last thing Dad said – either to me or to himself – was: 'You can't turn a ship under full sail at the drop of a hat.'

'That might be true,' I replied, 'but destiny is on our side.'

FIVE OF HEARTS

*... Now I needed to have
nerves of steel and not to count my chickens before
they hatched ...*

When I woke up the next morning I tried to remember what Baker Hans had said about the shaven girl just before he died. Dad soon started thrashing around in his bed, however, and the new day got the upper hand.

We met Mama in the lobby after breakfast, and now it was Dad's turn to go on up to the hotel room again. Mama insisted on taking me to the pastry shop alone. We agreed to meet Dad a couple of hours later.

As we were leaving, I gave Dad a private wink as a way of thanking him for the day before. I tried to communicate that I would do my best to bring Mama to her senses.

Once we had ordered at the pastry shop, Mama looked me straight in the eyes and said, 'I don't expect you understand why I left you both, Hans Thomas.'

I wasn't going to be thrown by this opening, so I replied calmly, 'Do you mean to say you know why?'

'Well, not exactly . . .' she admitted.

But I wasn't going to let her get away with half an admission. 'You probably have no idea why you just packed your suitcase and left your husband and son without a trace except for some smeary pictures in a Greek fashion magazine.'

A delicious plate of cakes and some coffee and a fizzy drink were placed on the table, but I wasn't going to be bribed by this, so I continued: 'If you are trying to say you don't understand why you didn't send so much as a postcard to your own son in eight whole years, then you'll understand if I say thank you very much and leave you sitting here with your coffee.'

She removed her sunglasses and started to rub her eyes. I didn't see any tears, but maybe she was trying to squeeze some out.

'It's not that simple, Hans Thomas,' she said, and now her voice sounded as though it was about to break.

'One year has 365 days,' I continued. 'Eight years have 2,920 days, and that's not including February 29. But on neither of these two leap-year days did I get a peep out of my mother. It's quite simple, in my opinion. I'm pretty good at mathematics.'

I think the bit about the leap-year days was the *coup de grâce*. The way I managed to include my birthday made her take both my hands in hers, and now the tears ran down her face in streams, without her rubbing her eyes.

'*Can* you forgive me, Hans Thomas?' she asked.

'It depends. Have you thought of how many games of solitaire a boy can play in eight years? I'm not quite sure myself, but it's a lot. In the end, the cards become a kind of replacement for a proper family. But if you think of your mother every time you see the Ace of Hearts, then something is wrong.'

I said this about the Ace of Hearts to see her reaction, but she just sat looking completely baffled.

'The Ace of Hearts?' she gasped.

'Yes, the Ace of Hearts. Didn't you have a red heart on the dress you were wearing yesterday? The question, though, is who the heart is beating for.'

'Oh, Hans Thomas!'

She was really confused now. Maybe she thought her son had become mentally disturbed because she had been away for so long.

'The point is that because the Ace of Hearts has got herself mixed up in trying to find herself, Dad and I have had serious problems resolving the family solitaire game.'

You could have knocked her over with a feather.

I continued: 'At home on Hisøy Island we have a drawerful of jokers, but they're no good when we have to roam Europe looking for the Ace of Hearts.'

She smiled warmly when I mentioned the jokers.

'Does he still collect jokers?'

He's a joker himself,' I replied. 'I don't think you know the man. He's a bit of a card, you know, but lately he has had more than enough to do trying to rescue the Ace of Hearts from the fashion fairy tale.'

She leaned over the table and tried to pat me on the cheek, but I just turned away. Now I needed to have nerves of steel and not to count my chickens before they hatched.

'I think I understand what you're saying about the Ace of Hearts,' she said.

'That's good,' I replied. 'But don't even think of saying that you know why you left us. The explanation for that mystery is really buried in something which happened with a magical pack of cards a couple of hundred years ago.'

'What do you mean?'

'I mean that it was in the cards that you should travel to Athens to find yourself. It all has to do with a rare family curse. Clues were left in a Gypsy woman's fortune-telling and an Alpine baker's sticky bun.'

'Now you're pulling my leg, Hans Thomas.'

I shook my head knowingly. First I glanced round the pastry

shop; then I leaned over the table and whispered, 'The truth is, you've got mixed up in something which occurred on a very special island in the Atlantic Ocean long, long before Grandma and Grandpa met each other up at Froland. Moreover, it wasn't accidental that you travelled to Athens to find yourself. You were drawn here by your own reflection.'

'Did you say reflection?'

I took out a pen and wrote ANITA on a napkin.

'Can you read that word backwards?' I asked.

'ATINA . . .' she read aloud. 'Ooh, it sounds just like Athinai. I never thought of that.'

'Of course not,' I replied patronisingly. 'There's probably quite a few things you haven't thought of. But that's not important now.'

'What is important, then, Hans Thomas?'

'The most important thing now is how quickly you can pack your suitcase,' I replied. 'In a way, Dad and I have been waiting for you for more than two hundred years, and now we're about to lose patience.'

Just as I said this, Dad came sauntering in from the street outside.

Mama looked at him and threw her hands up in despair. 'What have you done with him?' she asked. 'The boy just talks in riddles.'

'He's always had a lively imagination,' Dad said, pulling up an empty chair. 'Otherwise he's a good boy.'

I thought this was a pretty good answer. Dad couldn't have known what kind of confusion tactics I had been using to persuade Mama to return to Arendal with us.

'I've only just begun,' I said at this point. 'I still haven't told you about the mysterious dwarf who has followed us ever since we crossed the Swiss border.'

Mama and Dad exchanged meaningful glances. Then Dad said, 'And I think you'd better wait with that, Hans Thomas.'

*

By late afternoon we had realised we were one family who couldn't bear being in different parts of the world any longer. I must have awakened the motherly instinct.

Already when we were in the pastry shop – but particularly later on that day – Mama and Dad started hanging around each other's neck like young lovers, and before we said good night I noted the start of some serious kissing. I thought I'd better put up with this, considering what they had been missing for more than eight years, but on a couple of occasions I was forced to turn away out of sheer politeness.

It's not really important to say any more about how we finally managed to pile Mama into the Fiat and head north.

I think Dad wonders a lot about how Mama could be so easily won over, but I had known for a long time that the eight painful years would be behind us if only we found her in Athens. Nevertheless, I did take note of the fact that she had to be the world's fastest at packing a suitcase. She also had to break a contract, which is one of the worst things you can do south of the Alps. Dad said she would easily get a new contract in Norway.

After a couple of hectic days we were back in the car, taking the quickest route back, through Yugoslavia to the north of Italy. I sat in the back seat as before, but now there were two adults up front. This meant that I had a real problem finishing the sticky-bun book, as Mama had a habit of turning round without warning. I hardly dared think what would happen if she saw the little book I had been given by the baker in Dorf.

When we reached northern Italy late that night, I had my own room and could read the sticky-bun book without disruption. I read well into the early hours of dawn, when I fell asleep at last with the book on my lap.

SIX OF HEARTS

... as real as the
sun and the moon ...

Albert had talked all night, and at times I had pictured him as that twelve- or thirteen-year-old boy.

He sat in front of the fireplace staring at something which a long time ago had been a blazing fire. I hadn't interrupted him while he had told me his story – in the same way he had sat fifty-two years ago when Baker Hans had told *him* about Frode and the curious island. I got up and walked over to the window which faced Dorf.

A new day was breaking outside. The morning mist drifted over the tiny village, and heavier clouds floated above the Waldemarsee. On the other side of the valley the sun had just begun to creep down over the mountainside.

My head was full of questions, but because I didn't know where to start, I said nothing. I walked back across the floor and sat down in front of the fire next to Albert, who had so kindly taken me in when I had collapsed outside his little cabin.

Thin trails of smoke still rose from the ashes in the fire, like wisps of the morning mist outside.

'You'll stay in Dorf, Ludwig,' said the old baker, in a way that could have been taken as a question or an order, or possibly both.

'Of course,' I replied. I had already understood that I would be the next baker in Dorf. I also realised that I would be the one to carry the secret of the magic island into the future.

'But that's not what I was thinking about,' I added.

'What's on your mind, son?'

'I was thinking about the Joker Game – because if I am the unhappy soldier from the land in the north . . .'

'Yes?'

'Then I know that . . . I have a son up there,' I said – and being no longer able to hold it in, I hid my head in my hands and wept.

The old baker put his arm round my shoulders.

'Yes, that's true,' he said. '*The soldier does not know that shaven girl gives birth to beautiful baby boy.*'

He let me cry, and when I looked up again he said, 'But there is one thing which I have never understood; maybe you can explain it to me.'

'What's that?'

'Why was the poor girl shaven?'

'I didn't know that she was,' I replied. 'I didn't know they were so cruel to her, but I heard that they did that sort of thing after the liberation. Girls who had been with enemy soldiers lost their hair as well as their honour. That's why . . . that's the only reason why I haven't contacted her since. I thought she might forget me. I thought it would just hurt her even more if I contacted her again. I didn't think anybody knew about us, but obviously I was wrong there, too. When you have a child . . . there's no hiding the truth.'

'I understand,' he said, and sat staring into the empty fireplace.

I got up and paced restlessly round the room.

Could all this be true? I thought to myself. What if Albert was crazy, like they whispered down at the Schöner Waldemar.

I suddenly realised I had no proof that what Albert had told me was true. Every single thing he had said about Baker Hans and Frode could be the ramblings of a confused old man. I had not seen any Rainbow Fizz or any old playing cards.

My only clue was the few words about the soldier from the land in the north, but even they could have been made up by Albert. Yet there was the bit about the shaven girl – my only true grounds for belief – but then I remembered I could very well have said that in my sleep. It wouldn't have been so strange for me to talk about a shaven girl when I was so worried about Line. I was probably also worried that she might be pregnant. And then – yes, then Albert could have taken a few of the disjointed words I had said in my sleep and baked them into his story. He had been pretty quick to ask about the shaven girl . . .

The only thing I was completely sure of was that Albert hadn't sat up all night to make a fool of me. He had believed in every word he said, but that could be the real problem. The village gossip might be true. Albert might be out of his mind, living in his own little world – in both senses of the word.

From the moment I had arrived in the village he had called me his son. Maybe *that* was the root of Albert's fantastical story. Albert desired a son to take over the bakery down in the village. So, without being aware of it himself, he had invented the whole confused story. I had heard of cases like that before. I had heard of crazy people who could be complete geniuses in a special field. Albert's field had to be inventive storytelling.

I paced back and forth across the floor. The sun continued to creep down over the mountain.

'You are very uneasy, son,' the old man said, interrupting my thoughts.

I sat down beside him. Then I remembered how the evening had begun. The night before, I had been sitting in the Schöner Waldemar when Fritz André had started talking about Albert's many goldfish. I had seen only one goldfish myself – and I didn't think it was that strange that the old baker had brightened up his lonely existence with a goldfish. However, when I had come home late last night, I had heard Albert walking about in the attic, and when I confronted him about it – yes, then we had sat down and the long night had begun.

'All the goldfish . . . you told me Baker Hans had taken some gold-fish from the mysterious island. Are they still here in Dorf? Or – or do you just have the one?'

Albert turned round and looked deep into my eyes. 'So little faith you have, my boy.'

The moment he said this, a shadow clouded his brown eyes.

I was impatient now, and maybe it was because I was thinking of Line that I replied rather more sharply than I meant to. 'Well, answer me, then! What happened to the goldfish?'

'Follow me.'

He stood up and went into his cramped bedroom. He pulled down a ladder from the ceiling – just as he had told me Baker Hans had done when he had been a boy.

'We're going into the attic now, Ludwig,' he whispered.

He climbed up first, and I followed him. If the whole story about Frode and the curious island was pure invention, I thought to myself, then Albert is a really sick man.

As soon as I peered over the edge of the trapdoor into the attic, I knew that everything Albert had sat up all night telling me was as real as the sun and the moon. Up here in the attic there was a multi-tude of goldfish bowls, and in every one of them swam goldfish all the colours of the rainbow. The attic was full of the most remarkable objects. I recognized the Buddha statue, the glass statue of a six-legged moluk, the swords and rapiers, and many more of the objects which had been downstairs when Albert had been a boy.

'It's . . . it's absolutely fantastic,' I stammered as I took my first steps across the attic floor, and I wasn't just thinking of the goldfish. I now had no doubts that whole story of the magic island was true.

A blue morning light flooded in from an attic window. The sun didn't reach this side of the valley before midday, but all the same there was a golden light in the attic which wasn't coming from the window.

'There!' whispered Albert, pointing to a corner under the slanted ceiling.

Then I saw an old bottle, and from that bottle a glittering light fell on all the goldfish bowls and the other objects lining the floor, benches, and cupboards.

'That is Rainbow Fizz, son. Fifty-two years have passed since anyone touched it, but now we will carry the old bottle downstairs together.'

He bent down and picked up the bottle from the floor. When he tilted it, I saw something inside which was so beautiful my eyes began to water.

Just as we were about to turn and climb back down into the bedroom, I noticed the old pack of cards in a little wooden box.

'Can I . . . look?' I asked.

The old man nodded formally, and I carefully picked up the pile of tattered cards. I made out the Six of Hearts, the Two of Clubs, the Queen of Spades, and the Eight of Diamonds. I counted the cards.

'There are only fifty-one,' I exclaimed.

The old man glanced around the attic.

'There!' he said eventually, and pointed to a card lying on an old stool. I bent down and placed the card on top of the others. It was the Ace of Hearts.

'She still has a habit of losing herself, but I always find her again somewhere in the attic.'

I put the cards back where I had found them, and we went downstairs.

Albert fetched a little liqueur glass, which he placed on the table.

'You know what's going to happen,' he said simply, and I understood it was my turn to taste Rainbow Fizz. Before me – exactly fifty-two years ago – it had been Albert sitting in this room tasting this mysterious drink, and before him – fifty-two years earlier – Baker Hans had drunk Rainbow Fizz on the magic island.

'But remember,' Albert said seriously, 'you get only the one tiny sip. Then a whole solitaire has to be laid before you can remove the cork again. In this way the bottle will span several generations.'

He poured a tiny splash of the drink into the little glass.

'Here you are,' he said, handing it to me.

'I don't know ... whether I dare.'

'But you know you have to,' replied Albert. 'Because if these drops don't deliver what they promise, then yes, Albert Klages is nothing more than a mentally deranged old man who has sat up all night telling stories. But the old baker won't have that hanging over him, you understand, and even if you don't doubt the story now, the doubt will come one day. That's why it is so important that you *taste* what I have told you with your whole body. That's the only way you can become a baker in Dorf.'

I lifted the glass to my mouth and swallowed the few drops. Within seconds my body turned into a whole circus of different tastes.

It was as though I was in all the markets of the world. At the market in Hamburg I put a tomato in my mouth, in Lübeck I took a bite of a juicy pear, in Zürich I devoured a bunch of grapes, in Rome I ate figs, in Athens it was almonds and cashew nuts, and at the bazaar in Cairo I munched dates. Many more tastes swept through my body. Some of them were so unusual that I thought I was walking around the magic island picking fruit from the trees there. That was the tufa fruit, I thought to myself, that had to be ringroot, and that was kurberry. And there were even more. It was as though I was suddenly back in Arendal. I was sure I could taste cowberries and the smell of Line's hair.

I don't know how long I sat by the fireplace tasting. I don't think I said anything to Albert, but the old man finally got up and said, 'Now the old baker has to get some sleep. But before that I must put the bottle back up in the attic, and you should know I always lock the trapdoor after me. Oh yes, you're certainly a grown man, and fruit and vegetables are nutritious and tasty, old warrior, but you don't want to turn into a vegetable yourself.'

I can't be sure today if these were his exact words. I only know that he gave me some words of warning before he went to bed – and they were something about Rainbow Fizz and Frode's playing cards.

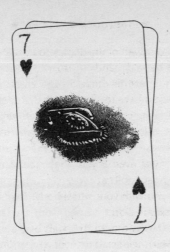

SEVEN OF HEARTS

... *The sticky-bun man shouts*
down a magic funnel ...

O nly when I awoke late the next morning did it really
dawn on me that the old baker I had met in Dorf had
been my own grandfather. The shaven girl could be
none other than Grandma back home in Norway.

I couldn't be more convinced. The Joker Game hadn't said in
exact words that the shaven girl was Grandma or that the baker
in Dorf was my own grandpa. But there couldn't have been that
many girls in Norway called Line with German boyfriends.

The whole truth still wasn't known, however. There were a lot
of sentences from the Joker Game which Baker Hans had never
remembered and had therefore never been told to Albert or anyone else. Would these sentences ever be found so the whole game
of solitaire could be completed?

All traces had been lost when the magic island had sunk into
the ocean, and it hadn't been possible to learn any more before

Baker Hans had died. It would also be impossible to try to blow life into Frode's playing cards again to see whether the dwarfs could remember what they had said 150 years ago.

There was only one possibility left; if the Joker was still on earth – then *maybe* he could still remember the Joker Game.

I knew that I had to get the grown-ups to make a detour through Dorf, even if it was out of the way and Dad's holiday would soon be over. And it had to be done without showing them the sticky-bun book.

I really just wanted to walk into the little bakery and say to the old baker, 'I'm back – I've returned from the land in the south, and I've got my Dad with me. He's your own son.'

Grandpa was soon the main topic of conversation at breakfast. I decided to wait with my dramatic revelation until towards the end of the meal. I was aware that my credibility was wearing a bit thin after all the things I had let slip from the sticky-bun book already. Well, I'd allow them at least to eat their breakfast in peace.

When Mama went to get her second cup of coffee, I looked deep into Dad's eyes and said rather emphatically, 'It was good that we found Mama in Athens, but one card is still missing from the solitaire before it can be resolved completely, and I have found that card.'

Dad glanced worriedly over at Mama; then he looked at me and said, 'What is the matter now, Hans Thomas?'

I continued to stare into his eyes. 'Do you remember the baker in Dorf who gave me a fizzy drink and four sticky buns while you sat in the Schöner Waldemar getting drunk on Alpine brandy with the locals?'

He nodded.

'That baker is your own true father,' I said.

'Nonsense!'

He snorted like a tired horse, but I knew he couldn't just shy away from this.

'We don't have to discuss it here and now,' I said, 'but you should know that I am one hundred per cent sure.'

Mama returned to the table and sighed in despair when she realised what we were talking about. Dad had reacted in much the same way, but we knew each other a lot better. He must have understood he couldn't dismiss what I had said until he had investigated the case further. He knew that I was also a joker who could discover things of great significance now and then.

'And what makes you think that was my father?' he asked.

I couldn't tell him it was something I had read in black and white in the sticky-bun book. Instead, I said something I had thought of the night before.

'Well, first of all, his name was Ludwig,' I began.

'That's a very common name in Switzerland and Germany,' said Dad.

'Maybe, but the baker told me he had been in Grimstad during the war.'

'Is that what he said?'

'Well, not in Norwegian exactly, but when I told him I came from Arendal, he exclaimed that he had also been in *der grimme Stadt*. I presumed that he meant Grimstad.'

Dad shook his head.

'*Grimme Stadt*? That means 'that awful town', or something. He could well have meant Arendal ... but there were a lot of German soldiers in the south of Norway, Hans Thomas.'

'Sure,' I replied. 'But only one of them was my grandpa, and that was the baker in Dorf. You know these things.'

In the end Dad phoned Grandma at home in Norway. I don't know whether this was because of what I had said or simply because he owed his mother a phone call to tell her we had found Mama in Athens. When Grandma didn't answer, he rang Aunt Ingrid, and she told him that Grandma had suddenly taken off on a trip to the Alps.

When I heard this I whistled.

'The sticky-bun man shouts down a magic funnel, so his voice carried hundreds of miles,' I said.

The look of astonishment on Dad's face was so great that it could have held all the mysteries of the world at once.

'Haven't you said that before?' he asked.

'Yes,' I replied. 'It's not impossible that the old baker finally realised that he had met his own grandson. Besides, he saw you, too, and blood is thicker than water, Dad. Or possibly he thought, after all these years, that he might try to make a little telephone call to Norway – seeing as he had just had a boy from Arendal in his shop. And if he did that, then it's not inconceivable that old romance flares up in Dorf just as strongly as in Athens.'

So it came to be that we sped north in the direction of Dorf. Neither Mama nor Dad believed that the old baker was Grandpa, but they knew they would never get any peace if they didn't go and check it out for themselves.

When we reached Como, we spent the night at the Mini Hotel Baradello like before. The fair had gone – with the fortune-teller and all – but I comforted myself with the fact that I had a room to myself again. Although I was exhausted after all the driving, I decided to read the rest of the sticky-bun book before I fell asleep.

EIGHT OF HEARTS

*... such a fantastic miracle that it's hard
to know whether to laugh or cry ...*

I stood up and went outside the cabin. It was hard to walk straight, because different tastes fought for attention throughout my whole body. As the most delicious strawberry cream slid through my left shoulder, a bitter mixture of redcurrants and lemon stabbed my right knee. The tastes chased through my body so quickly and so frequently that I couldn't name them all.

There are people sitting all over the world eating different things right at this moment, I thought to myself. That meant many thousands of different tastes, and it was as if I were present at all those meals – as if I were tasting everything people all over the world were eating.

I started to wander up into the woods above the cabin. As the firework display of tastes slowly began to subside, I felt something I have never lost since.

I turned round and looked down at the village, and for the first time I realised how fantastic the world is. How is it possible that there are people on this planet, I thought to myself. I felt I was experiencing something completely new, but at the same time it was something which had been out in the open ever since I was a small child. I had been asleep; my life on earth had been one long hibernation.

I am alive! I thought to myself. I am a person bursting with energy. For the first time in my life I understood what it meant to be a person, and at the same time I understood that if I had continued to drink the strange drink, then this feeling would gradually slip away until at last it disappeared completely. I would have tasted the whole world so often that I would become one with it. I would no longer have any feeling of existing. I would become a tomato – or a plum tree.

I sat down on a tree stump, and a roe deer appeared between the trees. It wasn't that unusual really; wild animals were always roaming around in the woods above Dorf. However, I couldn't remember that I had ever *seen* how much of a miracle a living creature is. Of course, I had seen roe deer, I saw roe deer almost every day, but I had never understood how unfathomably mysterious every single roe deer is. Now I understood why this was so – I had never taken the time to experience these wild animals because I had seen them so often.

It was the same with everything – with the whole world, I thought to myself. As long as we are children, we have the ability to experience things around us – but then we grow used to the world. To grow up is to get drunk on sensual experience.

I now understood exactly what had happened to the dwarfs on the magic island. They had been unable to experience life's deepest secrets. Perhaps that was because they had never been children. When they started to catch up on what they had missed, by drinking the powerful drink every single day, it wasn't surprising that they finally became one with everything around them. Now I appreciated how much of a victory it must have been for Frode and the Joker to have given up the Rainbow Fizz.

The roe deer stood watching me for a second or two before it bounded away. For a moment there was an incomprehensible silence, then a nightingale started to sing its heavenly tune. That such a little body could produce so much sound, breath, and music was a marvel.

This world, I thought to myself, is such a fantastic miracle that it's hard to know whether one ought to laugh or cry. Perhaps one should do both, but it isn't easy to do both at the same time.

My thoughts wandered to one of the farmers' wives down in the village. She was only nineteen, but one day she had come into the bakery with a little baby girl who was two or three weeks old. I had never been all that interested in babies, but when I peeped into the basket I thought I saw a look of wonder in the little baby's eyes. I hadn't thought any more about it, but now as I sat on the tree stump in the woods and listened to the nightingale's song and a carpet of sunshine unfolded over the fields on the other side of the valley – yes, then it struck me that if the little baby had been able to talk, she would have said something about how wonderful the world was. I had had enough sense to congratulate the young mother on the birth of her child, but really it was the child I should have congratu-lated. One should bend over every single new citizen of the world and say, 'Welcome to the world, little friend! You are tremendously lucky to be here.'

I sat thinking how terribly sad it was that people are made in such a way that they get used to something as extraordinary as living. One day we suddenly take the fact that we exist for granted – and then, yes, then we don't think about it any more until we are about to leave the world again.

I now felt an intense strawberry taste surge through my upper body. Of course it tasted good, but it was also so strong and rich that I almost felt sick. No, I needed no persuasion not to drink Rainbow Fizz again. I knew that I had more than I needed with the blueberries in the woods and a little visit from a roe deer or a nightingale now and again.

As I sat there, I suddenly heard a rustling of branches beside me.

When I looked up, I saw a little man peering out from between the trees.

I felt my heart somersault as I realised it was the Joker.

He walked forward a couple of paces, and from a distance of ten or fifteen metres he said, 'Yum, yum!'

He licked his tiny lips. 'You have refreshed yourself with the delicious drink? Yum, yum! says the Joker.'

I still had the long story of the magic island in my head, so I wasn't frightened. The initial surprise of seeing him soon disappeared as well. I felt as though we belonged together – I was a joker in the pack of cards, too.

I got up from the tree stump and walked over to him. He was no longer wearing the jester's purple costume with bells; instead, he had on a brown suit with black stripes.

I stretched out my hand and said, 'I know who you are.'

As he shook my hand, I heard a faint jingle of bells, and I realised he had simply put a suit on over his jester's costume. His hand was as cold as the morning dew.

'I have the pleasure of shaking the hand of the soldier from the land in the north,' he said.

He smiled strangely when he said this, and his tiny teeth shone like mother-of-pearl. Then he added: 'Now it is this Jack's turn to live. Happy birthday, brother!'

'It's . . . it's not my birthday,' I stammered.

'Sssh, says the Joker. It's not enough to be born only once. Last night the baker's friend was born again, because the Joker knows, and therefore the Joker wishes him a happy birthday.'

He had a squeaky doll's voice. I let go of his icy hand and said, 'I . . . I have heard everything . . . about you and Frode and all the others . . .'

'Of course,' he said, 'because today is Joker Day, my boy, and tomorrow is the beginning of a whole new round. Fifty-two years will pass until the next time. By then the boy from the land in the north is a grown man, but before that he visits Dorf. Luckily, he has been given a magnifying glass on his journey. Fancy magnifying glass, says Joker. Made from the finest diamond glass, he says. Because one can put things in one's pocket when an old goldfish bowl is smashed. Joker clever boy, but it is this Jack who gets the most difficult task.'

I didn't understand what the dwarf meant, but then he moved closer and whispered, 'You must remember to write about Frode's playing cards in a little book. Then you will bake the book in a sticky bun because *the goldfish does not give away the secret of the island but the sticky bun does,* Joker says. Enough!'

'But . . . the story of Frode's playing cards will hardly fit in a sticky bun,' I protested.

He laughed heartily at this. 'It depends on how big the sticky bun is, my boy. Or how small the book is.'

'The story of the magic island . . . and everything else . . . is so long it will have to be a very large book,' I protested again. 'And so it'll have to be a giant sticky bun, too.'

He looked at me cunningly. 'One mustn't be so cocksure, Joker says. Bad habit, he repeats. The sticky bun needn't be so big if all the letters in the book are tiny.'

'I don't think anybody can write that small,' I insisted. 'And even if it was possible, hardly anyone would be able to read it.'

'Joker says just write the book. You might as well begin right away. Then you can make it small when the time comes. And he who has the magnifying glass will see.'

I looked across the valley. The golden carpet had already drawn in over the village.

When I turned back to face the Joker, he was gone. I looked round, but the little jester had darted away between the trees as artfully as a roe deer.

I felt quite exhausted as I made my way back down to the cabin. At one stage I almost lost my balance when a powerful spurt of cherry shot through my left leg just as I was about to step on a rock.

I thought about my friends in the village. If only they knew. Soon they would be gathering in the Schöner Waldemar again. They had to have something to talk about, and there was nothing more nat- ural to gossip about than an old man living alone in a wooden hut away from everyone else. They probably thought he was a bit strange, and for safety's sake they declared him crazy. However, they were part of the biggest mystery themselves – it was all around them, they just didn't see *it*. Perhaps it was true that Albert had a big secret, but the biggest secret of all was the world itself.

I knew that I would never drink wine in the Schöner Waldemar again. And I also knew that one day it would be me they would gossip about down there. In a few years I would be the only joker in the village.

Eventually I dived into bed and slept until late afternoon.

NINE OF HEARTS

... the world is not mature enough to hear about Frode's playing cards ...

I felt the last pages of the sticky-bun book tickle my right index finger, and now I noticed that these pages were written with normal-sized lettering. I could put the magnifying glass down on the bedside table and read the book without it.

It won't be long now until you visit Dorf and collect the secret of Frode's playing cards and the magic island, *mein sohn*. I wrote everything down I remembered from when Albert with me spoke. Only two months after this *nacht*, the *alte* baker died and I the next baker here in the village became.

I wrote the story of the Rainbow Fizz at once, and I decided to write the story in Norwegian. That was so you *verstechen* would, but also so that the locals could not that – book find and read. Now have I *alles* Norwegian forgotten.

I thought that I contact you up there in Norway could not. Didn't know how Line accept me would, and dared not I to break the old prophecy. Because I knew yes, that you one day to the village come would.

The book I wrote on a normal typewriter. It was very impozzible smaller letters to write. But then – only a few weeks ago, heard I that them in the bank here in the village a wonderful machine have got. It was *ein* machine which copy could – so *dass ein* page smaller and smaller could be. When I copied my page eight times, the writing was so small that a very little book put together could. And you, *mein sohn,* you have indeed a magnifying glass off Joker got?

When I should the whole story write, had I only the sentences which Baker Hans remembered had. But yesterday I got a letter. There all the Joker Game written was – and that letter *natürlich* from the Joker was.

As soon as you in Dorf have been, will I Line telephone. And maybe one day we all can meet.

Oh – we bakers in Dorf are all some jokers who carry a *fantastisch* story. And that story must never get wings to fly like other stories. But like all jokers – both in large and small solitaire games – have we the task to tell the people about what an unbelievable fairy tale the world is. We know it is not easy to open their eyes so people see that the world is something big and unbelievable. But before they see what lies quite open in the day is a puzzle; the world is not mature enough to hear about Frode's playing cards on the magic island.

Once – in the land of tomorrow – can the whole world about my sticky-bun book hear. Until then must some drops of Rainbow Fizz drip once every fifty-two years.

And *ein* other ding must you never forget: Joker is in the world. If all the cards in the great solitaire totally blind become, will Joker never give up the belief that some people their eyes open all the same have.

So farewell, *sohn.* Maybe you have your mother found in the land in the south. And so you are here to Dorf when you are grown sure to come.

The last pages in this sticky-bun book are the Joker's notes of the great Joker Game which all the dwarfs on the magic island recited many, many years ago.

The Joker Game

Silver brig drowns in foaming sea. Sailor is washed ashore on island which grows and grows. The breast pocket hides a pack of cards which is placed in the sun to dry. Fifty-three pictures are company for the master glassblower's son for many long years.

Before the colours fade, fifty-three dwarfs are cast in the lonely sailor's imagination. Peculiar figures dance in the master's mind. When the master sleeps, the dwarfs live their own lives. One beautiful morning King and Jack climb out of the prison of consciousness.

The images jump out of the creative space into the created space. The figures are shaken out of the magician's sleeve and appear out of thin air bursting with life. The fantasies are beautiful in appearance, but all except one have lost their minds. Only a lonely Joker sees through the delusion.

Sparkling drink paralyses Joker's senses. Joker spits out the sparkling drink. Without the lie-nectar the little fool thinks more clearly. After fifty-two years the shipwrecked grandson comes to the village.

The truth lies in the cards. The truth is that the master glassblower's son has made fun of his own fantasies. The fantasies lead a fantastic rebellion against the master. Soon the master is dead; the dwarfs have murdered him.

Sun princess finds her way to the ocean. The magic island crumbles from within. The dwarfs become cards again. The baker's son escapes the fairy tale before it is folded up.

The fool slips away behind dirty boat sheds in the homeland. The baker's son escapes over the mountains and settles in remote village. The baker conceals the treasures from the magic island. The future lies in the cards.

The village shelters neglected boy whose mother has passed away. The baker gives him the sparkling drink and shows him the beautiful fish. The boy grows old and his hair turns white, but before he dies, unhappy soldier comes from land in the north. The soldier guards the secret of the magic island.

The soldier does not know that shaven girl gives birth to beautiful baby boy. The boy must run away to sea because he is the enemy's son. The sailor marries beautiful woman who gives birth to a baby boy before she travels to land in the south to find herself. Father and son search for the beautiful woman who can't find herself.

The dwarf with cold hands points the way to remote village and gives the boy from the land in the north a magnifying glass on his journey. The magnifying glass matches chip in goldfish bowl. The goldfish does not reveal the island's secret, but the sticky bun does. The sticky-bun man is the soldier from the land in the north.

The truth about the grandfather lies in the cards. Destiny is a snake which is so hungry it devours itself. The inner box unpacks the outer box at the same time as the outer box unpacks the inner. Destiny is a cauliflower head which grows equally in all directions.

The boy realises that the sticky-bun man is his own grandfather at the same time as the sticky-bun man realises that the boy from the north is his own grandson. The sticky-bun man shouts down a magic funnel, so his voice carries hundreds of miles. The sailor spits out strong drink. The beautiful woman who can't find herself finds her beloved son instead.

The solitaire is a family curse. There is always Joker to see through the delusion. Generation succeeds generation, but there is a fool walking the earth who is never ravaged by time. The one who sees through destiny must also live through it.

TEN OF HEARTS

*... there is a fool walking the
earth who is never ravaged by time ...*

It wasn't easy getting to sleep at the Hotel Mini Baradello after reading the last pages of the sticky-bun book. The hotel didn't seem so 'mini' any more. Hotel Baradello and the surrounding town of Como joined together to form part of something infinitely bigger.

With regard to the Joker, it was just as I had thought. The dwarf at the garage was the same cunning trickster who had darted in between the boat sheds in Marseille, and he had been in the world ever since.

Now and again he had appeared before the bakers in Dorf; otherwise he had probably wandered the world without settling anywhere. One day he was in a village, the next day he was somewhere else entirely. The only thing hiding his true self was a thin suit which he wore over his violet costume with the jingling bells. With an outfit like that, he couldn't just move to a normal suburban area. It would also look rather odd if he lived in a place for too long and didn't change in ten, twenty, or a hundred years.

From the magic island, I remembered that the Joker could run and row without getting tired like ordinary mortals. For all I knew, he could have run after Dad and me all the way from when we first saw him at the Swiss border. Then again he could quite simply have jumped on a train.

I was sure the Joker had frolicked around in the great game of solitaire, having escaped from the mini-solitaire on the mysterious island. He had an important mission here just as he had there: large and small men alike are to be reminded at regular intervals that they are remarkable creations bursting with life but have far too little understanding of themselves.

One year he was in Alaska or the Caucasus, the next he was in Africa or Tibet. One week he showed up at the harbour in Marseille, the next week he was running across the Piazza San Marco in Venice.

So now all the Joker Game pieces were in place. It was wonderful to see how beautifully all the sentences Baker Hans had forgotten joined together to form a whole.

One of the Kings' sentences had eluded Baker Hans: *'Generation succeeds generation, but there is a fool walking the earth who is never ravaged by time.'* I would have liked to let Dad read precisely this sentence to prove that the picture he had drawn of the ravages of time was not as bleak as he would have it. Not everything is ripped to shreds by time. There is a Joker in the pack of cards who runs up and down the generations without losing so much as a milk tooth.

Ha! I felt this promised that mankind's wonder at existence would never die. This appreciation might indeed be a rare gift, but it would never be wiped out. It would show up time and time again, as long as history and mankind existed for jokers to frolic around in. Ancient Athens had Socrates, Arendal had Dad and me. There were sure to be more jokers in other places and other times, even if there weren't multitudes of us.

The very last sentence Baker Hans had heard in the Joker Game, and which had been repeated three times because of the King of Spades's impatience, was: '*The one who sees through destiny must also live through it.*'

Maybe this sentence was directed at the Joker, who lived through one century after another. But I thought I had also seen my destiny, thanks to the long story I had read in the sticky-bun book. But doesn't everybody? Although our lives on earth can seem negligibly short, we are part of a common history which outlives us all. We don't just live our own lives. We can visit ancient places like Delphi and Athens. There we can walk around and sample the atmosphere of those who lived on earth before us.

I looked out of the hotel window, which faced onto a back yard. It was pitch black outside, but a brilliant light shone inside my head. I felt as if I had received a rare comprehensive view of the history of mankind. That was the great solitaire. Now only one little card was missing from my family solitaire.

Would we meet Grandpa in Dorf? Might Grandma already be with the old baker?

The darkness in the back yard was just beginning to turn blue when I fell asleep, fully clothed, on the bed.

JACK OF HEARTS

. . . a little man rummaging around in the back seat . . .

Nothing was said about Grandpa as we drove north the next morning until Mama declared that this idea about the baker in Dorf was just about as much as she could tolerate of boyish pranks.

Dad gave the impression that he didn't believe any more than Mama did about the baker in Dorf, but nevertheless he defended me now, and I appreciated it greatly.

'We'll drive the same way home,' he said, 'and we'll buy a big bag of buns in Dorf. At least we'll be nice and full. And as far as boyish pranks go, you must admit that you have been spared this for many years.'

Mama put her arm over his shoulder and said, 'I didn't mean it like that.'

'Careful now,' he murmured. 'I'm driving.'

So she turned to me instead. 'I'm sorry, Hans Thomas. But

please don't be too disappointed if this baker doesn't know any more about Grandpa than we do.'

The bun feast would have to wait until we reached Dorf much later that evening, but we needed to eat something in the meantime. Later that afternoon Dad pulled into Bellinzona and parked in a back alley between two restaurants.

While we ate pasta and roast veal, I made my biggest mistake of the whole trip: I started to tell them about the sticky-bun book.

Perhaps it was because I couldn't keep the great secret that it all happened ...

I began by telling them I had found a tiny book with microscopic writing in one of the sticky buns I had been given by the old baker. Therefore, it had been perfect that I'd already received a magnifying glass from the dwarf at the garage. Then I told them roughly what the sticky-bun book was about.

I have asked myself many times since then how I could have been so stupid as to break the formal promise I had given the old baker, when we were only a few hours from Dorf. I think I know the answer now: I so much wanted it to be Grandpa I had met in the little Alpine village – and I really wanted Mama to believe it, too. However, I just ended up making everything much more difficult.

Mama glanced at Dad before returning her attention to me. 'It's good that you have a lively imagination. But the imagination must have limits as well.'

'Didn't you tell me something like this on the roof terrace in Athens?' Dad piped up. 'I remember I was envious of your imagination – but I have to agree with Mama that all this about the sticky-bun book is stretching things pretty far.'

I don't know why exactly, but I started to cry. I felt as though I had carried so much on my own, and now that I had spilled the beans to Mama and Dad, they didn't believe me.

'Just wait,' I sniffed. 'Just wait until we get back to the car. Then I will *show* you the sticky-bun book, even though I promised Grandpa to keep it a secret.'

Dinner was finished at top speed, and I hoped that Dad would at least keep an open mind to the possibility that I might be telling the truth.

Dad left a hundred Swiss franc note on the table, and then we rushed out into the street without waiting for the change.

As we approached the car, we saw a little man rummaging around in the back seat. It is a mystery to this day how he managed to open the car door.

'Hey, you!' shouted Dad. 'Stop!'

With that, he ran at full speed over to the red Fiat. However, the man who had been half inside the car dashed out onto the street and hurried around the next corner. I could have sworn I heard the sound of bells as he disappeared.

Dad followed; he wasn't a bad runner. Mama and I stood by the Fiat and waited almost half an hour before he came lumbering round the same corner he had taken at furious speed.

'As if he sank into the ground,' he said. 'The devil!'

We started to check the luggage.

'I'm not missing anything,' Mama said after a while.

'Neither am I,' said Dad with one hand inside the glove compartment. 'Here's my driving licence, our passports, my wallet and my chequebook. He's even left the jokers. Maybe he was just after a drink.'

They both got inside the car, and Dad let me into the back seat.

I had a sinking feeling in my stomach, because I remembered I had only hidden the sticky-bun book under a sweater. Now it was gone!

'The sticky-bun book,' I said. 'He's taken the sticky-bun book!'

I broke down again.

'It was the dwarf,' I sobbed. 'The dwarf stole the sticky-bun book because I couldn't keep the secret.'

It ended with Mama joining me in the back seat and sitting for a long while with her arm around me.

'Poor little Hans Thomas,' she said over and over again. 'It's all my fault. We'll go back to Arendal, but first I think you should try and get some sleep.'

I sat bolt upright. 'But we are driving to Dorf?'

Dad swung onto the highway.

'Of course we're going to Dorf,' he assured me. 'A sailor always keeps his word.'

Just before I fell asleep, I heard Dad whisper to Mama, 'It was a bit strange. All the doors were locked, and you have to admit he was a *little* guy.'

'That fool can probably move through locked doors,' I said. 'And that's because he is an artificial person.'

Then I fell asleep in Mama's lap.

QUEEN OF HEARTS

. . . then suddenly an elderly
lady came out of the old pub . . .

I awoke a couple of hours later and jumped up in the back seat
to discover we were high in the Alps.

'Are you awake now?' Dad asked. 'We'll be in Dorf in about
half an hour. And we'll spend the night at the Schöner
Waldemar.'

A little later, when we drove into the village – which I felt I
knew better than anyone else in the car – Dad pulled right up in
front of the little bakery. The grown-ups tried to exchange secretive glances, but I saw through them.

The bakery was completely empty. The only sign of life was a
little goldfish which swam round and round inside a glass bowl
with a big chip out of it. I felt like a fish in a glass tank, too.

'Look,' I said, pulling the magnifying glass out of my jeans
pocket. 'Don't you see, it's exactly the same size as the chip in the
glass bowl.'

It was the only piece of visible evidence I had to prove I wasn't telling any old cock-and-bull story.

'Well, I'll be blowed,' exclaimed Dad. 'But it doesn't look as if it's going to be that easy to find the baker.'

I wasn't sure whether he said this to conclude the discussion in a kind way, or whether deep down he had believed everything I had said and was suddenly terribly disappointed that he hadn't met his father there and then.

We left the car and trudged in the direction of the Schöner Waldemar. Mama started to quiz me about who I usually played with in Arendal, but I tried to shake her off. The baker and the sticky-bun book was certainly no game.

Then suddenly an elderly lady came out of the old pub. When she saw us, she came hurrying over.

It was Grandma!

'Mother!' Dad cried out.

If nobody else heard him, then at least the angels in heaven must have, it was such a heartrending cry.

Grandma threw her arms around us all. Mama was so bewildered she didn't know what to do with herself. In the end, Grandma hugged me tightly and cried.

'My boy,' she wept. 'My sweet boy.'

'But – why . . . how . . .' Dad stammered.

'He died last night,' said Grandma sadly, looking at us all.

'Who died?' Mama asked.

'Ludwig,' whispered Grandma. 'He called me last week, and then we spent a few days together here. He told me he had had a visit from a young boy in his little bakery. Only when the boy had gone did he realise that it could have been his own grandchild and the man driving the red car could be his son. It is all so terribly sad, and yet at the same time wonderful. It was so good to see him. Then he had a heart attack. He . . . he died in my arms at the village infirmary.'

Now I broke down completely, weeping bitterly. I felt as though my own misfortune had clouded everyone else's. The three adults did all they could to comfort me, but I could no longer be comforted.

Grandpa was not the only one who was gone. I felt as though the whole world had disappeared with him. He could no longer confirm everything I had said about Rainbow Fizz and the magic island. But maybe – maybe that had been the intention. Grandpa was an old man, and I'd only had the sticky-bun book on loan.

When I had pulled myself together a few hours later at the Schöner Waldemar, we sat in the tiny dining room with the four tables.

Now and then the fat lady came over to me and said, 'Hans Thomas? *Nicht wahr?*'

'Don't you think it was amazing that he knew Hans Thomas was his own grandchild?' asked Grandma. 'He never even knew he had a son.'

Mama nodded in agreement. 'It's quite extraordinary,' she said.

It wasn't quite so simple for Dad, however. 'I think it is even more mysterious how Hans Thomas knew it was Grandpa,' he said.

All the adults looked at me.

'*The boy realises that the sticky-bun man is his own grandfather at the same time as the sticky-bun man realises that the boy from the north is his own grandson.*'

They all stared at me seriously, they seemed almost worried, but I continued: '*The sticky-bun man shouts down a magic funnel, so his voice carries hundreds of miles.*'

In this way I received some kind of compensation for all the doubt which had surrounded my judgment. I also understood that I would never be able to share the sticky-bun book with anyone.

KING OF HEARTS

*... the memories float further
and further away from that which once created
them ...*

There were four people in the car when we headed north again, two more than when we had driven south. I thought it wasn't such a bad trick, but I also felt as though the King of Hearts was missing.

Once again we passed the little garage with only one petrol pump, and I think Dad had a deep desire to meet the mysterious little man again. However, the little fool wasn't to be found. It didn't surprise me, but Dad cursed and swore.

We made a few enquiries around the neighbourhood, but the people there could tell us only that the garage had been shut down ever since the oil crisis in the seventies.

This is where the great journey to the philosopher's homeland came to an end. We had found Mama in Athens, and we had met Grandpa in the little Alpine village. But I also felt that my soul had been wounded, and that wound branched from the depths of European history.

Only after we had been home a long time did Grandma confide in me that Ludwig had managed to bequeath everything he owned to me. She said that he had also joked about me one day taking over the bakery in Dorf.

Several years have now passed since Dad and I made the long journey from Arendal to Athens to find Mama, who had lost herself in the fashion fairy tale.

I remember as if it were only yesterday that I sat in the back seat of the old Fiat. I am absolutely positive that I was given a magnifying glass by a little man on the Swiss border. I still have the magnifying glass, and Dad can confirm that the dwarf at the garage gave it to me.

I can swear that Grandpa had a goldfish in his bakery in Dorf, because we all saw it. Both Dad and I also remember the white pebbles in the forest above the wooden cabin in Dorf. Time has passed, but it can't erase the fact that I was given a bag of sticky buns by the old baker. I still have the pear taste of the fizzy drink in my body, and I haven't forgotten that Grandpa said something about a drink which tasted even better.

But was there really a little book in the sticky bun? Did I really sit in the back seat and read about Rainbow Fizz and the magic island? Or did I just sit and imagine the whole thing?

As time passes – and the memories float further and further away from that which once created them – the doubt always comes sneaking into my mind.

Because the Joker stole the sticky-bun book, I have had to write everything down from memory. Whether I have remembered everything or whether I have added bits here and there, only the Delphic Oracle knows.

It must have been the old prophecy from the magic island which made me finally realise that I had met my own grandpa in

Dorf. Because I didn't realise whom I'd met until we'd found Mama in Athens. But what had made him understand?

I have only one answer: Grandpa wrote the sticky-bun book. He had known about the old prophecy since the end of the Second World War.

Maybe the greatest mystery was where we had met—in a tiny bakery in a mountain village in Switzerland. How did we get there? We had been fooled into taking that long detour by a dwarf with cold hands.

Or was the greatest mystery that we met Grandma in the same village on our way home?

Maybe the greatest mystery of all was how we managed to free Mama from the fashion fairy tale. The greatest thing of all is love. Time can't pale that as easily as it fades old memories.

Now all four of us are living happily on Hisøy Island. I say four, because I now have a little sister. She was the one wading through the leaves and horse chestnuts on the road outside. Her name is Tone Angelica, and soon she'll be five years old. She talks like a waterfall all day long. Maybe she is the greatest philosopher.

Time is turning me into an adult. Time is also making the ancient temples crumble and even older islands sink into the sea.

Was there really a sticky-bun book in the biggest of the four buns in the bag? No question crosses my mind more often. As Socrates said, the only thing I know is that I know nothing.

But I am positive there is still a Joker roaming around the world. He will make sure that the world never rests. Whenever possible—and wherever possible—a little fool will jump out wearing long donkey ears and jingling bells. He will look deep into our eyes and ask, Who are you? Where do we come from?